"Less than a week ago, I knew who I was," Noah said.

"I knew what I wanted to be and do with my life," he continued. "I trusted the people I thought were family and the people I was working for. Now I don't know who to trust or who I am."

His words alone froze what Rachel had been going to say on her tongue.

"Apparently, some of them knew before the DNA test that I might be the long-lost heir or they wouldn't have asked me to take that darned DNA test. Why didn't they speak up then? Why all the secrecy?" Noah turned his head to the side to face her and held out his hand. "You're not part of the Adair family. Tell me." He paused before continuing. "Who can I trust besides you? Right at this moment, I think you are the only person I know who hasn't lied to me."

Wave after wave of guilt washed over her as she took Noah's hand and squeezed it. "Noah, I..." She swallowed hard to clear her throat of the knot forming there so that she could say the words she knew she should.

* * *

We hope you enjoyed The Adair Affairs—The notorious and powerful political family is back with even more secrets.

* * *

If you're on Twitter, tell us what you think of Harlequin Romantic Suspense! #harlequinromsuspense

Dear Reader,

When I was asked to participate in The Adair Affairs continuity, I was thrilled to revisit some of the characters I met in The Adair Legacy books. As a reader and a writer, I love to see the characters I've grown to know and love show up in other books. It means I don't have to say goodbye to them quite yet.

What better place to set a book than near San Diego, California? I visited San Diego once and fell in love with the beautiful city nestled against the coast. Looking out over the water dotted with sailboats made me feel peaceful and happy. The weather in Southern California is perfect, never too hot or too cold, and you can grow just about anything.

I hope to return to San Diego someday. Maybe I'll charter one of those sailboats to take me out on the ocean. If I do, I'll be sure to write the experience into one of my books so that you can come along with me.

In the meantime, happy reading!

Elle James

HEIR TO MURDER

Elle James

HARLEQUIN® ROMANTIC SUSPENSE

Special thanks and acknowledgment to Elle James
for her contribution to The Adair Affairs miniseries.

ISBN-13: 978-0-373-27917-3

Heir to Murder

Recycling programs
for this product may
not exist in your area.

Printed in U.S.A.

New York Times and *USA TODAY* bestselling author **Elle James** is a former IT professional and retired army and air force reservist. She writes romantic suspense, mysteries and paranormal romances that keep her readers on the edge of their seats to the very end of every book. When she's not at her computer, she's traveling to exotic and wonderful places, snow-skiing, boating or riding her four-wheeler, dreaming up new stories. Learn more about Elle James at ellejames.com.

Books by Elle James

HARLEQUIN ROMANTIC SUSPENSE

The Adair Affairs Series

Heir to Murder

Deadly Allure
Secret Service Rescue
Deadly Liaisons
Deadly Engagement
Deadly Reckoning

HARLEQUIN INTRIGUE

Thunder Horse Redemption
Triggered
Taking Aim
Bodyguard Under Fire
Cowboy Resurrected
Christmas at Thunder Horse Ranch

Visit Elle's Author Profile page at Harlequin.com or ellejames.com for more titles.

This book is dedicated to my family, who supports me in my writing endeavors. They are my strongest allies, my biggest fans and my cheerleaders who push me to succeed. I love you all!

Chapter 1

"Jackson?" A soft feminine voice called out through the doorway of the sixteen-stall stable at Adair Acres. The structure sat in the middle of one hundred and eighty acres of the most beautiful land Southern California had to offer. With sprawling citrus orchards, vineyards and pastures of alfalfa and the best horseflesh money could buy, it was an oasis of grace and beauty tucked in the gently rolling hills.

"Jackson?"

Noah Scott didn't respond to the voice, refusing to acknowledge the name he'd been born with. He threw a blanket over the black stallion's back and returned to the tack room for a saddle.

"There you are." His half sister, Landry Adair, met him as he exited the tack room with a saddle in hand.

Standing five feet ten inches tall, she was almost as tall as he was. With her hair pulled back in a low ponytail, she looked more like a girl than the twenty-six-year-old daughter of the deceased billionaire, Reginald Adair. She smiled at him with her bright blue eyes so much like his own. "Rachel called. She'll be here in a few minutes for her riding lesson."

"Tell her I'm taking the day off." He tossed the saddle over the stallion's back with a little more force than usual.

Diablo danced sideways, his ears slanting backward.

"She's driving all the way out here, expecting *you* to give her a riding lesson."

Noah ran a hand along the horse's neck, murmuring soothing sounds until the animal settled and let him reach beneath him to snag the girth. "Hell, *you* can give her the riding lesson."

"She prefers having you as her instructor, Jackson."

"Noah. My name is Noah."

Landry nodded. "Noah. I have to admit I have a hard time thinking of you as Jackson."

"Because that's not who I am." A couple days ago, Noah had known who he was and what he wanted to do: continue his import-and-export business on the side while working with his cousins at Adair Acres, where he could be around the horses and cattle he loved.

Now, he was reeling with the knowledge he wasn't who he thought he was. His real name was Jackson Adair. The long-lost son of the man who'd owned the ranch he'd been working. The man he thought of as his uncle.

Jackson Adair. How would he ever get used to it?

He'd spent the past thirty-seven years as Noah Scott. A man didn't change his name overnight. Hell, his entire life. He didn't bother facing Landry Adair, his half sister; instead, he focused his attention on the girth he cinched around the horse's belly. Once the girth was tight enough, he let the stirrup drop in place on the stallion he'd adopted as his favorite since coming to work at Adair Acres three months ago.

Landry touched his arm. "Are you going to be okay?"

"I'm fine."

He led Diablo out of the barn.

Before he could mount, Landry spoke again. "I'm here for you, if you need someone to talk to." She smiled, hesitantly. "After all, we're related. I'm your sister."

"Half sister," he corrected automatically, regretting it as soon as he noted the slight frown between her arched brows. Landry had always been nice to him and, though he had thought they were cousins, she'd been more like the little sister he'd never had growing up. Now that he knew it was true, it changed everything about their relationship.

But should it?

God, how could this happen to him? How could he have spent the past thirty-seven years of his life oblivious to the truth?

"If it makes you feel any better, none of us knew, either. We had some suspicions but that was pretty recent," Landry said as if reading his thoughts. "Now that we do know, we're glad you're the missing Jackson we'd always heard about. We love you. I can't think of anyone I'd rather have as my oldest brother." She emphasized *brother*, negating his attempt to make the distinction.

A knot formed in Noah's throat. Landry accepted him as part of her family. He'd yet to get a real reaction from her brothers, Carson and Whit. They might not be as thrilled to have to share their inheritance with him. Maybe he was being paranoid.

Now that the truth had been revealed and the terms of Reginald's will spelled out to him, he found it incredibly hard to believe he had a share in the ranch he'd come to work for.

Gathering the reins, he started to raise his foot to the stirrup, but a hand on his arm stopped him.

"I wish my father could have been here to know it was you all along," Landry said softly. "He only had good things to say about you. He'd have been proud to call you his son."

"Well, we'll never know that now, and guessing what he might have said or felt is as empty as guessing what the weather was the day I was born." He glanced down at her hand on his arm. "If you'll excuse me, I want to check on a fence in the north pasture."

Landry stepped back. "Of course. You need time to sort this all out. If you need to talk, you know where to find me."

Noah swung up into the saddle, nudged his horse's flanks and rode away from the Adair barn, all his motions from rote memory.

Thoughts and memories ricocheted through his mind as he gave the stallion his head. Soon they were racing across the fields, nothing but the sound of the horse's hooves and the creak of saddle leather to interrupt the chaotic feelings rattling around inside his head.

He leaned forward, the wind in his hair, the breeze taking the heat out of the warm morning sun already bearing down on his back.

For the hundredth time since he'd learned of the results of the DNA test, he shook his head. It couldn't be true. He wasn't one of Reginald Adair's children. The woman he knew as his mother wouldn't have hidden him as a baby from his biological father and mother. Hell, Reginald was *her* brother. And Ruby, Reginald's first wife, had been her sister-in-law.

All his life, Emmaline Adair Scott, the woman he'd called Mother, had sheltered him, kept him secluded from other children and other families. He'd assumed she'd done it to protect him because she loved him so much. Now…holy hell, she'd been hiding him from his *real* family. They'd never lived in any one place for very long. His mother had him in small private schools in France, or homeschooled him to keep anyone from suspecting he wasn't her child.

If not for the summer his mother had taken ill and required major surgery, she'd have kept him from the rest of the Adair family. But she couldn't care for him while she was laid up for several months. His grandparents had sent him to stay at his uncle's ranch in California.

That summer, surrounded by the Adair siblings, was the first time he'd felt part of a family. Reginald Adair had been kind to him. For a few short weeks, he understood what it might have been like to have a father to look up to. A man who cared about him and wanted to teach him the things a father taught his sons.

Working with and hanging around Reginald's children, whom he'd thought were his cousins, he'd finally gotten a feel for what it would be like to have siblings and be a member of a large family. Growing up as an only child, he'd always wished he had a brother to go fishing with or a sister to tease and protect.

He'd envied Reginald's children, wanting what they had. Not the money or the lifestyle of the rich, but a big family, people he could count on to always be there for him.

If he really was Reginald Adair's long-lost son, he had two half brothers and a half sister. The two boys and the girl, now grown, he'd come to respect and care for when he'd been there that summer so long ago.

If? His thoughts churned. The DNA test had been conclusive. There was no *if* about it. He was Reginald's son.

In this day and age, how could someone get away with stealing a child and hiding him for all those years? Everything he knew about his life had been a lie. All the times he'd asked his mother about his father, she'd lied to him. She'd told him that his father died before she'd given birth. All the while his father and his mother had been alive and well, grieving the disappearance of their son.

That his fake mother was related to his father—and knew how devastated he'd been by the loss of his son—was impossible to fathom.

All those years, growing up isolated in France, he could have known the joy of having brothers and sisters, sitting at a table filled with family, laughing, joking and sharing each other's lives.

All the years he could have spent with his family, getting to know and love them, were lost. Now that he knew who his real father was, the man was gone. Murdered before Noah had the chance to get to know him as a father.

As his horse galloped over acres and acres of grassland and rolling hills, all Noah could think was that he'd learned who his father was too late to get to spend time with the man. To get to know him.

Reginald Adair was dead. Shot to death in his office almost four months ago, and the authorities still hadn't identified a suspect in the murder case.

Noah would never have the opportunity to know his father.

The stallion had the bit between his teeth and ran like the wind, pounding the hard-packed earth, never seeming to tire.

Noah let him run until they neared one of the streams running through Adair Acres, the one with the waterfall and the large pool, surrounded by evergreen trees and rocky ledges to stretch out on.

When Noah pulled back on the reins, Diablo pulled harder against him, increasing his speed instead of decreasing.

It became a battle of the wills between the man and the stallion.

Noah dug his feet into the stirrups and pulled back as hard as he could on the reins until the horse's bottom jaw nearly touched his chest. Not until then did he finally slow, dancing sideways, whinnying, air huffing from his nostrils in angry puffs.

The big horse came to a jolting halt, reared up on his hind legs and pawed at the air.

"Whoa, Diablo," Noah said soothingly. He feared some of his anger and disturbed feelings had rubbed off on the horse.

As the horse rose on his hind legs, Noah leaned forward, his feet in the stirrups.

Diablo dropped to the ground, landing hard, jolting Noah in the saddle. Then he kicked up his hind legs, arched his back and bucked, trying to unseat the man as he dragged hard on the reins.

"Whoa, fella." Noah held his balance for the first eight seconds. When Diablo pulled a quick twist, however, Noah wasn't ready and was sent flying through the air to land hard on his back, knocking the wind from his lungs.

Diablo reared again and took off like a crazed animal, running hell-bent for leather back to the barn.

When Noah could breathe again, he pushed to his feet and dusted off his jeans. "Damned horse."

Since it was a good thirty-minute hike from the barn, Noah debated starting back. One glance around at where he was and he changed his mind. The one place in the world that calmed his soul was this spot on the Adair ranch.

The creek, filled with crystal-clear water, ran between the rolling hills, cutting through rocky crevices and long, flat pastures. And if he followed its path upstream, he'd find the waterfall and the naturally formed pool where he and his cousins—siblings—used to swim. With the air warming nicely, swimming was a distinct possibility, and it would delay his return to the ranch house, where he'd have to face up to his new role in the Adair family.

And what that role was, he had no idea.

Pushing all thoughts of his new status among Reginald Adair's offspring, he hiked upstream to the pool, kicked off his boots, pulled his shirt over his head and shucked his jeans. Without giving much thought to how cold the water might be, he dove in.

As soon as he hit the surface, the cool water shocked him out of his musings and reminded him he was alive and the pool was all his to enjoy without interruption. The media wouldn't swarm him and his family wouldn't be following him around to see what he would do next like some trick pony in a sideshow.

It was just him, the chill water and sound of the cicadas chirping. He swam the length of the pool and back several times until his body warmed despite the coolness of the water. The sun found its way through the trees overhanging the rocky shoreline, speckling the water and making it shine like diamonds.

Noah wished he could stay out there, away from everything. Away from having to make decisions about what he was now going to do with his life. Before the DNA test, he'd been content to work on the ranch as a ranch hand and operate his import-and-export business out of the guesthouse on Adair Acres.

Knowing he had a controlling interest in the property, he wondered if he would be expected to do something other than work the ranch. He had never fit in with the corporate world and he didn't want to live in a city.

Hell, he had everything he'd ever wanted in life.

Why did it have to cause him so much heartache and introspection? He wished he had someone to talk to, someone who wasn't a member of the Adair family. An unbiased individual he could bounce his thoughts off of without worrying whether he was encroaching on their territory or stealing their inheritance.

An image of Rachel Blackstone appeared in his thoughts. The pretty socialite with wavy dark brown hair that kissed her shoulders and a slim body with all the right curves sprang to mind. He'd spent weeks teaching her how to ride, always maintaining his distance, regarding himself as her social inferior. She was a member of San Diego's social elite. A child of the privileged class. He had been the ranch hand, the poor cousin to the megarich Adairs.

Rachel had never made him feel inferior. She'd always talked to him as an equal, asking questions about his life as if she really cared.

For a few brief moments, he'd considered asking her out on a date. When he gave himself enough time to think it through, he realized it was ridiculous to think he could mingle in the same social sphere. He didn't attend charity balls. He'd eaten out at nice restaurants, but not as nice as the ones she'd be used to. What did he have to offer as a ranch hand, making a living teaching rich girls how to ride horses and running his small business as a sideline?

Now that he was one of the Adairs, would she see him differently? He was still the same person inside even if his name had changed.

Noah struck out again across the pool, swimming

hard, hoping if he wore himself out, he would be too tired to think so much.

Head down, concentrating only on the next stroke, he was startled by a voice calling out his name.

"Noah!"

He stopped in the middle of the pool and glanced up at a rocky ledge.

As if conjured by his thoughts, Rachel Blackstone sat on the smooth boulder, her slim, jean-clad legs dangling over the edge.

Suddenly conscious of his state of undress, Noah sank low in the water. "How long have you been there?"

"Long enough to admire a very handsome naked bottom gliding through clear water." She winked.

Heat rose up his neck and into his cheeks as he treaded water, sure to keep the lower part of his body well beneath the surface. "Sorry. I didn't expect company."

She laughed, the sound joyful and as pure as the air. "I'm not sorry. I was enjoying the view."

"If you'd just turn your back, I'll get dressed and we can be less awkward."

She raised her brows. "I don't feel the least awkward." When he remained where he was in the water without responding, she pouted. "Modesty is way overrated." Then she turned her back. "I promise not to look."

Noah swam over to the shore and emerged on the bank next to the pile of his clothing. Still dripping, he tugged his jeans over his wet thighs. When he had them on, he collected his boots, shirt and belt and climbed onto the boulder where Rachel sat with her back to him.

Her dark hair swung across the top of her shoulders and down her back as she flexed her shoulders and tipped her face toward the sun. "About done?" she called out.

This wasn't the first time they'd been to the pool together, but this was the first time she'd seen him without his clothes on and it had every blood cell in his body humming swiftly through his veins. He wanted to touch her but held back. She was far too beautiful and tempting. Rather than touch her with his hands, he leaned over her shoulder and whispered against her ear, "Close enough."

Noah's breath stirred tendrils of Rachel's hair along the side of her neck. She spun around on her bottom, discovering that she was within easy reach of his broad and very naked chest. Droplets of water gleamed in the sunlight, daring her to capture them with her tongue.

Rachel licked her lips and dragged her gaze from his chest to his eyes. "Do you swim naked in the pool very often?"

"When it's warm and I'm alone."

"Ever considered swimming here with a woman?"

He shook his head. "No, but now that you mention it…" As he tipped his head toward the water, his lips tilted upward on the corners. "Care to?"

When he looked at her like that, with that sexy gleam in his eyes and a teasing half smile, she was tempted to throw off her clothes and drag him back into the water.

"Uh, not now." As soon as she'd said the words, regret settled in. For the past few weeks, she'd had him teaching her how to ride horses, though she was an accomplished rider and had been riding since she was a small child. But he didn't know that. And it had been at Landry's request.

Landry had been her best friend since they'd attended private school in San Diego. When Landry had asked Rachel to keep an eye on Noah, Rachel hadn't seen it as much of a hardship. The man was so darned sexy she was surprised a dozen women weren't standing in line for riding lessons with him.

Noah shook out his T-shirt and raised it above his head.

Rachel captured his arm with her fingers. "Don't put that on because of me. You aren't offending my sensibilities…and…and you need to let your skin dry more." Mostly, she wanted to stare at his muscular body while she had an excuse.

"In that case, I won't." He tossed the shirt to the side and stretched out on his back beside her, lacing his hands behind his head. "What brings you out this far?"

"I had a date for riding lessons."

He shook his head. "You don't need riding lessons."

"I don't?"

Again he shook his head. "Let me guess, you've been riding since you were a small child, right?" His gaze rolled her way, his brows rising in challenge.

Rachel chewed on her bottom lip before finally nodding. "Yeah. I got my first pony when I was four."

Noah snorted. "Figures. I find it harder and harder to know when someone is telling me the truth or a lie." His lips thinned and he stared up at the sky.

"Hey. You're far too cynical for one so young."

"I'm not young. I'm thirty-seven years old and the

person I trusted most has been lying to me for all thirty-seven years. What's one more person lying to me?"

Her heart squeezing tight in her chest, Rachel didn't refute his statement. The guilt weighed heavily. Instead, she lay on her back beside him and stared up at the leaves hanging over her, the sun sneaking through the gaps.

"If you didn't come for the riding lesson, did you come out to stare at the long-lost son of Reginald Adair?"

"No, I came to see how you were doing." That was true. But only half of the truth. She'd come to tell him that she'd been spying on him for the past several weeks as a favor to Landry. Surely he'd understand how careful the Adairs had to be. The family was rich. Noah could have been a scamming relative looking for a way to make off with some of the Adair fortune.

Since the DNA test, conjecture had been settled. Noah Scott was in fact Jackson Adair and justified in any claim on Reginald Adair's legacy.

For the past month, Rachel had spent more time at Adair Acres than in San Diego where she was heavily involved in philanthropy, raising money for those in need. She'd put much of her work on hold in order to help Landry and her brothers spy on Noah.

She had to admit, it was much more interesting staying at Adair Acres than at her home, which had become just a big empty space since the deaths of her parents when she was a little girl.

Her chest knotted. Now that she didn't need to spy on Noah, she didn't have an excuse to stay. She'd miss having the Adair family around her, and her afternoons of riding lessons with Noah.

Her purpose for coming to Adair Acres that day was to confess her part in Landry's plan to find out as much as she could about the man they suspected might be the missing Jackson Adair. She steeled her nerves and opened her mouth.

"Less than a week ago, I knew who I was," Noah said. "I knew who I wanted to be and what to do with my life. I trusted the people I thought were family and the people I was working for. Now, I don't know who to trust and who I am."

His words froze what Rachel was going to say on her tongue.

"Apparently, some of them knew before the DNA test that I might be Jackson or they wouldn't have asked me to take that darned test. Why didn't they speak up then? Why all the secrecy?" Noah turned his head to the side to face her and held out his hand. "You're not part of the Adair family. Tell me…" He paused before continuing. "Who can I trust besides you? Right at this moment, I think you are the only person I know who hasn't lied to me."

Wave after wave of guilt washed over her as she took Noah's hand and squeezed it. "Noah, I…" She swallowed hard to clear her throat of the knot forming there so that she could say the words she knew she should. Words that would reveal her for the liar she was and dash his hopes of having someone unbiased to confide in.

Before she could say anything, he rolled over and planted his hands on the boulder on either side of her arms. "When I was growing up, I wished I had a big family, siblings to play with, to love and to share my life and theirs. One simple DNA test and poof! I have it all. But in my head, I'm still the poor cousin working for the rich Adairs. This life, the fancy cars, the social scene, flying around the world at a moment's notice… It's not who I am. I don't belong here. I feel like I need to leave and start over somewhere else."

Rachel sat up, bringing him with her. "Noah, no. You are a member of the Adair family. You have just as much of a right to be here as they do. It's not your fault someone stole you from your parents." It broke her heart to see the man torn by his desire to stay where he finally had a home and family, and leaving because he didn't fit in. "Things will work out."

"Whit and Carson can't be happy about me."

"Landry is thrilled. She knew how much it meant to her father to find you." Rachel lifted both his hands in hers and held them between hers. "You just have to give Whit and Carson time to get used to having you around permanently. They already know you—it's just a matter of accepting you as their brother."

"I don't know. I didn't come here to cause the Adairs trouble and heartache."

"You can't leave now. They lost their father and Patsy, their mother, is going to jail. Landry and her brothers may not know it, but they need you as much as you need them."

Noah shook his head. "Why would they need me?"

"Because you were the missing link to their father's past. The reason he had such a hard time accepting them. You have to stay and let them get to know you and you them."

Noah's fingers closed around hers and he stared into her eyes. "Okay. I'll stay. But not for them, but because you asked me." He smiled and leaned forward, pressing his lips to her forehead. "Thanks."

His mouth was soft, his gesture gentle. It could have been the kiss of a brother to a sister, but Rachel didn't have sisterly feelings toward this man.

Over the past few weeks of riding lessons, she'd fallen deeper and deeper under his spell. He wasn't like any of the men she'd dated. He was patient, caring and considerate of her feelings. The man didn't have a shallow bone in his body and he didn't give a damn about who could best influence his career or portfolio.

Though Noah thought he didn't know who he was, Rachel knew exactly who he was: a real man who could be taken at face value and who would love his family dearly.

When he bent to kiss the tip of her nose, she tipped her head back. His lips missed their target, capturing her mouth in a soft brush of a kiss. Before he could pull away, she wrapped her hands around the back of his neck and pulled him closer, opening her mouth to him. It was up to him to make the next move.

Chapter 2

Noah swept past Rachel's lips to caress her tongue in a long, sensuous stroke. She tasted of mint and tea and her body was soft against his harder lines. For the past few weeks, he'd dreamed of wrapping his arms around her and holding her close just like this.

He leaned her back against the boulder and explored her mouth, touching, tasting and teasing.

Her slender hands, behind his head, separated and skimmed across his naked shoulders, down his back to his waist and lower to slip into the back pockets of his jeans.

His groin tightened and his kiss became more urgent. He wanted more of her. Leaving her lips, he blazed a path with his mouth across her chin, down the long, slender line of her neck and lower to the V in her button-up blouse.

He reached between them and flipped the buttons loose, one after the other, until her blouse fell open, exposing a lacy black bra. Her breasts swelled over the low cups. As he settled a kiss over each, her back arched off the boulder, rising to meet him.

He cupped one breast and pinched the nipple through the lacy fabric, rolling it between his thumb and forefinger. Rachel moaned, the sound making every nerve in Noah's body come alive.

Pushing the cup of her bra aside, he exposed a rose-tipped nipple and captured it between his lips, tonguing it into a tight little bud.

Her fingers curled into his hair, drawing him closer.

After tasting one, he pushed aside the other cup and tasted the fruit of her other breast, laving his tongue across the tip until it too beaded in a tight knot.

When Rachel's leg slid up the side of Noah's, he fought for control. Just because he was now her social equal didn't make it right to take advantage of her. With a huge amount of effort and constraint, he stopped himself before he went further.

Once he pushed himself up to a sitting position, he drew Rachel's blouse together and grabbed his T-shirt. "We should get back before someone comes looking for us."

Rachel sat up, straightening her clothes, twin flags of color high in her cheeks. "The way Diablo raced past me, I'd say it won't be long before someone comes searching for your body."

Noah pulled his boots on and stood, extending a hand to Rachel. "I'm sorry I took advantage of your kindness."

She raised a hand. "Please. I'm not sorry you did."

He grinned and cupped her cheek in his hand. He couldn't resist one last taste and he bent to kiss her again. When he stepped away, he willed his pulse to slow. The woman had his insides humming, begging for more. "I hope you tied your horse up, or we'll both be walking."

"As a matter of fact, I did tie her up." She led the way to a copse of trees where her white Arabian mare stood patiently.

Noah cupped his hands and stooped low. "You first."

"No, I can ride on the back. You take the saddle."

"No. I feel pretty stupid getting tossed off my horse, when I'm the one who is supposed to be teaching riding lessons. I deserve to suffer a little for that."

"Is that what happened?" Rachel chuckled. "In that case, you should ride on the back." She stepped into his hand and he lifted her up into the saddle.

Then he put his foot in the stirrup and mounted the horse to sit behind her and the saddle, wrapping his arms around her middle. Her waist was narrow and he liked the way it felt, small but firm.

Thankfully, Rachel set the horse off in an easy gallop, minimizing the jarring gait of a trot.

Noah held on, enjoying the feel of her in his arms. She smelled of honeysuckle and the outdoors and she was soft in all the right places. She calmed him and made him feel natural and at home.

Fifteen minutes later, as they neared the barn, she slowed the horse to a walk. When they rode into the barnyard, Landry emerged, leading another horse. An older woman followed, her brow furrowed, light brown hair pulled back in a neat twist at the back of her head. There was something oddly familiar about her facial structure, but Noah couldn't put his finger on it.

"Oh, thank goodness," Landry called out. "I was just about to go looking for you two. When Diablo came back without his rider, I worried you'd been hurt."

The woman behind her pressed a hand to her mouth and stared up at Noah.

Noah slipped off the horse and held up his hands to Rachel. Capturing her around the waist, he swung her out of the saddle and set her on her feet. When he turned to face Landry and the woman, he noted that the woman's eyes had filled and she caught her lip between her teeth. "Is this…?" she said, and stopped, choking on a sob.

"Yes, ma'am." Landry tied the horse she'd been leading to a post, hooked the woman's arm and urged her forward. "This is my good friend Rachel Blackstone and my brother, Jackson Adair, better known as Noah Scott. Noah…" She paused, her gaze intense. "This is your mother, Ruby Adair Mason."

Noah's heart stopped and then bounded ahead in a pulse-pounding race to catch up. He'd known his real mother was still alive, but he hadn't gotten past the initial shock of his new identity to think about actually meeting her.

As she stood in front of him, he could finally see himself in her. Emmaline, the woman who'd raised him, looked like an Adair with her dark hair and blue eyes. Although he had blue eyes, Noah had never looked like an Adair. His hair was light, where Emmaline, Reginald and his children had dark brown hair and his facial structure was totally different. More like the woman standing in front of him.

Ruby reached out to touch his chin and then hers. "You have the cleft in your chin like mine." She smiled through watery eyes. "And blue eyes like your father."

At a loss for what to say, he took her hand and held it in his. She was thin, almost frail and he was afraid to squeeze hard on her fingers for fear of breaking them. He knew he should say something, but what? "Nice to meet you." It was lame, but he really was glad to meet the woman who had given birth to him. She had never lied to him and, like him, she was a victim in the whole situation.

"Well, you two will have a lot to talk about." Landry backed away. "Rachel and I will take care of the horses and we have some baby shower planning to do for Elizabeth and Whit's upcoming bundle of joy. I could have a lunch and tea prepared for you two up at the big house, if you like."

Elizabeth and Whit Adair were expecting a baby. Landry, Georgia and Rachel had volunteered to give her a baby shower.

Noah shook his head. He didn't feel comfortable at the main house and had chosen to live in the guest-house. But even there seemed too intimate for a first meeting with his mother.

Ruby laid a hand on his arm. "If it's okay with you, I know of a nice little sandwich shop just this side of San Diego. We could get a bite to eat there and I wouldn't be far from my hotel."

"I'll drive," he offered.

Ruby shook her head. "If it's all the same to you, I

prefer to take my own car. That way I can go straight from the restaurant to my hotel."

"Fair enough. I could meet you there in forty-five minutes. I'll need to shower after my ride and dress in something that doesn't smell like horse."

Ruby smiled. "You could come as you are. I wouldn't mind."

Her smile was genuine and Noah liked it. "I'd rather shower."

"Then I'll see you in forty-five minutes." Ruby gave him the name of the sandwich shop and turned to leave, hesitated and faced him again. "I'm really happy to finally see you." Tears flooding her eyes, she hurried away.

Noah's heart felt like a huge knot in his chest as he walked toward the guesthouse. Too many revelations were hitting him all at once and he didn't know quite how to process them all. Part of him wanted to put off the lunch with Ruby, but his curiosity about her won out. He wanted to learn more about the woman who should have raised him and loved him.

He couldn't help thinking how his life might have been had he never been stolen away and raised by his aunt. Knowing what happened and where his mother's life had taken her after she and Reginald Adair had divorced would help him understand who Ruby Mason was.

After shedding his clothing in the bathroom, he stepped under the cool spray of the shower and washed the creek water out of his hair with a squirt of shampoo. Once he had scrubbed his entire body, he shut off the water and dried himself, dressed in his best jeans and a pullover polo shirt the color of his eyes.

He felt as though he was going to an interview with an important person and he didn't want to disappoint her. This was his mother. The woman he hadn't seen since he was too small to remember.

Noah keyed the location into his cell phone and brought up the map. Driving through the gates of Adair Acres, he followed the directions to just outside of San Diego. He parked his truck in front of a bistro with little tables and checkered tablecloths. The sun was shining, but the trees overhanging the front patio provided enough shade to make it comfortable outside.

Ruby sat at a table on the terrace, behind a short wrought iron fence. When she spotted him dropping down out of his truck, she rose, twisting her hands together, her teeth gnawing on her lower lip.

Noah's own pulse picked up as he closed the distance, passing through the garden gate into the bistro's patio area.

Ruby smiled tremulously. "I wasn't sure you'd come. I wouldn't have blamed you if you'd changed your mind."

"I told you I'd be here. I keep my promises." He held her chair as she took her seat, then settled in the one across the tiny table from her. "I hope you weren't waiting long."

She grimaced. "I came straight here and ordered a cup of tea. It helps to calm me."

"I'd ask you why you were so nervous, but I find that I'm possibly as unnerved by what's happened as you are."

She sighed shakily. "It's just that I've searched for so long. I'd hoped…but I didn't think I'd ever find you. And now…" She glanced across the table at him, her eyes filling again with tears. "I promised myself I wouldn't cry again, but I can't help it. I've dreamed of this day most of my life, and almost thought it would never happen. And here we are." She leaned forward, a smile curling her lips through the tears. "I can't believe how big you've grown."

"I should hope I'd grown big. I'm thirty-seven."

"Thirty-seven." She swallowed hard. "Thirty-seven years I didn't get to spend with you, watching you grow into a man." Ruby sucked in a deep breath and let it go, her shoulders straightening, her lips firm. "That's thirty-seven years I need to catch up on. I have so many questions I'd like to ask, but I don't know where to begin."

"I have a few of my own. Maybe we can just cover the basics in this meeting. I'm still adjusting to all of this."

"Of course, of course." She touched her hand to her face, her cheeks flushed. "Where to begin?" She pulled her wallet out of her purse and extracted a small photograph from it and held it out to him. "This is a picture of you taken a couple weeks before—well, before it happened." She handed him a photograph of a baby boy with blue eyes and a tuft of bright blond hair.

Noah stared down at the photo. "It looks a lot like the ones my mother, er, aunt had in an album. I can't understand how she could steal a child and live with herself."

"From what I was told, Emmaline didn't steal you. Your grandparents did the stealing and gave you to her."

"I know. But she knew I didn't belong to her. She should have returned me as soon as my grandparents handed me over."

Ruby took the photo from him and stared at it, her gaze far away. "She'd just lost her own baby. I know how awful that feels. I can understand her wanting to keep you. You were probably like a gift that she couldn't bear to give back. Not after her baby died. Postpartum depression can be bad, but giving birth only to lose your baby afterward had to have intensified her grief."

Noah shook his head. "You of all people shouldn't be so forgiving. There's no excuse for taking and keeping another family's child."

"I'd have done anything to have my baby back," Ruby said, her voice breaking on the last word. "There's nothing worse than losing your child. God, I left you outside to go answer the stupid telephone."

Noah reached across the table and took Ruby's hands. "You can't blame yourself. You couldn't have known someone would take your baby." Though he was talking about himself, it felt as if the child that had been stolen was someone else. And though the woman whose hands he held was his mother, he hadn't had the benefit of growing up with her. She was a stranger. And that saddened him.

He couldn't change the past. All he could do was accept the present and build a future with the knowledge and the people he now knew were his family.

Gently squeezing her hands, he urged, "Tell me about you."

She sniffed and glanced up at him. "What do you want to know?"

"Everything." He smiled. "From the time I disappeared until now."

She laughed and pushed the fine hair out of her face. "There's not a whole lot to say. After you disappeared, your father couldn't forgive me for leaving you unattended. For that matter, I blamed myself. I don't know if you are aware, but Reginald and I married because I was pregnant with you."

Noah nodded. "I'd heard as much."

She shrugged. "Since you were gone, there wasn't any reason for us to stay married. We divorced, I moved away from North Carolina to Florida and he moved to California. In Florida, I met a wonderful man I fell in love with and married." Her smile was wistful and happy.

"What about other children?" he asked. "Do I have any half brothers or sisters?"

Ruby shook her head. "My husband had a daughter he brought into our marriage." Her smile widened. "She accepted me as her mother from the moment I came to live with them. Georgia isn't like a stepdaughter—she's more than that. I think you'll like her."

Noah was still awed by his newfound family. Going from a man with only a mother who kept him secluded from the rest of his relatives to having an entire family and extended family, he was blessed. "Georgia is your daughter? Is she Carson's fiancée?"

"She is." Ruby grinned. "Such an unlikely pair. But so in love."

Noah chuckled. "She'll give Carson a run for his money. They seem happy together."

Ruby's face brightened. "I think so. Carson needed her and she needed him. And now that I've found you, I have my entire family in one place. I couldn't be happier, myself."

"Will you be going back to Florida anytime soon?"

Ruby nodded. "Yes."

Disappointment knifed through Noah. "I'm really sorry to hear that. I'd hoped to get to spend more time with you."

She laughed. "I'm only going back to sell my house. I have nothing to keep me in Florida. Since my husband passed away, it's just me. Georgia isn't leaving California and now that I've found you…"

Noah found himself leaning forward. He didn't want distance to keep him from knowing this woman. "Does that mean you'll be moving?"

"It does. I want to be close to my children." Her voice caught. "You don't know how happy that makes me to say that—children." She patted his hand. "Don't worry, I won't move in with you or Georgia. You have your own lives. I'll get a little place of my own. But with any luck I'll see you sometime?" She glanced across at him, her eyes wide, hopeful.

He was touched by the warmth in her gaze. "Count on it."

"What about you? I've told you about my life—what about yours? I want to know all about you. Where did you grow up? What was it like for you going to school?

Did you play sports, have you ever been married?" She stopped asking long enough to take a breath. "Oh, who am I kidding? I can't catch up on all thirty-seven years in one lunch. And we haven't even ordered."

"We have time."

"I hope so. Because I really want to know you."

"And I want to know you." He lifted the menu. "What do you think you'd like to eat? We can talk while we wait for our food."

They ordered and talked, catching up on the big events of each other's lives and some of the little ones that made them who they were. By the time they'd consumed their sandwiches and a couple cups of tea, Noah was more comfortable and relaxed around this woman who was his biological mother.

When the plates were cleared and the check paid, Ruby pushed back from the table. "I should get going. I've taken up enough of your time." She stood and slipped her purse over her arm.

"I've enjoyed it and hope we can do this again soon," Noah said, and meant it.

"Me, too. I know I can't have back the years I missed, but there are so many more ahead of us. I don't want to waste a single one of them."

Noah tossed a couple of bills onto the table and escorted Ruby out to the parking area. "Where did you park?"

"On the side. The front was full when I arrived."

At the side of the building, a small sedan sat at a slant on the sloped parking spot.

Ruby stood beside the car. "I'm really glad we had

this time together." She looked up at him. "Do you mind if I hug you?"

He smiled. "Not at all." He bent as she wrapped her arms around his shoulders and he gathered her slim body in a hug.

Although awkward at first, Noah felt the love and tenderness in her gesture and his heart swelled.

"I've always loved you," she whispered. "And I never gave up hope." Her arms tightened briefly, and then they fell to her sides. Ruby climbed into her rental car and started the engine, lowering the window.

"When will you head back to Florida?" Noah leaned against the door frame, not really wanting her to leave.

"Not for a couple more days. Do you mind if I come to visit you?"

"Not at all. I'd be honored."

She backed out of the parking space and then stopped. She shifted into Park, opened the door, jumped out and ran back to wrap her arms around him one more time. "Please tell me you won't disappear again. Please."

He hugged her, holding her tight. "I promise."

Ruby leaned back, rubbing tears from her eyes. "I just couldn't bear to lose you again."

"I'm not going anywhere."

She stepped back, straightening her hair. "I know that. It's just…" With a sigh, she said, "It's happened before."

"I'm all grown up."

"Yeah, and someone killed Reginald. Now that the world knows you're related to him, you could be in danger."

He pushed his shoulders back. "I can take care of myself."

"I'm sure Reginald thought he could take care of himself, as well. Be careful."

"I will."

This time when Ruby climbed into her car, she drove away, leaving Noah staring after her.

His life felt surreal. He'd been talking to his mother all afternoon, and she was a stranger.

He wished he could talk to Emmaline, the woman who'd raised him as her son. When the DNA results had been confirmed, she'd disappeared. How could she hide at a time like this? Noah had so many questions only she could answer.

But then she'd kept a stolen baby that belonged to her brother, hiding the secret for thirty-seven years. It would explain why she'd isolated him from the rest of her family for so long. There had to be a law against doing that. When she'd been found out, she probably ran, afraid of going to prison.

His mind was churning and he didn't want to go home. He surveyed the scene below him. The bistro was perched on a hill overlooking the beautiful harbor town of San Diego, and Noah thought of Rachel.

She lived in the city, only a few short minutes away. After he'd kissed her that afternoon, Noah wondered if she'd want to see him again. She calmed his soul at the same time she stoked the flames of desire.

The more he thought about it, the more he wanted to see her. Perhaps she could help him make sense of his life. Even if she couldn't, he wanted to explore where their relationship was going. One kiss wasn't enough with Rachel.

Digging his cell phone out of his pocket, he entered her number and waited.

She picked up on the second ring. "Hi, Noah? Did you have a nice visit with Ruby?"

"I did." He ran his fingers through his hair, his pulse pounding in his veins. He'd never asked Rachel out on a date, having felt he wasn't in her social stratosphere. She might still consider him nothing more than the hired help and turn him down. But if he didn't ask, he'd never know. "Look, I'm still in town. Would you like to have dinner with me?"

"As in a date?"

Noah drew in a deep breath and let it out. "Yes."

She laughed. "I thought you'd never ask. I'd love to have dinner with you, but let me do the cooking. You can come to my place. I grill a mean steak."

"I didn't mean for you to have to cook."

"I love to cook. So is it settled? You're coming to my place."

"When?"

"Two hours."

"Good, I have a few errands to run while I'm in town." His heart lighter than it had been in days, he smiled into the phone. "I'll see you then."

His world might have turned upside down, but the one person he knew he could count on and trust was Rachel.

Chapter 3

"Why didn't you tell him over the phone?" Landry Adair asked.

Rachel glanced around her beautiful apartment, decorated with homey touches and cheerful artwork, unlike the estate she'd grown up in only a few miles away. The home her parents left her was large, sprawling, lavishly decorated and made her feel achingly lonely. She only lived there when she entertained others of the socially elite.

Any other time she stayed in her apartment in a quaint, older section of San Diego. The apartment was just the right size for a single woman.

Realizing that she was stalling, Rachel sighed.

"Like I said, I started to tell him while we were out riding, but...well I got sidetracked." He'd kissed her and every thought of telling him that she'd been spying on him had flown out of her head. By the time she could think again, they were back at the barn and his mother was there. "And I refuse to tell him over the telephone. I'll tell him tonight."

"At least we made good progress on the plans for Elizabeth's baby shower. Don't forget, we need to get together soon with Georgia to finalize them. Why don't you come out to the ranch later this evening?"

Rachel knew they needed to finish planning, but she had a different commitment for the evening. "Noah's coming to my apartment tonight."

"That's interesting." Landry's bright blue eyes sparkled as she swept the long brown hair with the soft gold highlights back from her forehead. "How'd that come about?"

"He asked me out to dinner. I thought it would be better if we had dinner at my place."

"I didn't know you two were dating."

"We weren't. This is a first. I could have gone out to a restaurant with him, but just couldn't. If he gets angry, and we're here alone, it's just me, not a roomful of strangers staring."

Landry chuckled. "And if he walks out, you don't have to worry about finding a ride home."

"Something like that." Rachel paced across the floor of her living room, her cell phone pressed to her ear. The sun shone bright through the ground-level windows of her town house apartment. The sky was crystal clear and the harbor, with the mix of motorboats and sailboats, couldn't have been more beautiful. Still, those things didn't hold her attention. All she could think about was the fact she had to tell Noah that she had been spying on him for Landry and her brothers.

Georgia Mason, Carson's fiancée, had been the one to notice the similarity between her stepmother's and Noah's facial structures and cleft chins. Until she'd pointed it out, none of them had seen it. They knew Noah as their cousin. Landry, Whit and Carson had decided it would be best to keep an eye on him. If he was the long-lost son Reginald Adair had been searching for almost four decades, had he known and was he aware of the inheritance his father had left him? They wanted to be sure he wasn't some gold digger looking for a way to claim money that didn't belong to him.

When she'd hired Noah to give her riding lessons, Rachel didn't know much about him. Spying on him seemed harmless and a way to help her friend and the family she cared so much about.

What she hadn't counted on was falling in love with the kind and gentle man who knew his way around horses more than he did around humans. He was patient with the animals, and with her and all her questions. She hadn't told him she already knew how to ride, pretending she'd only done so on the rare occasion and that she was nervous around the large animals.

They'd ride out for hours, several times a week, stopping to rest by the creek she'd found him skinny-dipping in earlier that day. God, she'd wanted to join him, to feel his naked body against hers.

With the whopping lie between them, she didn't feel she had the right to slip into the water and seduce him. Hadn't she already tricked him into revealing so much of his heart and soul to her?

His comment about not knowing who to trust had struck far too close to home.

Rachel couldn't go another day without confessing. If he refused to see her again, it was the price she paid for not being up-front with him to begin with.

"Why do you have to tell him?" Landry asked.

"I'd rather he heard it from me than finding out from someone else."

"Whit, Carson and I wouldn't tell him."

"Not intentionally." Rachel couldn't risk it. And she wouldn't feel right being with him when a lie stood between them.

"Look, Rachel, since I was the one who roped you into spying on him, I should break it to him."

"No. That would make it worse. I own up to my mistakes. The sooner the better."

"If that's the way you want it," Landry conceded. "Just promise you'll let me know how it goes."

"I will." Rachel ended the call and glanced at the clock, her heart ratcheting up a notch. One hour and thirty minutes before Noah arrived.

She hurried around the apartment, straightening bright yellow and red throw pillows, dusting surfaces of the rich mahogany antique curio cabinets and occasional tables. Some of them had come over from Europe with her great-grandmother. She'd found them hidden in the attic of her estate, collecting dust. They would never have matched the elegant, modern furnishings of the larger estate. But they were perfect for her little apartment. She'd pulled them out of the attic, lovingly repaired what was broken and moved them into her apartment, giving them the home they deserved. And she'd collected over the years. She liked that her furniture had seen many generations of use. With a final swipe of the dust cloth over her already immaculate living space, she admitted it was as good as it would get.

Later, with less than an hour to spare, she began preparation of their meal.

She knew enough about Noah to realize he wouldn't be impressed with Cornish hens or a pilaf—he'd want a hearty supper fit for a man who worked outside all day long. Steak, baked potatoes and a fresh green salad would do the trick. Thankfully, she'd been to the grocer that morning with Noah in mind.

Pulling the ingredients from her refrigerator, she prepared a marinade in a rectangular dish and laid the steaks inside to soak. She covered the dish and left it on the counter to give the steaks time to warm up to room temperature for when Noah arrived. She'd fire up the grill on her balcony and have it hot and ready to go when Noah walked through the door.

Rachel loved to cook but had very few occasions to do it. She stayed busy with her social obligations, organizing charitable events and philanthropies. The money she'd inherited from her parents gave her a hefty cushion to live off of the rest of her life, if she chose not to work another day.

She'd gone to college and graduated with a degree in International Business with a minor in Marketing. It helped her run the charitable foundations her mother and father had started and set up to run in perpetuity.

As much as she enjoyed helping others, she'd love nothing better than to cook and care for one man. As soon as she'd started going to Noah for riding lessons, she'd begun to see that he was just the kind of man she wanted. The kind of man she could see spending the rest of her life with.

But was she the type of woman he could see himself spending the rest of his life with? For weeks, she'd basically lied to him.

Tonight, she'd tell him the truth. If he couldn't forgive her or trust her after that, well then, that was the end of the time she'd spent with him. Sure, as Landry's best friend, she'd see him occasionally, but the long days riding out over Adair Acres with Noah would stop.

She swallowed hard on the lump forming in her throat. She hoped and prayed it wouldn't come to that. In the meantime, she would look her best to deliver her confession.

In her bathroom, she touched up the curls in her hair with a curling iron, applied a light dusting of blush to her cheeks to mask their paleness and added a little gloss to her lips.

Dressing for her confession was more difficult. What did one wear to a declaration of wrongdoing? She pulled a pretty yellow sundress out of the closet, held it up to her body and tossed it aside. Too cheerful.

A red dress was too flamboyant and jeans were too casual. She finally settled on a short black dress with thin straps. Though it could be construed as what she'd wear to her own funeral, it hugged her figure to perfection and made her feel a little more confident. She knew she looked smooth, sleek and pretty.

As she held the dress up to her body, a knock sounded

on the door. She squealed and the hanger slipped from her fingers. "Just a minute!" she called out.

Grabbing the dress off the floor, she unzipped the back and stepped into the garment. Quickly, she slipped it up over her hips and the straps over her shoulders.

"I'm coming," she said, hurrying toward the door as she zipped the dress as far up the back as she could, while running across the living room.

She had her hand on the doorknob, twisting it before she realized she hadn't put on a pair of shoes or sandals. Too late to go back for shoes, she opened the door and her breath caught.

Noah's broad shoulders filled the doorway. Wearing crisp blue jeans and a soft blue polo shirt that matched his eyes and complemented his sandy blond hair, he made her heart slam hard against her chest and then beat so fast she thought she might pass out. "I'm sorry, I was just getting dressed and I forgot shoes, and I haven't started the grill…"

He stepped through the door and closed it behind him. "My fault. I finished my errands earlier than I expected. I could have waited at a park or stopped for coffee, but…I wanted to see you." Already standing close to her, he reached out, cupped her cheek and gazed down into her eyes. "Hey."

"Hey, yourself." She laid her hand against his and leaned into his palm. "I'm glad you came early." And she was. The right clothes, food and shoes didn't mean anything when he was standing in front of her, looking so handsome.

For a moment she thought he was going to kiss her.

He leaned forward, his head dropping low, his lips hovering over hers.

She held her breath, her chin tipping up. She could practically feel his lips on hers. Then the reason she'd invited him to her place popped into her head and she knew she couldn't have that kiss without first revealing what she'd done. But before she could tell him her news, she decided to feed him first. Her tongue snaked out and wet her suddenly dry lips. "If you can wait thirty minutes, I'll cook the steaks and potatoes."

"Where's your grill? I can get that started."

Grills and steaks were the last things on her mind. She could barely think past his broad chest and the way he filled the room in which he stood. "On the balcony," she managed to say, but she couldn't budge. Her feet seemed stuck to the floor.

Noah chuckled. "I don't know about you, but I have the uncontrollable urge to kiss you."

"Same here," she confessed. If only telling him she'd spied on him was easy. "Maybe we should get started cooking, or we won't have anything to eat tonight."

As soon as she stepped away from the hand on her face, she regretted moving at all. She liked how warm and work roughened his palm felt against her skin and wondered what it would feel like if he ran those hands all over her body. She'd gotten a small teaser that afternoon. It wasn't enough. She wanted more.

Ready to retreat to the safe zone of her kitchen, she spun on her bare heels and would have walked away.

Noah's hand closed on her shoulders. "Um, sweetheart, did you have a little trouble getting dressed?"

"What?" Hearing him call her sweetheart made her knees weak.

His fingers brushed the bare skin of her back. "Let me get that zipper for you."

Once again, his rough fingers skimmed across her skin and a shiver of anticipation rippled through her.

"I find myself wanting to skip dinner altogether." Rather than zip the dress up her back, his fingers hesitated.

Rachel closed her eyes, willing herself to control the raging desire rising up like a tsunami inside. "Me, too," she said, all her self-coaching flying out the window with Noah's fingers touching the middle of her naked back.

She leaned against his hand, filling her lungs with much-needed air and letting it out a little at a time, hoping to slow her racing heart.

"Is it wrong to go straight to dessert?" He whispered the words against the back of her neck, his warm breath stirring tendrils of her hair, causing her nerve endings to ignite.

"Who needs steak?" she said, turning in his arms, her determination to hold off until she spoke to him crumbling.

"I can wait to eat."

Resting her hands on his chest, she gazed up into his eyes. "Why now?" she asked.

"Because I ate a late lunch, and I can't think of anything else but kissing you." He bent to brush his mouth across hers.

"No, I mean we've been seeing each other at the ranch for weeks. Why the sudden interest in me now?"

He shook his head, tucking a lock of her hair behind her ear. "Not sudden. I've always been interested. I just didn't know if you returned the interest until today. I was taking it slow."

She snorted. "Slow? You made turtles look speedy." Her eyes narrowed. "And now?"

"And now my life has been turned upside down. The truth as I knew it is a lie, and I don't know anyone anymore. You are the only constant in my life and I guess I was afraid if I didn't do something soon, I'd lose you."

"Oh, Noah, I'm not going anywhere. I was waiting for *you* to show interest in *me*." She bit her bottom lip, knowing now was the time to tell him her part in the events that led up to his DNA test and the revelation that he was Reginald Adair's son. "Noah, I need to tell you something—"

He didn't give her the opportunity. He swept his mouth across hers and deepened the kiss, pushing his tongue past her teeth.

Rachel melted into him, her arms circling the back of his neck. This was where she'd wanted to be. Forgotten were the marinating steaks and the potatoes waiting to be popped into the microwave.

Noah's fingers slid down her back to where she'd half zipped her dress. Instead of sliding the zipper up, he dragged it downward and slipped the straps off her shoulders.

The dress dropped to the floor around her feet and she stood in only a pair of sexy black lace panties. Nothing else.

She dragged his shirt up out of the waistband of his jeans and over his head, tossing it to the floor. Next she unbuckled his belt and slid it through the loops. It joined the shirt. Then she loosened the top button on his fly.

Noah lifted her by the backs of her thighs and backed her against the wall. "If this is going too fast, say the word and I'll stop."

Too fast? He wasn't moving fast enough. "Please, don't stop." She wrapped her legs around his waist and wove her fingers into his hair, bending to press her lips to his temple.

He captured one beaded nipple between his lips and sucked it into his mouth, tonguing it until it tightened into a bud.

Her heart racing, she arched her back and urged him to take more.

Holding her against him, he spun around and carried her to the middle of the living room and settled her on the Persian carpet in the middle. She'd never lain naked on the carpet and felt the deliciously soft texture against her skin.

The sun sinking low on the horizon spread a golden glow over Noah's naked torso, casting him in bronze as he dropped over her, settling between her legs. A shadow moved over him and then disappeared as if something had briefly blocked the sun through the window. Perhaps a bird, a plane or a passing truck on the street outside.

Rachel had been so intent on drinking in his tapered muscles and gleaming chest she wouldn't have noticed the shadow if it hadn't blocked the golden glow.

Then he was kissing her again and she forgot who

she was, that this was supposed to be a dinner date to confess her sins.

Noah caught her mouth in a long, lingering kiss. He scraped his mouth over her chin and down the length of her throat and over her collarbone, angling toward the swells of her breasts.

She rose up to meet him, her breasts beaded and already sensitive to his touch. He tongued one, rolling the nipple between his teeth, then performed the same ritual on the other. Moving downward, he blazed a path of kisses and nips over her belly and down to the apex of her thighs.

Her breathing grew more ragged the lower he swept.

Hooking his fingers into the elastic waistband of her panties, Noah dragged them down her legs and off before tossing them to a corner.

Rachel's knees fell to the side and she raised her hips.

Noah parted her folds and touched her there with his tongue, tapping gently.

Like fireworks exploding in rapid succession, her nerves ignited and sent sparks shooting to the very outer edges of her skin. Her breath caught and she held it as his tongue swirled, flicked and dipped lower, until she catapulted over the edge of reason.

Noah was climbing up her body, his member nudging against her entrance, where he paused.

"Why are you stopping?" she cried, ready to take him inside.

His jaw tight, he gritted between clenched teeth, "Protection." He reached into the back pocket of his jeans and removed his wallet, fumbling through. "Damn."

"You don't have any?"

"No." He stared down at her, a muscle twitching in his jaw. "I don't suppose you do?"

Rachel shook her head, her racing heart barely slowing at the possibility of calling a halt to what she craved so much.

Noah tossed his wallet to the side and bent to kiss her, then rolled to his side and lay on the floor beside her, draping an arm over his forehead. "I'll come more prepared next time."

Rachel turned onto her side and rested her cheek against his chest. "I could run to the drugstore," she offered.

"We can wait." He brushed his fingers over her nipple. "*I* can wait."

"But what if *I* can't?" She caught his hand and pressed his open palm to the full swell of that breast he'd teased.

He dragged in a deep breath and let it out. "There's nothing I want more than to make love to you. But you invited me to dinner, not to take advantage of being alone with you in your apartment. And besides, we probably shouldn't be half-naked in front of your open windows." He winked. "What will the neighbors think?"

"To hell with the neighbors." She pulled him closer to kiss his lips. "But I did invite you to dinner. The least I can do is feed you."

Noah reached over her to the sofa, where a light throw blanket lay. He snagged it and handed it to her.

"It's getting dark outside and the lights on in here will make us even more easily visible to prying eyes."

"Thanks." Her cheeks burning, she wrapped the blanket around her while Noah zipped his jeans, tucking the evidence of his passion inside.

"I'll be just a minute." Rachel rose, grabbed her dress and panties and made a beeline for her bedroom, glancing at the windows as she did. It had gotten darker and there was a woman walking her dog beneath the streetlight. All she'd have to do was turn and she'd have gotten an eyeful.

Her cheeks burning even hotter, Rachel entered her bedroom and closed the door behind her before she dropped the blanket. Holy hell, she had just had the best foreplay of her life and would have gone all the way with Noah had either one of them had protection. And she still hadn't accomplished what she'd intended to. She ducked into the bathroom to splash water over her heated face, wondering how she'd tell him now that they'd made love on her living room floor.

Noah gathered his shirt and slipped it over his shoulders. He moved around the town house as he threaded his belt through the loops on his jeans.

A soft brown leather sofa could have been considered masculine, but the bright pillows in orange, yellow, red and teal tones gave it a cheerful, more feminine appearance. The two overstuffed chairs on either side of the sofa used the same color palette as the pillows, tying the furniture together. The Persian carpet was a modern design made of high quality wool.

Oil paintings strategically placed along the walls

could have been selected by an interior designer to complement the furnishings and accent tables. Everything was tasteful and the overall impression was one of light, broken up by rich colors and textures. It was a warm and inviting home and reflected its owner.

Noah wandered over to the floor-to-ceiling window and searched for the mechanism to close the curtains. When he couldn't find a string or rod, he started to grab the edge of the curtains and drag it over. In the process, he noticed a button on the wall. He pressed it and the curtains started sliding slowly. As he waited for them to close all the way, he glanced out the window. A figure moved in the shadows, just out of reach of the solitary streetlight on the corner. He wouldn't have been concerned if the figure had moved on as if walking home. But it remained just out of the light, standing still, not moving.

A ripple of awareness slid across Noah's skin. Though it seemed ridiculous and paranoid, he felt as though the person outside was staring at him as he stared back. The curtain closed, shutting out the shadow and cocooning Noah and Rachel inside the town house.

Noah shook off the strange feeling and counted it as an overactive imagination. Not everyone in the world had huge secrets, hidden agendas and nefarious motives.

A buzzing sound caught his attention and he found a cell phone on the table beside the sofa. It looked exactly like his so he lifted it and read the writing on the display screen.

It was a text from his half sister, Landry.

Are you going to tell him before or after dinner?

Noah stared at the phone. *Tell him what?* was the first thought in his head. The second being, *Tell who what?* Perhaps she had the wrong number. He was about to respond to her text telling her that when another text flashed onto the screen.

Remember to tell Noah it was my idea and not to blame you.

Confused, he stared down at the phone. It looked like his with the same black protective case and the same make and model. Then he remembered he'd left his phone in his truck. This phone probably belonged to Rachel.

As he came to that conclusion, the meaning of the words made more sense. Landry was asking Rachel if she'd told him something. Obviously it was something that he might not like, if she was looking to take the blame for it.

Now the phone had his full attention. Like a sleepwalker, he couldn't stop himself. He held the phone in both hands and slowly keyed, What should I tell him?

He knew it was wrong and that he was violating Rachel's privacy by reading her text messages, but after all the lies he'd been told and all the secrets he hadn't been a party to until now, he had a sinking feeling in his gut that this was going to be another one to add to the mounting list.

What could Rachel and Landry have done that was so bad he'd get mad? He'd always thought of Rachel as someone he could trust, someone who wasn't a member of the family, who didn't have a stake in Reginald's will.

He almost set the phone aside, not wanting to have his faith in Rachel shattered. As he moved his hand to do that, another text popped up on the screen.

Be straightforward. Tell him about spying on him and why we did it.

A lead weight settled in the pit of Noah's belly.

Chapter 4

Dressed now in the soft lemon-yellow sundress and feeling more in control of her thoughts and her body, Rachel stepped out of the bedroom, a smile curving her lips. "I bet you're hungry."

Noah had his back to her and seemed to be staring down at something in his hand, his body stiff and unbending.

"Noah?" A cold sensation trickled down her spine as she crossed the room to where he stood and touched his arm.

He jerked away.

Her heart pinched in her chest. "Is something wrong?"

"I thought it was mine." Turning, he held out a cell phone. "But it wasn't. Landry texted you." He stared straight into her eyes.

Rachel could feel the blood leaving her face. She didn't have to look down at the phone to get the gist of what he'd discovered. "I was going to tell you tonight."

"Before or after we made love?" he asked, his voice soft, barely above a whisper, but the anger behind it as hard and as sharp as a steel-edged knife.

"Before. But—"

Noah held up a hand. "Save it. I need to go back to where I belong." He snorted. "Trouble is that I don't know where I belong anymore. I don't think there is a soul in this world I can trust."

"Please, Noah. I can explain."

"What's to explain? You were spying on me." He jammed his shirt into the waistband of his jeans and buckled his belt. "You did a good job of fooling me. You're a good actress, Rachel. And I suppose you always knew how to ride a horse. And you were probably acting when you pretended to like me."

"No. I mean yes, about the riding, but no, I really do like you."

"You and Landry must have had a really good laugh about me." He bent to grab his wallet from the floor.

"No, Noah, it wasn't like that." Once again, she touched his arm. "It started out as a favor. But my feelings changed. I got to know you. You're kind, gentle and patient and I could see what a good person you are, and I genuinely like you."

This time, when he jerked his arm away, his lip curled back in contempt. "The sad thing is that I really want to believe you."

"You can. Just give me another chance."

"No. I'm done playing games with you and the

Adairs. I may be related by blood, but I'm not like them and have no desire to be like them. And I guarantee, I won't let my guard down ever again." Noah reached the door, yanked it open and marched out.

"I didn't mean to hurt you," Rachel called out, her voice trailing off on a sob as Noah slammed the door behind him.

The phone in her hand buzzed and she looked down at it through a wash of tears.

Did you get my last text?

Rachel sank to the floor, tears trickling down her cheeks as she read through the messages. It couldn't have been worse timing. After several minutes, she texted Landry— He knows.

And?

Rachel stared at the word and couldn't move her hands to respond.

More tears escaped.

Landry's ringtone sang out and Rachel nearly dropped the phone. When she finally held it steady, she pressed the talk button and pressed the phone to her ear.

"Rachel, honey, are you okay?" The sound of her friend's voice only made the tears flow heavier. "Sweetie, are you there?"

She swallowed her sob and croaked, "I'm here."

"He didn't take it well, did he?"

"No. I feel like my heart has been ripped out of my chest. Is that normal?"

"Oh, baby, you've got it bad."

"I know." She sniffed and reached for a tissue in the box on an end table. "I wasn't supposed to care. He was just the interloper."

"But you do."

"Yeah." She dabbed at her puffy eyes. "I do, and he's part of your family now."

"Do you want me to come over?"

"No. I'll be all right. No one ever died of a broken heart." She laughed, though it sounded more like a sob. "I'll be okay."

"You don't sound okay. I'm coming over," Landry insisted.

"No, that's not necessary. I really can't stay here." Rachel lurched to her feet, too upset to be alone. "Do you mind if I come over to your place?"

"Not at all. Come. Stay the night. We can crack open a bottle of wine. I could call Georgia over and maybe we can put our heads together and finalize Elizabeth's baby shower. That might take your mind off Noah."

Rachel doubted it. Baby talk would only make her want to be with Noah even more. She could picture sandy-haired, blue-eyed little boys with those cute little clefts in their chins. She had to stop thinking that way. It would never happen now. "Let's keep it just you and me, if you don't mind."

"Not at all."

"Wait." Rachel stopped on her way to her bedroom. "What will Derek think about giving you up for a night?"

"Don't you worry about him," Landry said. "I love that man like no other, but he can live without me for a night. He'll understand. You've always been there for me. It's my turn."

Rachel glanced around the town house. There was nothing holding her there. No reason to stay and plenty of reasons to leave. "I'm on my way. I'll see you in thirty minutes."

"Are you sure you're up to driving?" Landry asked. "I could come get you?"

"No. I'll manage." Rachel ended the call and stood in the middle of the living room trying to think through her next step. She wanted to go to Landry's place. Staying in the room where she and Noah had shared their passion just made her want to cry. She had to get away.

Grabbing her purse, she slung the strap over her shoulder, dug her car keys out of the bottom and headed for the door. She was halfway outside when she remembered she hadn't put on any shoes. Back in the town house, she dug out a pair of sandals and headed out the door, locking it behind her.

Night had settled in around San Diego and streetlights shone out over the city below. From her hillside townhome, Rachel could see much of the city and the harbor below dotted in lights.

She climbed into her car and pulled down her driveway, blinking through the tears welling up yet again. She never cried this much. And never over a man. She'd learned long ago not to fall in love. Hadn't her mother taught her that?

Rachel's multibillionaire father had cheated on her mother more often than either her mother or Rachel knew about. When her mother finally decided enough was enough, she'd filed for divorce.

Rachel's father had the lawyers, the sleazy private investigators who'd lie for a case of beer and the financial backing to smear her mother through the sludge at the bottom of the San Diego Bay. He'd even tried to turn Rachel against her mother.

When the divorce was final and the dust had settled, Rachel's mother had bought a small vineyard on the edge of San Diego and retired from the social circles and the people she'd thought were her friends. She'd since passed away and left Rachel the vineyard and a nice little nest egg.

Not that she needed it. Her father had had a massive heart attack while making love to a woman half his age. He'd left her his entire fortune and the job of managing the charities her mother had set up.

Rachel teetered on the edge of society, using her social status to help in her efforts to raise money for the charities near and dear to hers and her mother's hearts, especially for the navy SEALs and the families of those men who gave so much for their country. Helping them was her way of giving back what her father never could.

Soured on men, she'd agreed to spy on Noah, not knowing what she knew now.

He was a genuinely good man. The kind of man a woman could trust not to cheat on her or lie. Unfortunately, she'd done what she despised in others. She'd lied to him about her real reason for hanging around him. What had started out as an effort to help her friend had become more complicated the more Rachel got to know Noah.

Her breath caught on a sob and she forced it down as she drove to the end of her driveway. When Rachel reached the road, she couldn't pull out on the street. A large dark sedan parked in front of her driveway, blocking her exit.

Already upset about the events of the evening, she didn't feel like confronting the driver, or anyone for that matter. The interior of the vehicle was dark, but she could see the shadowy shape of someone inside.

Rachel honked her horn. The vehicle remained where it was. Not a light came on inside or out.

Anger shifted to concern. Was the driver injured or unconscious? Was that why he wasn't moving?

Pushing her own heartache aside, Rachel unclipped her seat belt and climbed out of her Jeep. "Hello!" she called out loudly enough to be heard by the driver inside the car.

The person didn't move and the interior remained too dark to make out the face to see if his eyes were opened or closed.

Rachel edged toward the vehicle. If this was a ruse to get her out of her car to abduct her, she didn't want to get too close. But she had to get close enough to tell whether or not the driver was in physical distress.

As she neared the front fender, the engine roared to life and the car shifted into Reverse, backing up so fast the tires squealed, leaving a thin layer of rubber on the pavement.

Alarmed, Rachel backed a step up onto the driveway. She was partly relieved the car had moved, even though the movement was odd. Why would a person wait until she'd almost reached the car before he revved the engine and backed out of the way?

Convinced the driver was on drugs or drunk, Rachel glanced over her shoulder at her Jeep.

The squeal of rubber on asphalt made her turn back to the big sedan. It screeched to a halt and the headlights flashed on, the high beams blinding her.

Raising her hand to block the light, she backed another step up the driveway.

The engine revved again and tires spun on the pavement, the vehicle rocketing forward.

Stunned, Rachel froze as the heavy sedan barreled straight for her. When the car bumped up over the curb, slamming metal against concrete, Rachel finally snapped out of it, but too late to avoid impact.

She knew it was going to hit her—all she could do was minimize the impact. As she'd seen done in the movies by trained stuntmen, she slammed her hands on the hood of the vehicle and swung her legs up and to the side like a gymnast on a vault. She slid across the hood, smacked into the glass and rolled off to the side, landing flat on her back. Her head bounced on the concrete.

Pain flashed through her and the streetlight on the corner blinked out.

Noah headed for Adair Acres, the only home he knew. He drove through the gate, past the guesthouse and straight for the stable. At least the horses weren't deceitful and out to question his every move. They could care less how much money he had or how he planned to spend it. All they wanted was to be treated with respect and be fed regularly. Why couldn't life be that simple?

The last person he could count on had just proved to him that he couldn't trust anyone at all. He shoved the gearshift into Park, climbed down from his truck and strode into the stable.

Diablo nickered from his stall, pawing at the door for attention.

Noah grabbed a brush from the tack room and led the stallion out of his stall, tying his lead to a post. Then he brushed the horse from nose to tail, one long, smooth stroke at a time.

At first Diablo tossed his head and stamped his hooves. Either he was able to sense Noah's unrest and it made him uneasy, as well, or he was impatient for another ride out across the fields, the wind in his mane.

Forcing himself to slow down and take it easy, Noah soothed the horse and continued brushing with calmer motions until the stallion stood steady, accepting the attention.

When he was done, he stroked the horse's velvety soft nose. "I trust you more than any of the Adairs, and you threw me this morning."

Diablo nickered, almost as if chuckling at his accomplishment in unseating Noah.

"Yeah. I deserved it. I was pushing you too hard when it was my own problem." Noah sighed. "The question is what should I do?"

"If you're waiting for the horse to answer, you might be waiting awhile." Carson Adair, with his light brown hair cropped short and military bearing from years in the Marine Corps, stood ramrod straight, his arms crossed over his chest in the open doorway to the stable.

"He's the only one who makes sense."

Carson's lips twisted and he nodded. "You have a point. Things have been insane around here." Carson's eyes narrowed, his brows drawing together. "Landry tells me you talked with Rachel."

Noah grabbed the horse's lead, walked him back to his stall and settled him in. "Are there any more spies I should be aware of? Hell, if you'd just asked, I'd have told you everything I know. Even as cousins, I thought we were family."

"Like you, we don't know who to trust. They still haven't caught our father's killer."

Noah stepped back as if he'd been slapped. "Good Lord. Did you think I'd done it?" Noah closed and secured the stall door before facing Carson. "Should I add 'potential murderer' to the title of 'gold-digging secret son' as a caption on my dossier?"

"He was *your* father, too."

"It takes more than a sperm donation to be a father."

Carson snorted. "Tell me about it. Reginald Adair was too busy looking for you to be much of a father to the rest of his children."

"At least you had each other." Noah carried the brush into the tack room.

"He might not have been much of a father to us, but he left a significant chunk of his estate to a son no one seemed to be able to find. When Georgia suggested you might be that missing son, naturally, we thought you might have ulterior motives."

"Naturally." Noah snorted. "Like I might have ingratiated myself with the family in order to knock off the old man?"

"Think about it. Our father is shot to death and you

came back to Adair Acres. The will was read and then Georgia pointed out how much you looked like her stepmother. The pieces all fell into a strange place. What would you have done if you were us?"

Noah let Carson's words flow over him and settle into the crevices of his mind before answering. "I would have asked me what the hell I was up to."

Diablo nickered and tossed his head over the top of the stall's gate.

With Carson's explanation making more sense than he liked, Noah needed to keep moving. He walked to the stack of hay on one end of the stable, broke off a couple sections of one bale and carried it back to Diablo's stall, dropping it into the manger.

Noah dusted the hay from his hands and shirt. "Did you really think I could have killed your father?"

"Not once we heard your alibi, but you could have hired someone to do him in."

The irony of the situation was not lost on Noah. Reginald's kids had such mixed feelings about losing their father. He'd barely given them much thought, his entire focus spent on finding his missing son—an obsession he couldn't shake for thirty-seven years.

The older Adair's murder had hit Noah harder. Reginald had welcomed him to come work at the ranch. He'd been his only male role model Noah's entire life. He used to imagine being part of the larger Adair family. Whit, Carson and Landry may not have been close to Reginald, but they cared about one another and made it clear they'd do anything for their siblings.

"Look, you have a right to be angry with us. We shouldn't have spied on you, but we wanted to protect each other and our heritage. Don't blame Rachel. Landry talked her into doing it. If you don't believe me, ask Landry."

Noah didn't want to believe Carson, but the sincerity of the former Marine was hard to dispute. He'd always respected the man and now was no different.

"It's like I told Rachel," Noah said. "I don't know who to trust anymore."

"I don't blame you. We still haven't found Dad's killer. It could be anyone. We're all struggling to figure this out."

Noah sighed. "Is that why you came here, tonight?"

Carson gave him half a smile. "Yeah. Landry and I felt responsible. If I'm not mistaken, Rachel has a thing for you. I'd hate to see something we asked her to do cause a rift between the two of you. I almost lost Georgia due to my own pigheadedness."

Carson and Georgia had their share of issues to overcome. But they had and they were together now, and happy.

Noah began to suspect he might have overreacted to Rachel's deception.

"I bet if you just talk to Rachel, you'll see that she didn't mean any harm by spying on you. She and Landry are like sisters. If Landry had known then that Rachel would fall for you, she wouldn't have asked her to spy on you. And no matter what you might think, Rachel wouldn't hurt anyone intentionally."

Guilt hit Noah in the chest, making his heart hurt. Rachel had tried to tell him the truth. Now that he'd had time to calm down and think about it, he had to admit to himself that she'd tried more than once, the first time being out on the ranch by the creek.

Oh, hell. She'd tried that night and he'd kissed her so long she didn't have time tell him before he carried her to the living room floor and made love to her.

He glanced across at Carson. "I have to go." He pushed past Carson, headed for his truck.

"Where are you going?" Carson called out.

"To find Rachel."

"Hey, man, good luck with that. Rachel's a good person. I'm sure she'll forgive you."

An hour ago Noah thought he might never forgive Rachel for the part she'd played spying on him for the Adairs. Now he was hurrying to apologize to her for blowing up.

As he raced down the long drive to the ranch gate, he fumbled with his cell phone in the dark. He scrolled through his contacts, hit Rachel's phone number and waited. It rang five times and her voice mail picked up.

"Hi, this is Rachel. I'm unable to come to the phone at this time. Leave a message and I'll get back to you as soon as possible." Her voice was light, cheerful and made Noah realize what an idiot he'd been. At the very least, he should have given her the opportunity to explain herself.

He ended the call without leaving a message. What would he say? *I'm sorry?* He was still torn by the fact she'd lied to him. But he couldn't blame her for helping a friend and he understood why the Adairs wanted to keep an eye on him.

He paused as the electronic gate swung open and he dialed Rachel's number again.

Before it could connect, another call came in. Landry's name flashed in the display window.

Driving through the open gate, he ended the call to Rachel and answered Landry's. "Landry."

"Oh, thank God," she gushed. "I wasn't sure you'd answer your phone."

The tension in Landry's voice caught Noah's attention and he pressed the cell phone to his ear and squeezed the device. "What's wrong?"

"I can't get ahold of Rachel," Landry said.

Though he hadn't had any success contacting her, Noah hadn't been too concerned. "Maybe she's in the shower."

"No, she said she was leaving her apartment fifty minutes ago. She should have been here twenty minutes ago."

"Could she have stopped for gas?"

"It wouldn't take her twenty extra minutes to put gas in her car."

"Look, Landry, I'm headed that way. I'll stop by her apartment and see if she's there."

"Thanks. You'll let me know if she's not?"

"I will."

"Oh, and, Noah?"

"Yes, Landry?"

"Don't blame Rachel for spying on you. I asked her to."

Noah's jaw tightened. "She didn't have to say yes."

"She's my friend. At the time I asked, she didn't know you."

Unable to let go of all of his anger, he argued, "She could have told me sooner."

"I asked her to wait until after the DNA results were in. Please, don't be mad at Rachel. She's upset enough as it is. Just try not to be mad at her."

He didn't want to argue on the telephone while driving. Besides, Landry sounded worried enough, which worried him even more. "I'll try."

"I guess that's all I can expect. I'm sorry." Landry paused. "Find her, Noah."

Noah pressed the accelerator to the floor and the truck leaped forward. He told himself Rachel was fine, that she'd changed her mind on visiting Landry and stayed at home to get in the shower.

The more he thought about it, the less reasonable that theory sounded. His gut told him all was not well. He hit the redial on Rachel's number and it rang over again to her voice mail.

Halfway to San Diego and several calls to Rachel later with no response had him speeding twenty miles per hour over the posted limit.

His phone rang and he took his eyes off the road long enough to note Landry's name on the display screen. Oh, good. She'd be calling to say Rachel had arrived and that she was fine.

"Did she make it there?" he asked without saying hello.

"No."

His pulse ratcheted and he tightened his grip on the steering wheel until his knuckles turned white.

"She's been in an accident."

His heart plummeted and his foot left the accelerator. "What happened?"

"She was hit by a car. She's being taken to the hospital as we speak."

Chapter 5

Pain shot through the back of Rachel's head to the front. She tried to open her eyes, but the light seeping through the gap in her eyelids only caused the pain to intensify.

"Hey, sleepyhead…" A warm, rich tone wrapped around her and a large, gentle hand squeezed hers.

This time when she opened her eyes, she pushed past the pain and stared up, as if through a haze, into blue eyes. "Noah?"

"Yeah, it's me, babe." He smoothed the hair back from her forehead, his fingers warm and gentle.

She closed her eyes again and moaned. "I'd give my eyeteeth for a painkiller."

"I'll let the nurse know."

"No, wait." She reached out to grab his arm.

Noah covered the hand on his arm. "I'm waiting."

"I'm sorry." Forcing her eyes open again, she stared up at Noah until her vision cleared. "I should have told you."

"Don't worry about it. Just rest and get to feeling better."

"Easier said than done." She moaned. "I feel like I have an elephant sitting on my head."

"The doctor said you had a minor concussion and a few bruises and scrapes, but no broken bones. You're lucky. You should be fine in a couple days."

"When can I go home?"

"We'll talk about that later. Let me get the nurse to bring some pain medication for that headache." He slipped out of the room and returned a few minutes later with a nurse carrying a small cup with pills in it. She cranked the bed up to a sitting position, handed her the medicine in the cup and got her a cup of water with a straw.

Rachel cracked her eyelids open, blinked several times and got dizzy with the amount of movement.

When the nurse stopped in front of her and held out the cup with the straw, it was all Rachel could do to hold the medicine.

"Here, let me." Noah took the cup with the straw from the nurse and added, "Thank you."

The woman left the room and Noah held the cup close to Rachel's mouth. "Take the pills, they'll make you feel better."

She popped the pills into her mouth, the bitter taste on her tongue almost gagging her.

Noah positioned the straw for her to take between her lips without having to move her head.

She had to swallow twice to get the pills to slide down her dry throat. Then she washed them down more with several additional sips. That little bit of effort left her head aching and she sank back against the pillows, closing her eyes.

"How long have I been out?"

"A few hours. It'll be morning soon."

"Landry—" She struggled to get up.

"Is the one who called me. She went downstairs to the cafeteria for some coffee."

"I'm so sorry to keep you two up."

"What do you have to be sorry about?" He set the water on the table and sat in a chair he pulled up close to the bed. Taking her hand, he asked, "Do you know what happened to you?"

She frowned, the effort making her head hurt worse, so she relaxed her brow and tried to think. "The last thing I remember is getting into my Jeep to go to Landry's."

"A neighbor found you on the ground by the road, your Jeep parked in the driveway. Do you remember getting out?"

Flashes of light blinded her and pain knifed through her head. She squeezed her eyes shut as the memories returned, like unraveling the threads of a blanket. "There was a car."

Noah encouraged. "Go on."

"It was parked in front of my driveway." She opened her eyes and stared into his as the terror of the night before flooded back. "When I got out to tell him to move, he backed up and…and ran me over."

"You're okay now," Noah said, his voice strained but comforting. His jaw tightened and a muscle flickered in the side of his cheek. He lifted her hand in his and held it to his cheek. "I'm surprised you weren't hurt more seriously."

She stared at Noah, but she wasn't seeing him as the memory ran through her head like the replay of a sporting event. "He aimed for me. He backed up and aimed for me, running up over the curb to hit me."

"How did you keep from being crushed?"

Her lips twitched. "From watching action movies."

"Action movies?" He laughed. "How did that help?"

"When I saw it was going to hit, I planted my hands on the hood and vaulted onto it. When he turned back to the street, I slid off and hit the ground. That's all I remember until now."

He shook his head, a smile tipping the corners of his lips. "Apparently you did the right thing. Other than a bump on the back of your head, you were pretty much unscathed. It could have been so much worse."

"But why?" She raised her arm to block the light shining into her eyes. "Why would someone run me down?"

"We were hoping you'd shed more light." Landry stepped into the room, carrying two cups of coffee.

The pungent scent drifted across the room, tempting Rachel. "Is one of those for me?"

"Not unless the doc gives you the okay."

Rachel closed her eyes, the effort to keep them open almost too much. "That's okay, it smells good, but I'm not sure what my stomach can handle right now."

"Rachel, the police were here earlier wanting to question you on the accident."

"Do you remember what the vehicle looked like?" Noah asked.

"It was a dark four-door sedan," she replied.

Noah squeezed her hand. "Did you happen to see a license plate?"

"No."

"Can you identify who was driving?"

"No. The windows were dark and there weren't any interior lights to light up his face. Then the headlights came on and it blinded me." The headlights bearing down on her flashed through her memory. Her fingers curled into the sheets. "The car ran up over the curb. I didn't have time to get out of the way. I knew it was going to hit me." Her entire body trembled.

Noah sat on the edge of the bed and gathered her in his embrace, easing his arm around her carefully so that he didn't hurt her.

Landry stood on the opposite side of the bed and held her hand. "I'm so sorry, sweetie. I should have come to you."

"It's not your fault. I shouldn't have left," Rachel said, clinging to Noah's shirt, still shaking so hard her teeth rattled. "It was like a nightmare. I couldn't move fast enough."

Noah stiffened as he held her, his broad hand brushing down the length of her arm, in long, soothing strokes, as much to calm her as to temper the rage building inside him. "You two are missing the point.

Rachel wasn't hit because of what either of you did or didn't do. Someone purposely tried to run her over."

Landry stared at Rachel. "But who? Rachel is one of the kindest, most gentle people I know. She wouldn't hurt anyone. Why would anyone want to hurt her?"

"Do you have a jealous old boyfriend?" Noah asked Rachel.

She shook her head. "No. I've been so busy with my various philanthropies, I haven't had time to do anything but my riding lessons."

"Have you had any issues with anyone on your charity committees or whatever organizations you belong to?"

Again Rachel shook her head. "No. I don't try to be the boss. I just help out where I can, bringing in sponsors."

"I'm on some of those committees, Noah," Landry confirmed. "Everyone loves Rachel."

Rachel laughed, the sound more like a sob. "Apparently someone doesn't."

His chest squeezed at the miserable sound. Everything he'd seen of Rachel matched what Landry and Carson said. She wouldn't hurt anyone intentionally. She was basically nice and loved by most.

His arms tightened around her. He couldn't stand seeing her hurt. At the same time, he struggled with what he suspected were growing feelings for this woman.

He refused to get too involved in the drama and pain revolving around the people who were supposed to be his family. Rachel had proven she was one of them, having spied on him for their benefit. Still he didn't want harm to come to her.

"Has anyone tried to hurt you in the past?" Noah persisted.

"No," Rachel responded.

Landry let go of Rachel's hand and paced the floor. "It seems as though the Adair luck has rubbed off on you." She stopped in the middle of the floor and ticked off on her fingers. "First, my father was murdered in his own office. Then our mother going all crazy, trying to kill Whit's wife, and Derek's near miss with his ex's boyfriend. Seems like anyone having anything to do with an Adair is either being shot at, stabbed, framed or something equally horrible." Her brows rose. "And that goes for my aunt Kate, as well. We're a cursed family."

As Landry counted off the events, Noah wanted to refute everything she was saying, but he couldn't. In fact, someone had been lurking around Rachel's apartment. He remembered the shadow hovering outside Rachel's living room window. "I hate to agree with you, Landry, but until I stepped past riding lessons to seeing Rachel at her apartment, she hadn't had any trouble."

"Noah, I was just kidding."

"No. I think you have something. Since I've been at the ranch, the Adairs have had nothing but trouble. Everyone loved Rachel until I got involved with her."

"Uh, it takes two to get involved." Rachel lay back against the pillow, still holding on to Noah's hand. "Just so you know, I'm conscious—you don't have to talk like I'm not in the room."

"Sorry, sweetie." Landry smiled at her friend and then faced Noah again. She sucked in a deep breath and let it out. "I'm almost sad it turned out that you're my half brother. Now that everyone knows Noah is an

Adair, you will be suffering the Adair curse. You and anyone who dares associate with you." She rolled her eyes toward Rachel.

Noah faced Rachel, as well.

Rachel held up her hands. "That's ridiculous. Who would come after me just because I kissed an Adair?" As soon as the words left her mouth, her cheeks flushed a rosy red.

Landry grinned. "I knew you two had to be doing more than talking about horses on those long rides out on the ranch."

Noah narrowed his eyes as he considered Landry's suggestion of an Adair curse.

Rachel pointed a finger at Noah. "Don't frown at me. I'm not your problem to be solved."

"Actually, I'm thinking you are. If someone came after you because of me, who's to say he won't do it again?"

The color leached out of Rachel's face. For a moment she didn't say anything. Then she squared her shoulders and faced him, her chin lifting. "I don't need your sympathy or your protection. I can take care of myself."

Noah raised his brows. "Like you did last night?"

"I'm alive, aren't I?" she challenged. "Now that I know I could be a target, I'll be better prepared."

Noah shook his head before she finished talking. "I can't risk it."

"You don't have to risk it."

Landry laid a hand on her arm. "Noah's right. You live alone, without a security system on your apartment. If someone is after you, you don't stand much of a chance."

"I'll buy a gun," Rachel insisted.

Noah shook his head. "That takes too much time. You might not have a day, much less at least a week to find, register, buy and qualify with the weapon."

"Then I'll hire a bodyguard." Rachel turned to Landry. "Your aunt Kate was vice president of the United States. She should know of a good bodyguard."

"Even if Kate can recommend a bodyguard, that takes time, too," Noah said. "In the meantime, you'll be exposed."

"I'll get a dog," Rachel stated.

Landry shook her head. "Didn't you tell me that your apartment doesn't allow pets? Honey, you need to come stay out at the ranch. At least there we have a security system and plenty of us around to run interference should you get into trouble."

"No," Noah said.

Landry stared at him. "No? But she won't be safe in her own apartment."

"Agreed. She's not staying at her apartment and she's not going to the ranch house." Noah's gaze pinned Rachel's without wavering.

She frowned, her eyes narrowing. "Oh, no you don't. I won't do it."

"Yes, you will," he said.

"What do you mean? Won't do what?" Landry stared from Rachel to Noah and back. "Am I missing something?"

"I like living alone. I can take care of myself," Rachel insisted, her voice fading off.

Noah stood tall, firm in what he knew he had to do.

"If I'm the reason someone is after you, I need to be the one to protect you."

"You're under no obligation to protect me. It's not as though we are dating, engaged or married. You don't even *like* me," she wailed, and clasped a hand to her head, wincing. "You're making my head hurt." Rachel pointed to the door. "Get out."

Landry grinned. "Are you going to move in with Rachel?"

Rachel covered her eyes with her arm. "No, he's not."

"No, I'm not," Noah agreed.

"You're not?" Rachel and Landry said at once.

Rachel pushed to a sitting position and stared at Noah. "Good, because I don't need your help."

Landry's eyes widened. "You're not moving in with her and she's not coming to the ranch. How are you going to protect her?"

"Oh, I'll protect her, all right." He crossed his arms over his chest. "She's going to come stay at the guesthouse with me."

"Oh, no, I'm not." Rachel crossed her arms just like Noah.

Noah almost laughed at her stubborn expression as she sat in the hospital bed, her hair in disarray. If not for the danger of the situation, he would have laughed out loud. But there was nothing funny about Rachel being run over by some idiot in a sedan.

"You're coming to the guesthouse." Staring down at her, he spoke firmly. He wouldn't take no for an answer. "And that's all there is to it."

"I can't." She smiled at him smugly. "I promised

my neighbor I'd watch her dog for her while she was on vacation."

Noah frowned. "When?"

"Starting tomorrow." She glanced at the window. "Sorry, make that today. Damn." Rachel grabbed the sheet and started to throw it off of her lap. "I promised to check in with her at eight o'clock. Her plane leaves at eleven. She's going to visit her grandchildren in Virginia."

"She can find a kennel to care for the dog. You've been injured."

"I made a promise to Mrs. Davis I'd keep Sophia for her. She doesn't trust anyone but me. Besides to get a reservation in the best kennels you have to be on their lists months in advance."

"She'll have to deal with it. You're coming to the guesthouse with me as soon as you're released from the hospital."

Rachel started to shake her head and stopped, grimaced and pinched the bridge of her nose. "You're not listening. I can't. I have to be close to Mrs. Davis's house so that I can check on Sophia at the very least three times a day."

"Then I'll move in with you."

Her lips firmed and she dropped her hand into her lap. "My place isn't big enough for the two of us."

"It was last night," he said before he could stop himself.

Her cheeks reddened. "That was last night. You've stated your opinion of me since then, and I tell you, the apartment is not nearly big enough for both of us."

"Rachel, honey, the point to this exercise is to keep

you safe," Landry reasoned. "If you don't move to the ranch either in the main house or the guesthouse, you could be in danger."

"Then I'll move Mrs. Davis's dog into my house. I said I'd get a dog and there you have it."

Noah's brows dipped. "What kind of dog?"

Rachel squirmed in the bed before admitting, "It's a teacup Yorkie."

His lips twitching on the corners, Noah managed to say, "I can see how a dog that size will protect you."

"Sophia is a very fierce Yorkie. She bit the mailman once."

Noah snorted. "I bet he's terrified now."

Landry laughed out loud. "Seriously, Rachel. A Yorkie isn't a guard dog. The best she can do is bark to alert you."

"Better than any alarm system around, if you ask me."

"And if someone is about to break in? Then what? You wait for him to trip over the dog?" Noah couldn't believe he was having this argument with her. Couldn't she see that she needed protection and she wasn't going to get it from a dog the size of a rat?

The door to the room opened and a young woman in a white lab coat with a stethoscope draped around her neck walked in and gave Noah and Landry a stern look. "Are we having a party? I can hear the noise all the way out in the hallway."

"Pardon me." Noah's cheeks heated and he stepped back from Rachel's bed.

"We were just discussing what was best for Rachel," Landry said.

"Perhaps I can weigh in on the conversation?" The doctor smiled and held out her hand to Noah. "I'm Dr. Adams, Miss Blackstone's physician."

"Good, maybe you can talk sense into her," Noah said, shaking the woman's hand.

"Hello, Dr. Adams." Landry shook hands with the doctor. "Please, maybe she'll listen to you."

"Miss Blackstone has suffered from a mild concussion. When she's released from the hospital, she'll need someone with her for the next twenty-four to forty-eight hours."

Landry snorted and propped her hands on her hips. "See? You aren't staying by yourself."

"Then you can stay with me," Rachel was quick to point out.

Noah held up his hand. "We'll discuss this when you get clearance from Dr. Adams to leave."

"That will be soon, since I'm here to perform one last check and then sign the release forms. If you'd like, you could bring your car around the front of the hospital while Miss Blackstone and I go through checkout."

Feeling as though he'd been dismissed, Noah left the room, took the elevator down to the lobby and exited to the parking lot. He couldn't leave things the way they were. Deep down he was convinced Rachel wasn't safe and he couldn't just wait until the next bit of bad luck happened along to confirm. Next time, she might not be so lucky as to survive.

The sun had risen over the horizon. A few fluffy white clouds floated on what promised to be a bright and beautiful clear blue sky.

As he walked to his truck, he pulled his telephone

out of his pocket and dialed the nonemergency number for the San Diego Police Department. He was passed around several times before he landed with the detective working Rachel's hit-and-run case.

"Detective Grant speaking."

Noah gave him the information Rachel had imparted to him earlier.

"Thanks, Mr. Scott. I'll need Miss Blackstone to come in to a file a statement as soon as she's feeling up to it."

"Have you found out anything?"

"Nothing. We canvassed the area, talked to the neighbors. Most of them were asleep when the attack occurred. Her next-door neighbor, a Mrs. Davis, found Miss Blackstone when her dog's barking woke her. She looked out in time to see a dark sedan speeding away from the scene, but she didn't get a license plate or description of the assailant. If not for the dog, Miss Blackstone could have been there all night."

Noah agreed to swing by on their way to Rachel's apartment. He still wasn't convinced staying in San Diego at Rachel's apartment was the right thing to do, but he'd work on that angle when he had Rachel in his truck. He couldn't leave her alone until they found the culprit.

And he had to admit, he was feeling a large amount of gratitude to Mrs. Davis and her barking dog. He sighed. How could he tell Mrs. Davis to put the little dog into a kennel now? Not only would he be watching out for Rachel, but now he'd have to include the little dog that had quite possibly saved her.

By the time he'd completed his call, found his truck

and pulled up to the front of the hospital, Rachel was waiting in a wheelchair by the door with Landry standing beside her. Dressed in the yellow dress she'd worn the night before, she'd brushed her hair neatly back from her forehead. The sun glanced off the top of her head, bringing out the red and gold highlights in her light brown hair, making her look radiant and almost angelic, her green eyes sparkling in the cool morning air.

His heart hitched. Had she not been as quick thinking as she had been when the car came barreling toward her, she might not be alive today.

As mad as he'd been, he couldn't discount the knowledge he might have lost her the night before.

Noah climbed down and rounded the front of the truck.

"I can get in myself," Rachel insisted. "For that matter, why don't I ride with Landry?"

"You're riding with me," he said, brooking no argument.

"Fine." She glared at him. "You don't have to be so cranky."

Landry chuckled behind her. "Oh, sweetie, you give that man hell."

"You're not helping," Noah muttered.

"Rachel, do you want me to come by and stay with you during the day?" Landry bent to give Rachel a hug. "You know I will."

"Yes." Rachel grabbed her friend's arm and glared at Noah. "I would prefer that over having Mister Bossy Pants hovering inside my apartment."

"Too bad," Noah said. "As you mentioned, your

apartment is too small for the two of us. If I'm there, it'll be much too small for three."

Landry stared at Rachel. "Your apartment's too small? I thought it was one of the largest in the complex."

Rachel shifted her glare to Landry.

Noah laughed.

Landry's eyes widened. "Oh, I get it. It's too small for Mister Bossy Pants." She shrugged and gave Noah a weak grin. "I guess you're on your own. Call me if you need me for anything. And I mean anything." She laid a hand on Noah's arm. "Again, I'm sorry for setting Rachel up to spy on you. You're a good man, Noah." She winked. "I know that now, brother."

Noah helped Rachel out of the wheelchair and up into the truck, planting a hand on her firm derriere and liking it far too much.

"Hey. I told you I could do this on my own." She hopped into the seat and swung her legs into the cab.

"I know." He rounded the truck, his jaw tightening, his hand tingling from where it had touched her. He hoped the police found the hit-and-run suspect soon. He wasn't sure how long he could stand being this close to Rachel and not touching her.

Chapter 6

Rachel sat in the passenger seat, her head aching from her clash with the mystery driver in the dark sedan. But that didn't really account for the way her stomach churned just by being in close quarters with Noah.

Last night he'd told her he didn't trust anyone, including her. Had he changed his mind? For a moment, she dared to hope and glanced his way.

The dark scowl creasing his forehead didn't give her any indication.

"Wouldn't it be easier to print a public announcement that you and I aren't seeing each other? If I'm being targeted because of you, someone has it all wrong." She waved her hand between the two of them. "You and I aren't a thing."

"I didn't mention it last night because I didn't think

it had any bearing at the time, but I thought I saw a shadow lurking around your window."

She stared across at him, heat rising in her cheeks. "When?"

"When we were lying on the living room floor."

The wind was sucked from Rachel's lungs as her cheeks flamed. "Oh, my God. Someone was watching us?" She pressed her palms to her face, trying to breathe normally. "That's just creepy."

"I blew it off thinking I'd imagined it, but after you were attacked, I realize it might not have been all in my mind."

She wrapped her arms around her middle. "I'll never be able to open my blinds again."

"I wouldn't worry too much. You'd have to be right up against the window to see what was happening on the living room floor."

"But we were standing up by the door when it all started. I took off my shirt!" Rachel shook her head. "How embarrassing."

"Embarrassing is the least of your worries. Someone was spying on us."

She snorted. "Now that's rich. I thought I was the only one spying on you."

"Whatever happened to privacy?"

"I don't know, but I can understand why you were so angry with me. That's just too darned creepy."

Noah nodded, his face grim. "And the reason why I don't want you to stay at your apartment on your own."

"I'm staying at my apartment." She crossed her arms. "I have to watch out for Sophia."

"Agreed about Sophia."

Rachel shot a glance at him. "I thought you wanted to shuffle her off to a kennel?"

"I did, until I learned that she was the one who alerted your neighbor to your situation. Mrs. Davis found you because Sophia wouldn't stop barking."

Rachel smiled. "I knew I loved that dog for a reason."

His face softened and he chuckled. "Yeah, well, she gets a dog biscuit and a place to stay for her heroism."

"Thanks." Rachel melted toward the big man beside her. God, he was sexy when he laughed. And that he'd give credit to a dog...it made him twice as attractive. "I didn't want to break my promise to Mrs. Davis. She's a sweet older woman and that dog is her surrogate child, now that all her kids are grown and scattered across the country."

He handed her his cell phone. "Call her and let her know you'll be a few minutes late."

"Why?" Rachel glanced at the clock on the dash. "We have enough time to get from the hospital to my town house."

"We have to make a stop at the police station for you to file a statement." He took his gaze off the road for just a moment to look her way, concern etched in the lines of his brow. "If you're up to it."

Rachel shifted her gaze forward, away from those startling blue eyes and the urge to fall into them. As far as she knew, he was still angry with her for spying on him and she couldn't blame him. "If it means finding whoever did this to me, I'm up to it. The sooner we catch him, the sooner I get my privacy back."

A shiver slipped down her spine at the thought of

someone watching them make love through her living room window. She could kick herself for leaving the blinds open. But then she would never have guessed a simple kiss would go that far.

A warm wash of physical memory swept the cold shiver away. Her body heated all the way to the core and she squirmed in her seat, looking out the side window, turning her face away from Noah, knowing her cheeks would be flushed. The sun glinted off the window as they pulled into the police station parking lot.

Noah shifted into Park and climbed down.

Rachel unbuckled her seat belt and hurried to open her own door and get out before Noah could assist. Weak from her altercation with a speeding vehicle, she couldn't find the strength to resist her body's reaction to Noah's touch. She'd be better off avoiding him.

She shoved the door open and stepped onto the running board, misjudging the amount of weight her legs were up to holding. When she shifted off the seat, her legs buckled. She would have fallen flat on her face on the concrete had Noah not reached for her at just that moment.

He caught her beneath her arms and crushed her to his chest, his arms like steel bands around her.

For a long moment, she let him hold her, pretending she hadn't lied to him and that he wasn't disappointed and angry with her. Leaning into his chest, she inhaled the wonderful scent of man and a soft hint of aftershave that suited him to perfection. Her fingers curled into his shirt, scraping the hard muscles beneath.

Rachel's breath caught and held as she steadied herself and finally pushed away from him. Not until she stood on her own, with only his hands resting at her waist, was she able to suck air back into her lungs. "Thanks."

"Let me help you next time. You're probably a little shaky from the attack."

Oh, she was shaky all right. As much from being near to him as from being hit by a car. Whatever she did, she couldn't let him know how much he affected her. "Let's get this over with. I want to get home and shower the gravel out of my skin."

Detective Grant took her statement, had her sign it and made the whole ordeal as quick and painless as possible. No matter how fast it was, by the time she left the police station, her head ached and it seemed as though every bone and muscle in her body had been subjected to a meat grinder.

Noah stopped just outside the station door, gripped her arms and stared into her face. "Are you okay?"

She nodded, feeling the blood draining from her head, a gray fog creeping in around the edges of her vision. She shook her head. "No."

Noah bent and swept her up into his arms, carrying her for the remaining steps to his truck. He hit the button to unlock the doors.

The gray fog thickened as Rachel reached for the truck door. Her hand couldn't seem to close around the handle. "Sorry," she said, slipping deeper into an abyss of darkness.

"Hang in there," he whispered. "I'm taking you back to the hospital."

"No," she said. "I'll be okay. I just need a nap." She

fought for a second longer, finally giving in to darkness. At least there, her head didn't hurt.

Noah settled Rachel in the front seat of his truck, torn between taking her back to the hospital and driving the few short blocks to her town house.

After he had her buckled in her seat belt, she came to long enough to smile at him. "I'm okay. Really."

"Then stop passing out on me," he said with a little greater force than he intended, shaken more than he cared to admit by her sudden collapse.

"Did I?" She shook her head, looking confused. "Sorry. I'll try not to."

Only slightly mollified by her words, he hurried around the truck and climbed in, ready to head back to the hospital.

Rachel straightened in her seat. "I'm okay. Take me to my place, please."

"You could have a blood clot or something. I'm concerned."

"Don't be. I got a little weak. I think I need food. I get wobbly when I don't eat on time. If I recall correctly, I didn't have dinner last night or breakfast this morning."

Her statement made sense and Noah gave in, driving to her town house instead of the hospital.

As soon as he parked in the driveway and helped Rachel down from the truck, a diminutive elderly woman with elegantly coiffed white curls, a tasteful cream-colored pantsuit and matching orthopedic shoes hurried out of the town house next to Rachel's. "Oh, Rachel, sweetie. I'm so glad you're okay."

Rachel leaned against Noah's body.

He slipped his arm around her waist and held her up, willing the older woman to move out of his way so that he could get Rachel into the house.

Rachel reached out to touch the woman's arm. "I'm sorry I'm late, Mrs. Davis. I know you must have been worried about missing your plane."

"Oh, fiddle." The woman waved her hand in the air. "I've a mind to cancel my reservation and stay to make sure you're okay."

"No, don't do that on my account. Your daughter will be very disappointed." Rachel glanced up at Noah. "Besides, Noah will be here to take care of me and help with Sophia."

Mrs. Davis's gaze ran between Noah and Rachel. "Sophia doesn't much care for men."

"I'm sure she'll be fine with Noah. He has a way with animals," Rachel reassured the woman. "He's been working with the horses and cattle at Adair Acres."

Noah winked. "She's a hero for alerting you to Rachel's accident. I promise to be extra nice to Sophia."

Mrs. Davis's brows rose. "Even if she nips at your ankles?"

How annoying could a little dog be? Besides, she'd saved Rachel. "Mrs. Davis, I don't care if she takes a chunk out of my skin. She's top dog in my books."

Mrs. Davis frowned, appearing somewhat unconvinced. "She really doesn't like men. But if you're sure."

"We are," Rachel answered.

Noah tipped his head toward the town house. "I

need to get Rachel inside—she's still not at one hundred percent."

Mrs. Davis backed up. "I'm so sorry. You're usually so chipper, it's hard to think of you as anything else."

"I'll be over in a few minutes to get Sophia," Rachel said.

"Oh, no, dear. You relax." Mrs. Davis waved her hands. "I'll bring Sophia over with her leash, dishes and food."

Rachel smiled at the older woman. "Thank you, Mrs. Davis."

"No. Thank *you*!" She turned away and spun back. "Oh, my, I almost forgot. I have your key. After the ambulance came and took you away, I removed your purse from the car, turned off the engine and kept your keys and purse at my house." She held out her hand. "Here are your keys. I'll bring your purse over with the dog."

She handed the key to Noah, turned and hurried away.

Noah led Rachel toward the door, ready to pick her up and carry her should she show one sign of weakness. She was slim, toned and light. He didn't mind carrying her when she fit nicely in his arms. And the added bonus that she smelled like the honeysuckle growing on a fence in back of the stable, only made her harder to resist.

"You don't have to help me with the dog, you know," Rachel said as Noah paused at the door to insert the key. "I promised to take care of Sophia—not you."

"She's a dog after my own heart. We'll get along fine." Noah twisted the key in the lock and pushed the door open wide for her to enter. With a little bow, he waved her inside. "Besides, I wouldn't dream of leaving her out on the streets."

Once inside, he resumed his hold on her elbow, led her to the living room and settled her on the sofa.

The sight of the rug in front of sofa had his body humming and his blood thumping through his veins. His groin tightened and he wished the previous night had turned out differently.

Had Rachel not confessed her part in spying on him, he wouldn't have left in a rage and she wouldn't have been upset and needed Landry's company. They would have stayed in the town house the entire night. Whoever had run her down wouldn't have hit her, and she wouldn't have been hurt and spent the night in the hospital.

Now, more than ever in his life, he could see how one decision could lead to an entire chain of events.

Had his true mother not left him in the backyard to answer a telephone, he might have been raised by Reginald and Ruby instead of by Reginald's sister, Emmaline. Then Reginald wouldn't have had Whit, Carson or Landry, whom he was beginning to get to know. He hoped one day he could trust them, but until they learned who had killed Reginald, he wasn't sure who to trust.

Perhaps all the decisions and events were meant to be. If Landry hadn't been born and Georgia hadn't suspected he was Jackson Adair, he'd never have met Rachel.

He still wasn't sure he trusted her. One thing was certain, though—the previous night had taught him that he wasn't willing to let her go just yet.

He'd be much better off if he walked away while his heart and mind were still intact. He could conduct his import and export business from any city in the US or abroad. He wouldn't have to get involved with his family whom he wasn't sure he trusted and that sure as hell didn't trust him.

Rachel had managed to get past the loner inside him and bring him out of his shell. Not an easy feat when the woman who'd raised him had ingrained in him the need to hide himself and his feelings from others.

"Noah, you should go back to the ranch. I don't feel right taking you away from your work. And I'm not sure I want you to stay in my apartment."

"Why?"

"I'm not…" Her lips pursed and she stared off into the corner as if searching for the right word.

He let her struggle, his gut twisting. She wasn't what? Wasn't in love with him? He held his breath and waited for her to finish her statement, bracing himself for what might come next, amazed that it mattered.

Finally, she frowned and stared straight at him. "I'm not comfortable around you. You're so big and you make my home seem so small. Besides, you won't be comfortable here. You need to be out on the ranch in wide-open spaces. Not cooped up in town."

Noah breathed and smiled. He liked that he made her uncomfortable. At least she wasn't indifferent. And she knew him. Knew that he didn't like to be hemmed in, that he needed space or he got antsy and anxious.

The woman he'd thought was his mother had raised him in small towns in France, sending him to private schools. He wasn't encouraged to bring friends to his house and he probably never would have met his cousins had Emmaline not had emergency surgery and needed someone to take care of him while she recovered. That was when she'd sent him to live with Reginald one summer. The best summer of his life. Up until then, he'd been a loner, secluded and always dreaming of being a part of a large loving family.

A knock on the front door snapped him out of his reverie and he hurried to see who it was. He checked through the side panel beside the door before he opened it to Mrs. Davis.

The older woman had a purse and a big canvas bag over her shoulder and a hairy fur ball tucked under one arm.

"This is Sophia," she said.

The shaggy dog had red, black and silver-tipped hair. When Noah reached for her, she growled and snapped her sharp little teeth at him.

Mrs. Davis grimaced. "She doesn't trust strangers, especially men. Hopefully she'll get used to you in time."

Noah figured the dog would get used to him, but would he get used to her? He'd never been allowed to have a pet. His mother hadn't liked animals in the house and refused to let him keep an outside dog, claiming they didn't have a fence and it wouldn't be fair to the dog to keep it kenneled all the time.

Mrs. Davis marched into the town house and set the dog on the floor. "She only eats a cupful of dog food a day. No table scraps or her tummy gets upset. I play music for her at night so that she doesn't wake up barking at every little noise."

"I remember," Rachel said. "Does she still like Jason Mraz?"

The older woman grinned, seeming pleased that Rachel remembered that detail about her beloved dog. "Yes, she does."

Noah fought to keep from rolling his eyes. The way Mrs. Davis was shooting off directions, she might have been listing details for babysitting a human child, not a small dog.

"I'll bring her kennel over in case you have to leave her alone in the house," the older woman said. "I'll only be gone for four days."

"Sophia and I will have a good visit." Rachel leaned over and tapped the side of the sofa. "Won't we, Sophia?"

The little dog ran to her and sniffed her fingers, then jumped up on her lap.

"I'll be right back," Mrs. Davis left, closing the door behind her.

"All this fuss for a dog?" Noah shook his head.

Rachel held Sophia protectively. "Not just a dog. This is Mrs. Davis's companion. Sophia is her friend, her confidante and surrogate child. She'd be lost without her." Rachel hugged the hairy rat to her cheek. "Isn't that right, Sophia?"

A little pink tongue snaked out and swiped at Rachel's face.

Mrs. Davis rapped on the door and pushed it open, lugging a dog kennel.

Noah relieved her of the plastic box and set it beside the door.

"Well, I guess I'd better go. My plane leaves in two

hours and the taxi should be here any minute." She leaned close to the floor and held her hand down low.

Sophia sailed out of Rachel's arms and stopped at Mrs. Davis's ankles, leaning into them, her perky ears pinned back, big black-brown button eyes staring up at her with the most pathetic gaze Noah had ever seen on a dog. "Be a good girl, sweetie." She lifted the animal and hugged her close, then put her down. The older woman's eyes filled with tears as she turned away.

Noah found himself wanting to reassure the woman. "We'll take good care of her, Mrs. Davis."

"Thank you."

After she left, Noah gathered the big bag she'd left and dug out a dog blanket, fuzzy squeak toy, leash, food and water dishes and a plastic container of dry dog food.

Rachel started to get up. "Sophia usually goes on hunger strike when Mrs. Davis leaves, but she'll need water."

"Sit. I'll take care of it." Noah carried the bowl into the kitchen and filled it with cool water, then set it on the tile.

When he returned to the living room, Sophia sat by the door, staring at it as if waiting for Mrs. Davis to come back.

"How long will she stay there?" he asked.

"Sometimes minutes, other times hours." Rachel gave the dog a sad look. "Poor baby misses her mama when she's gone."

Noah could imagine what a great mother Rachel would be with a child just by the way she cared for

Mrs. Davis's little dog. She was kind and tenderhearted to a fault.

He stared at her wondering what her babies would look like. Would they have the pretty light brown hair and green eyes of their mother? He could picture little girls with wispy curls playing tea party with their stuffed animals.

When he realized where his thoughts had taken him, he shook his head, left Rachel in the living room and entered the kitchen.

He opened the refrigerator. Inside was a small container of orange juice and a couple little tubs of fruit-flavored yogurt.

"My refrigerator is empty. I'd planned on going to the grocery store today," she called out.

"What happened to the food from last night?"

A long pause met his question.

"I threw it out."

He didn't comment, guilt knotting in his belly. "Are you up to going to the grocery store?"

"Actually, I don't want to leave Sophia alone just yet, and I could use a nap. My head hurts."

Noah searched the cabinets for a glass, filled it with water and found a container of ibuprofen, shaking two out into his hand. He returned to the living room and handed the pills and the glass to her. "Take them and go to bed."

She placed the pills on her tongue and took a big swallow of the water, then gulped down the medication. "What are you going to do?" Rachel held out the glass.

"I'm going to run really quickly to the grocery store and get something besides orange juice and yogurt with green slime growing on it. I won't be gone more than thirty minutes."

"Oh." She cuddled Sophia. "Don't worry about me. I'll be fine. I have Sophia to protect me." Her smile made him melt and nearly forget that she had lied to him.

He turned away and crossed to the door. "Don't go outside and don't let anyone inside while I'm gone."

"What if someone knocks at the door?"

"Ignore it and they should go away."

Her gaze shifted toward the blinds.

Noah's gaze followed hers and his gut knotted. "Leave the blinds closed. Let people think you're not home."

"I'm sure this is all overkill," she said, holding Sophia even closer.

"Better overkill than dead."

Rachel's face blanched.

Maybe he was being too dramatic, but he didn't want her to go outside until he was back. And even then, he didn't want her wandering on the streets of San Diego, which had already proved dangerous to her.

"Stay," he reiterated.

Her brows dipped. "I'm not a dog."

He grinned at her remark. "And Sophia isn't, either. Not the way you and Mrs. Davis treat her." He left, locking the door behind him, testing it to make certain it wasn't easily opened.

When he climbed into his truck and drove away, he didn't like the feeling that washed over him. He felt as though someone had been watching him or watching Rachel's town house.

He raised his foot from the accelerator and nearly turned around in the middle of the street. Then he got a grip. It was morning, bright sun shining down on the city. Who would try something in broad daylight?

Chapter 7

Rachel waited until she heard the sound of Noah's truck leaving the driveway. Once he was well and truly gone, she set Sophia on the couch beside her and stood.

For a moment she swayed, her head fuzzy and pounding against her temples. She'd be glad when the painkillers kicked in.

Sophia leaped off the couch and circled Rachel's feet, nervous, probably afraid Rachel would leave her, as well.

Pushing through the fog of dizziness, Rachel hurried toward her bedroom, grabbed clean panties and a bra from her drawer and a shirt and jeans from her closet. She wanted to take a shower before Noah returned, afraid if she had one while he was there, she'd lose all sense of modesty and pride and beg him to join her.

She switched on the water and stripped off her soiled clothing while she waited for the water to warm. Sophia settled on the bath mat, curled into a ball and laid her head on her paws, watching Rachel out of one cracked eyelid.

"Afraid I'll leave you?" Rachel spoke softly to the little dog.

Sophia didn't budge, the flicker of one ear the only indication she was listening.

Rachel stepped into the shower and pulled the curtain closed. She let the spray pour over her, washing away the gritty smell of pavement from her skin. She washed her hair, careful not to disturb the lump at the back of her head.

As she stood beneath the spray, she thought back over the events of the past twenty-four hours. One day she was lying on a boulder kissing Noah. Not much later on that same day, she was kissing the pavement, and not in a good way.

The distant sound of Sophia barking barely made it past the steady beat of water droplets spraying against the shower curtain. When it did, Rachel frowned, turned off the water and listened.

Sophia still barked, but the sound was muffled as if it was behind a door.

"Sophia?" Rachel called out. When she reached for the curtain to fling it aside, something pushed against the other side, shoving her, the curtain and the curtain rod into the tub. Rachel's feet slipped out from under her and she fell against the tile wall, fighting to get untangled from the shower curtain. The plastic liner wrapped around her, sticking to her skin as she slid down the wall into a heap at the bottom of the tub.

Something slammed on top of her, holding the shower curtain over her face, keeping her from catching her breath.

Rachel fought, but the curtain had wrapped around her legs and arms. She could barely move and the weight on her face was relentless.

Sophia barked hysterically in another room.

Rachel bucked and tried to roll over. She heard a grunt. *Something* hadn't fallen on her. *Someone* had tackled her and now held her down, suffocating her.

Fear ripped through her and made her fight even harder, her pulse pounding so hard against her eardrums she could barely hear.

The doorbell rang. Loud knocking followed.

Deprived of oxygen, her brain started to shut down, her vision diminishing. Then as quickly as the attack started, the weight on top of her shifted and moved away. The bathroom door closed softly and Rachel could hear the sound of footsteps running down the hallway toward the rear exit.

Glass shattered in the front of the house.

"Rachel!" Noah's voice called out. More glass breakage followed.

When Rachel tried to open her mouth to answer, she sucked in the plastic of the shower curtain liner. Without the weight of another person on top of her, she should have been able to claw her way out of the tangled mess, but she couldn't catch her breath and her arms and legs were still trapped.

Heavy footsteps raced through the house. "Rachel!" Noah called out, his voice closer.

The bathroom door banged open and the shower curtain was being ripped away from her face.

Rachel gasped, dragging in deep, replenishing breaths.

Noah freed her from the web of the shower curtain and liner. As soon as she could move, she flung herself at him, wrapping her arms around his neck.

"Oh, my God, Rachel. I'm so sorry. I didn't think you'd be in danger for just half an hour. I shouldn't have left you for even a minute."

"I'm okay," she said, her voice hoarse, her body trembling. "I'm okay," she repeated as if to reassure herself as much as him. "I'm okay, now that you're here."

She pressed her cheek against his chest, wanting to get even closer. "I couldn't breathe," she whispered.

"I have you now." He gathered her gently into his arms and rose, lifting her, carrying her back into the bedroom.

Rachel's gaze searched the room, fear making her press into him. A small yip sounded in the other room and brought her out of her own fear. "Sophia." She pushed against Noah. "Where's Sophia?"

"I'll check on her. You stay here." He laid her on the bed and pulled a sheet over her damp, naked body. Before he left the room, he checked beneath the bed and in her closet. "It's clear. Are you going to be all right?" he asked.

"Yes. Please hurry. I'm more worried about Sophia."

Noah left the room and jogged down the hallway.

As soon as he was out of sight, Rachel's heart raced, pounding so hard her breathing grew ragged. She pulled the sheet around her, slid her legs off the bed and stood, holding on to the side of the nightstand as her knees wobbled.

Then Noah was back, standing in the doorway with Sophia cradled in his arms. "She's okay."

Profound relief left her weak and trembling. She collapsed to the floor, the sheet wrapping around her, trapping her arms. Panic struck again and she fought, kicking and tearing at the cloth, grunting and keening like an animal caught in the jagged teeth of a fur trap.

Sophia barked nearby.

Noah crouched on the floor beside her. "Shh, it's just a sheet. Let me unwind it. Shh."

His calm, soothing tones eventually made it through her haze of fear.

Sophia's bark changed to a worried whine.

"Breathe," Noah said, stroking the hair from her face as he unwound the sheet, one fold at a time. "You're safe now."

"I'm sorry," Rachel said, rocking back and forth. "I'm sorry."

Once he had the sheet off her, he yanked his shirt off and eased it over her head, guiding her arms through the holes. When she was completely covered in the soft blue polo shirt, she looked up at him.

"Thank you," she said, then fell against him, sobbing quietly.

Once again, he lifted her from the floor and settled her on the bed. This time he didn't wrap her in the comforter or the sheet; instead, he lay down beside her and spooned her body into his. Sophia walked across the bed and curled up against Rachel's belly.

Head aching, she lay for a long time until her heart rate returned to normal. Every time her eyelids drifted closed, she'd be back in the shower, struggling to breathe. Her eyes popped open and she lay still until she had control over her speeding pulse again.

"You know what this means, don't you?" Noah's deep and resonant voice rumbled in his chest, the vibrations warming her back.

She shook her head, confused by what had happened and what it all meant, but sure of only one thing. Noah would protect her.

"You and Sophia are moving into the guesthouse at Adair Acres with me. Today."

Noah had practically run through the grocery store, grabbing what few groceries they might need for the night and racing for the checkout. When he got there, only one clerk was on duty, slowly checking out a line of six people with baskets full of everything from gallons of milk to laundry detergent.

The longer he waited in line, the more convinced he was that he was taking too long. He'd glanced at his watch at the twenty-five-minute mark. It would take ten minutes to get from the parking lot back to Rachel's town house. At the rate they were going, he'd be another fifteen minutes in line.

Leaving the cart he'd filled with the few items he'd collected, he walked out of the store empty-handed. He'd wait until Rachel felt well enough to go through a drive-through restaurant with him before he tried to get out again.

He pushed the speed limit all the way back, rolling through a stop sign and running a yellow light in its last second. When he reached the town house, nothing looked out of place, but a creepy sense stole over him as he dropped from his truck onto the ground.

That was when he heard Sophia's hysterical barking coming from somewhere inside the house. And from the direction it was coming, it wasn't the living room, where he'd left Rachel.

He ran for the door and inserted the key in the dead bolt. It wouldn't turn. Not even budge. Worried now, he leaned on the doorbell. Rachel didn't answer or even call out. Then he pounded on the wooden panel, fear slicing through him. Fear that he'd left Rachel too long and he wouldn't be able to get to her in time.

He ran to the floor-to-ceiling living room windows, cocked his leg and slammed his foot into one of the lower glass panels, jerking it back before the jagged edges could rip his pant leg.

He leaned close to the gaping hole and yelled out her name. When she didn't respond, he panicked and kicked out the rest of the glass in the windowpane and ducked low, edging his way through the broken window.

His heart lodged in his throat as he ran through the empty living room into the hallway leading to her bedroom. The bed was empty and the bathroom door was closed. He pushed through the door and ground to a halt, his heart stopping when he saw her body wrapped like a mummy, lying at an awkward angle in the bathtub.

Then she moved and Noah's heart started beating again.

Now, as he lay in the bed, holding her in his arms, he relived that horrifying moment when he thought she was dead. His eyes stung and he had to swallow several times before he could breathe.

In the short time he'd been gone, someone had broken into Rachel's house and tried to kill her.

When he felt her stop shaking, he stroked a hand along her arm. "I'm going to check the town house. I'll only be a moment. I won't be far. All you have to do is say my name and I'll be here. I'll hear you."

She clutched the hand on her arm and then slowly let go. "Okay."

He sat up, swung his legs over the side of the bed and stood.

Rachel rolled over, curling into a fetal position. She wrapped her arms around her legs, her gaze following him as he backed out of the room.

Noah almost went back to her, but he had to make sure that whoever had entered the house was gone. He slipped from the room and down the hall in the opposite direction from the one he'd come. The back door to the town house stood slightly ajar.

He stepped through and scanned the surroundings. Nothing looked out of order; no one lurked in the shadows. If the person who'd attacked Rachel had gone out the back, he was long gone. Noah turned to examine the door, careful not to touch it and leave his own prints. The wooden doorjamb had been scratched as if someone had dug into it with a sharp knife. The keyhole had been tampered with, as well, the edges jagged.

Reentering the town house, Noah pulled the door closed with the tip of his shoe, knowing that if the intruder had gained entry once, he could do it again even more easily the next time.

A quick tour of the house revealed nothing else out of order. Noah had found Sophia in a broom closet, probably placed there by the intruder. Thankfully, she hadn't been harmed or Rachel would have been even more traumatized.

And danged if Noah wasn't starting to like the yappy little dog. She'd proved herself to be a good living alarm system. With a window broken out, the back-door lock ruined and the place having been breached once, it was no longer safe for Rachel to stay there.

Noah hurried back to the bedroom and stopped in the doorway, his heart thumping hard against his ribs.

Rachel wasn't in the bed where he'd left her.

Noah spun, ready to charge through the house looking for her. A soft, whimpering yip behind him made him stop in midturn. The sound came from the other side of the bed between the mattress and the closet door.

Another little whining sound brought Noah through the door and around the corner of the bed.

Rachel was huddled on the floor in his light blue polo shirt, holding Sophia tucked between her chest and her knees.

"Come on, babe." He extended a hand. "We're getting out of here."

She reached up with one of her hands, clutching Sophia in the other and let him pull her to her feet.

"Can you manage to get dressed?"

She nodded. "As long as you hold Sophia."

Noah would do anything Rachel asked at that point just to see her eyes light up and a smile return to her pretty face. "Sure."

Rachel handed the little dog to him.

Sophia shook like a leaf in high winds. She curled into his shirt and tucked her little head behind his elbow.

Rachel pulled a pair of slacks off a hanger.

"Do you want me to leave the room?" Noah asked.

"No."

"You could change in the bathroom," he offered. "I'll stand guard."

A shiver shook her body so hard she winced. "I can't go in there."

He nodded.

She stood in front of him and slid the trousers up her legs and over her naked hips.

Noah tried not to stare, but he couldn't resist. She had beautiful, long, slender legs and the curve of her hips was perfect. He felt guilty that she turned him on even after she'd almost been killed. He fought his attraction. She didn't need him pawing at her now. She needed to feel safe and protected.

When she pulled his shirt over her head, he groaned and spun away. "I can only take so much stimulus."

"Sorry."

"Don't be. You're a very attractive woman."

She didn't say anything, but he could hear her moving around the room, shifting hangers in the closet and the wispy sound of clothing sliding over her body.

To drown out the sound of her dressing, he retrieved his cell phone and dialed the police station to report the most recent attack. The detective they'd spoken to earlier that day promised to be there within the next ten minutes.

Noah hung up, wondering how they'd stay put for ten minutes. He wanted to get Rachel out of the town house, away from the terrifying incident.

A soft voice called out from behind him, "I'm dressed."

When Noah faced her, Rachel sat on the bed wearing a silky white blouse and charcoal-gray trousers. She slipped her feet into strappy flat sandals, buckled the back strap and stood to relieve him of Sophia.

"We have to wait for the police before we can leave." He held out his hand and took hers. "Let's sit in the living room."

He led her to the living room and sat her on the sofa. The lock on the front door had been bent and something had been jammed into the dead bolt to keep it from turning easily with a key. Noah left it alone. The police would have to enter the way he had, through the window. Once they had the fingerprints they needed, they could fix the door lock.

Rachel held Sophia in her lap, stroking the animal's silky fur, her gaze shifting from the closed blinds to the glass on the floor by the broken window. When she tried to get up, Noah put out his hand and stopped her.

"I need to clean up the glass," she said. "I don't want anyone hurt."

"The police can take care of themselves. And I'll

deal with the mess later. It's important for us to not disturb any more evidence than we have so far."

"Should we wait outside?" Rachel asked.

"No."

They sat in silence until the detective and crime-scene investigators arrived. The detective took Rachel's statement and dusted for latent prints on the back door, the bathroom door and the shower curtain. Detective Grant had Rachel and Noah fill out a fingerprint card to help him rule out their prints in their search for the suspect's.

After the detective and the investigators finally left the town house, Rachel's face was pale and she was trembling again.

With swift, efficient movements, Noah found a suit-case and stuffed it full of shirts, jeans and an assort-ment of clothing from her closet.

Rachel threw panties and bras in with the other clothes and grabbed tennis shoes and a pair of cow-boy boots. She edged into the bathroom, her entire body shaking, and returned with a toiletries bag.

Noah was amazed at how she'd managed to face the bathroom after almost being smothered to death in there. And she did it carrying that darned dog while she gathered her makeup and toothbrush.

He hefted the now-loaded suitcase off the bed. "Ready?"

She nodded. No argument this time, no protesta-tions of independence.

It grieved his heart to see the shadows beneath her eyes and the fear when she moved toward the front door. No woman should have to be that afraid.

Noah vowed to find whoever had attacked her twice now and rip him apart. He stepped through the front door. Normally, he would marvel at the beauty of San Diego. The view from Rachel's front porch was priceless, the bay area like a picture postcard, the sailboats floating on steely-blue water in idyllic peace. But not that day. He glanced around, searching for danger before it struck Rachel again. He'd failed her once; he wouldn't fail her again.

When he felt fairly sure she would be safe, he curled his arm around her waist and used his body as a shield to get her to the truck and up inside.

Once she was settled, he climbed into the driver's seat and pulled out on the road, headed for Adair Acres.

At least there, she would be safer behind the gates. The guesthouse was wired with a security system. If someone tried to break in, not only would he receive a call, but the security service would dispatch a sheriff's deputy to the residence immediately.

Even with the technical advantages of the house, Noah wouldn't leave it to the security system to keep her safe. He'd stay with her until the danger had been neutralized.

He glanced across at Rachel as she sat in the seat beside him, clutching the little Yorkie in her arms. She stared straight ahead, her eyes wide, searching as if expecting something horrible to jump out at her.

Noah wanted to pull her into his arms and hold her until all the bad guys were brought to justice. Instead, he took her to the only place where he knew he could protect her, the place he now had a stake in, an inheritance he never asked for. Too bad he wasn't 100 percent sure he could trust his newfound family. He couldn't bring himself to trust anyone when Rachel's life hung in the balance.

As he pulled through the gate of Adair Acres, he viewed it from a different perspective. Would the gates and fences keep out the person responsible for attacking Rachel? Or was the person responsible someone on the inside?

Noah wouldn't risk it either way. He'd stay with her at all times.

An SUV stood in front of the one-story, Spanish-style guesthouse when they arrived. Landry got out, a frown creasing her brow.

Noah had barely gotten Rachel down out of the truck when his half sister leaped from the long front porch and enveloped her in a big hug. "Oh, honey, I heard what happened. Are you okay?"

"I'm okay," Rachel assured her. "Just tired."

A little yip sounded from between the two women as Sophia reminded them she needed to breathe, as well.

Landry backed away and laughed. "Sorry, Sophia. Is Mrs. Davis on vacation?" She took the dog from Rachel. "Come on. Let's get you inside." She led the way into the house.

Noah followed, carrying Rachel's suitcase and the canvas bag full of Sophia's things.

Landry was talking as she led Rachel through the house. "Let's get you settled in and I'll make you a cup of soup."

"That would be nice," Rachel said. "I am hungry."

Landry turned to Noah. "I can stay and get Rachel comfortable if you'd like to go check on the animals."

He hesitated, his gaze on Rachel. His distrust of everyone tugged at his need to do his job.

Rachel gave him half of a smile and nodded. "I'll be all right. Landry is my closest friend. I trust her."

Landry's brows rose. "You don't think I would hurt my Rachel, do you?" She slipped an arm around Rachel's waist. "We've been friends forever. She's like the sister I never had."

"If you're sure." He wasn't as convinced as Rachel seemed to be. "The past two times I left you, things happened."

"I was alone those two times," Rachel pointed out.

"She'll be with me," Landry said. "We can close the doors and set the alarms, if you're worried someone will attack here at the ranch."

"Please. I don't want to keep you from your work," Rachel said.

"I need to feed the animals and check on a horse with a sore hoof." He let out a long breath. "Okay, but only for a short time. It shouldn't take me more than an hour."

"By the time you get back, Rachel and I will have had a nice late lunch and I'll be sure she lies down for a nap."

Rachel frowned. "I'm not a child."

"No, but you've been injured." Landry patted her hand. "Let me baby you a little. It gives me some practice for when Derek and I get married and start a family."

Noah left the two women in the kitchen with Sophia lapping at a bowl of water Landry set on the floor. Before he headed outside, he spent a few minutes checking the house from top to bottom, beneath beds, in closets and in the bathrooms, especially behind the shower curtains.

He double-checked both showers twice. One had a shower curtain, the other had glass doors. After finding Rachel smothered in a shower curtain, he was determined to rid the guesthouse of all shower curtains and have shower doors installed. He pulled the shower curtain down, folded it and carried it with him as he checked the latches on all the windows and locks on the doors. When he reached the back door, he verified the alarm panel was working, set the code to turn it on and exited the house, pulling the door closed behind him.

He fished his phone out of his pocket and dialed Landry's number.

She picked up on the second ring. "Good grief, Noah. Have you even left the house yet?"

"I have. I'm right outside. I'll have my phone with me if you hear or see anything out of the ordinary."

"Will do. I'll keep a sharp eye out."

"Don't answer the door or let anyone inside," he warned.

"Noah, Rachel is not a prisoner."

"No, but be gentle, she's had quite a shock."

"If I didn't know better, I'd think you cared about her." She chuckled. "A lot."

"Just don't let anything happen to her. I won't be that far away, and I'll be back in less than an hour."

He was already walking toward the stable, pretty confident no one would hurt Rachel while she had Landry with her. And if anyone tried to break in, the security system would send a message to his phone and the sheriff's office. One hour. That's all he needed.

Yeah, and it had taken only thirty minutes of him being gone for someone to break into Rachel's town house and nearly kill her.

Chapter 8

Rachel sat at the small kitchen table and picked at the scrambled eggs and toast Landry had whipped up for her.

"What's wrong? Did I leave a piece of shell in the eggs?" Landry set a steaming cup of tea in front of Rachel and dropped into the seat across the table from her.

Shaking her head, Rachel managed to eat another bite of the eggs before setting her fork on her plate and lifting the cup of tea to her lips. The hot liquid swept down her throat helping to warm her body. She'd never felt so cold. A shiver shook her. "I don't know what's wrong with me. I was starving before…" She closed her eyes and inhaled a deep, calming breath.

Landry's hand closed over hers. "It's okay. You're safe now."

She pushed a hand through her hair. "I'd rather get run over a dozen times than be suffocated."

"I'd rather you didn't do either. I can't believe this is happening to you. It baffles me that anyone would want to hurt you. You're the kindest, gentlest human being I know."

Rachel smiled at her and squeezed her hand. "I'm glad I have people like you and your brothers as friends."

"Friends, hell. You're family, sweetie. We love you." Tears pooled in Landry's eyes and she brushed them away. "Look at me getting all teary eyed."

"I'm okay. Noah got there in time."

"Thank God." Landry tapped the table. "Now eat those eggs. You need to rebuild your strength."

Rachel forced the rest of the eggs and the piece of toast down her throat. "Noah has to be hungry, too. Maybe I should look at cooking something for when he comes back inside. He never got to eat the dinner I prepared last night and I'm almost sure he didn't get breakfast this morning."

"He's a big boy, he can look after himself."

"Not if he's too busy looking out for me. And he doesn't even like me." She lifted her teacup and sipped, trying to swallow her melancholy along with the hot liquid. It wasn't working.

Landry grinned. "Oh, honey, he likes you more than you think."

Rachel shook her head. "He was so angry last night. I seriously didn't think I'd ever see him again."

"Yeah, and then you had to go and let someone run you over. That changed the playing field." Landry chuckled. "I wish you could have seen his face when the nurse told him he couldn't enter your hospital room."

Rachel frowned. "But he was there when I woke up."

"Yeah. We had to pull strings and threaten to withdraw all the funding the Adairs funnel into the hospital to get them to let him in. I had to remind them that Noah Scott is actually Jackson Adair. They let him in. Although, I think he would have fought his way through had they not come around soon enough."

"Oh." Rachel stared into her tea. "He probably only felt guilty, or something, for leaving me."

Landry shook her head. "Guilt doesn't drive a man to hold your hand for hours. I think he even said a prayer or two during that time. Not to mention the trench he wore into the floor pacing when the nurse was taking your vital signs."

"It doesn't mean anything."

"What?" Landry snorted and leaned back in her chair, her eyes wide. "It means everything."

Rachel shook her head. "When I'm recovered and my attacker is caught, he won't want anything to do with me. I lied to him. The woman he thought was his mother lied to him. His grandparents who stole him from his real mother lied to him. How can a man trust anyone after that? Those people were family."

"You can still come out for riding lessons," Landry suggested.

"I doubt he'll agree to that. It would probably be best if I quit coming out to the ranch altogether."

Landry leaned her elbows on the table. "Is that what you want? To give up? To forget the feelings you have for him? Rachel, do you love Noah?"

Rachel continued to stare into her tea as if the swirling liquid could foretell her future. "He was so angry. He'll never trust me again."

"You didn't answer me." Landry leaned her elbows on the table. "Do you love him?"

"I want to be here for him. I'd like to be the one he can count on and trust. But I'm not. And I don't know if I can be with him for the long haul if he doesn't trust me."

Landry took the teacup from her and set it aside, then took her hands and held them. "Look at me, Rachel."

Rachel didn't want to, but eventually she glanced up into Landry's face.

"Do you love him?" Landry asked, one last time.

Tears gathered, clouding her eyes, and a knot formed in her throat. She nodded, unable to speak.

"If he loves you, like I'm pretty sure he does, he'll forgive you and learn to trust you again." Landry squeezed her hands. "Don't give up on him. Like all Adairs—me included—he has to be a little pigheaded for a while before he comes around to what's in his heart."

The doorbell rang, setting Sophia off in a barking frenzy. Normally the little dog ran to the door to see who it was. This time she barked from beneath the kitchen table, huddled against Rachel's ankles.

Rachel's heart hurt for the little dog. Sophia had been just as traumatized by being thrown into a broom closet and the move to two different houses. Bending over, Rachel scooped her up.

Landry rose from the table, biting her lip. "I promised Noah I wouldn't let anyone in."

"We should at least go see who it is." Feeling a little stronger after eating an entire meal, Rachel pushed to her feet, barely swaying this time.

The doorbell rang again and Sophia's shrill bark made Rachel's head hurt all over again.

Landry's cell phone rang and she glanced at the display screen. "It's Derek." She answered and smiled, staring across at Rachel. "You're at the front door of the guesthouse?" She moved toward the front of the house. "You have who? Ruby? Okay, we're coming. I'll have to get Noah's approval before I can let you in. I know. I promised him." She ended the call. "Derek has Noah's biological mother, Ruby, at the front door. Let me text Noah and let him know that we have visitors."

Rachel followed at a slower rate, her heart beating faster the closer she got to the front door. "Noah didn't want us to let anyone in."

"I'm texting him now. If he's okay with it, we'll let them in. If he's not, I'll send them out to the stable." Landry pressed Send on the cell phone as she reached the door. "Just a minute, Derek." She tapped the edge of her cell phone, waiting for Noah's response.

Her phone rang and she smiled as she answered. "That was quick. I thought I'd have to wait for you to finish shoveling horse manure or something. Your mother is here." She paused. "Ruby. Can I let her in? Derek's with her. I'd say safety in numbers. I really doubt a woman of Ruby's size could hold Rachel down in a bathtub. And if she is the attacker, we have enough witnesses here that she won't try anything." Landry winked at Rachel. "Okay. We'll be expecting you in twenty minutes." She rang off and reached for a painting beside the front door and folded it back like a door, revealing a control panel beneath. She hit a few buttons on the panel and closed the door. "That should disable the alarm long enough for them to get inside."

Landry opened the door and stood back.

Rachel had only met Ruby the day before, never having actually had a conversation with the woman. She was thin, a little shorter than Rachel with light brown hair and hazel eyes. Appearing fragile and pale, her face was gently wrinkled and sad until she smiled her welcome. Then her eyes lit and she seemed to come to life. "You're Rachel, aren't you? We met yesterday outside the stable."

Rachel held out her hand. Had it only been a day ago she'd first kissed Noah by the stream? So much had happened since then. She'd almost died twice.

"Yes, ma'am." She took the woman's slender fingers in her own. Her curiosity was piqued, knowing this woman had given birth to the man Rachel couldn't get out of her thoughts.

Landry shook Ruby's hand, as well, and then threw her arms around Derek, kissing him soundly.

Rachel's heart tugged with a sharp pang of envy. Their open demonstration of love was how it should be. She had to remind herself they had to overcome prejudices and preconceived notions, in addition to Derek's murderous former partner, before they could admit to their attraction and love for each other. Despite all their wealth, nothing came easy to the Adairs in the relationship department.

Seeing Landry so happy with Derek gave Rachel hope.

Ruby and Derek entered the house. Landry closed the door behind them and reengaged the security system.

"I can make some hot tea or iced tea, whichever you prefer," Landry offered.

"Iced tea would be lovely," Ruby responded. She took a seat on the sofa.

"I'll help," Derek offered. The kitchen was open to the living room with only a breakfast bar dividing the two spaces. Landry and Derek could keep an eye on Rachel, not that she needed it with Ruby. The woman was so thin and frail looking Rachel couldn't imagine she had it in her to hurt anyone. And what motive would she have to hurt her?

Rachel sat on the other end of the sofa and Sophia jumped up into her lap.

"Is that your dog?" Ruby asked.

Rachel ran her hand over Sophia's long silky hair as the little dog settled on her lap. "No. I'm keeping her while my neighbor visits her family in Virginia."

"I love dogs. I remember how excited I was when I'd had a baby boy. I couldn't wait until he was a little older so that he could have a dog to grow up with, like I did."

"Dogs are very loyal." Rachel scratched Sophia behind the ears. "I adopted a stray when I was ten. Or I should say he adopted me. My parents wanted to take him to the pound, but I talked them into keeping him."

Ruby smiled, her eyes glazing in memory. "My dog, Ginger, was a golden retriever and lab mix my folks let me adopt from the shelter. She was the one friend I could always count on to be there when I needed her."

Rachel glanced out the picture window at the horses in the pasture, her thoughts going back to a simpler time. "Max was the best dog. He was always there to greet me when I got home. He slept at the foot of my bed and he let me hug him when a storm frightened me. I think he was more afraid of the storms than I was, but together we weathered them just fine." It had been a long time since she'd thought of Max. It brought back fond memories of growing up, when her parents were still alive and she'd felt safe and loved.

"How did you meet my son?" Ruby asked.

Rachel's gaze dropped to the dog in her lap. "I asked him to give me riding lessons so that I could get close enough to him to spy on him."

"Is that so?" Ruby's eyebrows rose. "Why did you spy on him?"

"After Reginald's murder, Landry and her brothers didn't know who they could trust." It all seemed so convoluted. And so much had happened in the past few months. "When Georgia got here, she immediately saw the resemblance to you and suspected Noah was the missing Jackson Adair. We were all a little shocked. We didn't know whether he was friend or foe. If he knew he was Reginald's missing son, why hadn't he said anything? For all Landry and her brothers knew, he could have been Reginald's murderer or he might have been an imposter, setting himself up to steal Jackson's inheritance."

Ruby shook her head. "Isn't it sad to be so untrusting of others. Where I grew up, we didn't have much, but we had our friends and family. We could always count on them to be true and loyal. I didn't know there were people so dishonorable and cruel until I met and married Reginald." She held up her hand. "Not that Reginald was cruel to me, but his family…"

"Hated you." Landry returned to the living room with a tray of glasses filled with ice. Derek followed, carrying a pitcher of tea. "I'm sorry for what my grandparents and great-aunt did to you and Jackson. There's no excuse for stealing a woman's child and keeping him hidden for all those years. No excuse whatsoever." Landry placed a glass of ice on a coaster in front of Ruby.

Derek poured tea into it.

Together, they poured three more glasses and set the tray on a nearby table. Derek sat in a love seat that matched the leather couch. Landry snuggled next to him, slipping her sandals off and drawing her feet under her. "So, what do you think of Noah, now that you've met?"

The older woman's face lit up. "Seems so strange to call him Noah, but it suits the man he's become. He's so big and handsome—he has his father's eyes—and he's so polite." Ruby laughed. "I couldn't have asked for a nicer man."

"Emmaline might have kept him hidden," Landry noted, "but she taught the man some manners."

"And he's very good with animals," Rachel added.

"I'm thankful Emmaline loved him. I would have hated to think of him being abused or mistreated." She glanced around at the others. "I wanted him back, but most of all I wanted him healthy and happy wherever he was."

"From what we've observed, Noah didn't know Emmaline wasn't his mother. Noah grew up thinking she was all the family he had until she had to have emergency surgery and he was shuffled off to stay with us one summer." Landry smiled, her eyes glazing over. "I was just a little kid then, but I remember how happy he'd been running across the pastures and swimming in the creek."

"I missed all of that." Ruby's eyes teared. "I don't have any memories, pictures, old baseball hats, funky Christmas ornaments…anything…of Jackson growing up." She looked away, a tear slipping down her face. "Now that I've found him, all I can hope for is that he will let me be part of his life."

"Only Noah could make that promise," Rachel said quietly. As mistrustful as he was of everyone, he might not trust the woman claiming to be his biological mother.

Ruby nodded. "I know. First I have to gain his confidence. So many of the people he trusted have let him down."

"Like me." Rachel pushed to her feet. "If you'll excuse me, I'm really tired."

"Rachel, honey, I've turned down the covers on the bed in the middle bedroom." Landry started to rise.

Rachel held up a hand. "Don't get up. I can find my way."

Ruby stood. "I think I'd like to go out to the stable. Maybe I'll catch Jackson—Noah—out there." She closed the distance between herself and Rachel. "I don't know much about my son, but from what I've seen and heard, he's a fair and forgiving man."

"Yes, he is." But had he reached his limit of forgiveness with Rachel's confession? She almost didn't dare to hope.

"I'm banking on that forgiveness and sense of fairness. Because now that I've found my son, I want to be a part of his life. I didn't give up looking, I sure as heck am not giving up on him now." She hugged Rachel and whispered, "Don't give up on him."

Rachel hugged the woman and then broke away, hurrying toward the spare bedroom before she broke down and cried in front of everyone. She wasn't normally weak and weepy. Having almost lost her life twice might have something to do with it, but more than likely Noah's rejection had hit her the hardest.

As she crawled into the bed and settled Sophia beside her, she let the tears fall silently. When she'd spent them, she dried her eyes and thought about what Ruby had said.

Rachel had known Noah longer than Ruby, but in just one meeting, the older woman had seen in her son what Rachel had grown to love. The man was a loner, but he was fair, forgiving and compassionate. What had started out as just riding lessons between them had transformed into a solid friendship and, at least on Rachel's part, a deep, everlasting love.

She didn't want to go back to being just friends. They'd gone way beyond that when they'd kissed at the creek and made love on the floor of her town house. No. She didn't want to go backward; she didn't want to give up. Rachel wanted Noah for better or worse, for the rest of her life.

The only way she had a chance of getting that was to hang in there, forgive him for blowing up at her and let him have time to forgive her for spying on him. She'd learned a long time ago that trust once lost was very hard to regain. She had to prove to him she was worth trusting again.

She prayed he'd give her the chance.

Noah checked his watch again. It had only been the hour he'd promised when he left Rachel at the guesthouse with Landry. An hour wasn't nearly long enough to accomplish all he had to do in the stable, much less the rounds he needed to make to insure none of the fences were down or animals caught up in something like hay wire, field fence or briars.

The fences and outlying animals would have to wait until tomorrow for him to go out and check on them. Maybe he could get Whit or Carson to ride out on one of the ATVs.

In the meantime, the horse he wanted to inspect was in the corner of the pasture closest to the stable. No matter how much he shook the feed bucket, she wasn't coming.

He pulled his cell phone out of his pocket and hit Landry's number.

She answered on the first ring. "I thought you said you'd be back to the house by now."

"Why? Am I needed? Is everything okay?" His heart leaped and he dropped the feed bucket, ready to race back to the guesthouse and Rachel.

"Hey, settle down. Everything is fine here. Derek and I are sipping tea in the living room. Rachel and Sophia are asleep in the guest bedroom and your mother just left to find you."

Noah stood for a moment, willing his pulse to slow. "Are you sure Rachel's all right?"

"I just checked. She's sleeping. The poor girl needed it. She's all banged up and traumatized. I don't know how she's holding it together."

"Did you reset the alarm on the house?"

"I did. And I left the guest bedroom door open so that I could hear Rachel if she calls out."

Noah stared out at the horse in the corner of the pasture. "I want to check on Lady before I call it a day. She was limping yesterday afternoon. I checked her hoof then but couldn't find anything. I can see that she's still limping. I'll be in as soon as I can."

"Take your time. We're as snug as can be. Rachel's down for the count. I made her eat and she'll probably sleep until morning."

At the mention of food, Noah's stomach rumbled. "Is there anything left in the refrigerator?"

"Plenty. If you're really nice to me, I'll fix dinner for the four of us here."

"Thanks, Landry. You're a good friend to Rachel."

"And to you. After all, you're my brother." She paused. "Now, hurry up and get back here before you drive yourself—and me—crazy with worry."

Noah pocketed his cell phone and set off across the pasture with a lead rope and the bucket of feed. The sooner he caught the mare and led her back to the stable the sooner he'd be able to check her leg and hoof, feed her and return to the house and Rachel.

The mare proved to be skittish. Every time he got close, she trotted out of reach, favoring one hoof. The food wasn't tempting her. Noah figured she was hurting enough to kill her appetite.

He finally left the feed bucket in the middle of the pasture, eased the horse into the corner and inched up on her, talking soothingly until he was close enough to grab her halter and snap the lead in place.

Walking slowly, he led the horse across the pasture, collected the feed bucket and had made it back to the stable twenty minutes later. The doors to the building were closed. He thought he'd left them open. He was reaching out to open the back door when he smelled smoke.

The mare smelled it, too, and reared, backing away from the door.

Noah tugged on the door. The smell seemed to be coming from inside the stable. His stallion and two other horses were inside. He let go of the mare's lead and put his back into opening the door. The bar must have fallen into place on the inside. He could pull all day, but short of tying a rope to the back of his truck and pulling it off its hinges, that door wasn't going to open.

The sound of horses whinnying inside spurred him into action. He ran around the side of the structure, slipped through the wood fence railing and came to a skidding halt at the front of the stable facing the guesthouse. He tried the big double door. It too wouldn't open.

The small door leading into the tack room and through to the stable was on the other side of the big door. Noah ran to it and twisted the knob. It wouldn't open. He dug the key out of his pocket and shoved it into the lock. It wouldn't turn.

A voice cried out from inside.

Rachel? Noah shook his head. She was asleep back in the guesthouse, wasn't she? What had Landry said? Rachel was asleep…and Ruby was on her way out to see him at the barn.

Damn!

He pounded on the door. "Ruby?"

"Yes, Noah! It's me." She coughed. Smoke filtered through the cracks under the big stable door and between the wooden siding slats. "Help me! I can't get out."

Chapter 9

Noah cocked his leg and kicked the door close to the knob. The door frame cracked but held. He kicked again and a splinter of wood flew off around the lock mechanism.

One more kick and the door flung inward, smoke pouring out.

Ruby lay on the floor, coughing, her wrists and ankles secured with duct tape. She had a nasty bump on her forehead and her clothes were torn and dirty.

Noah scooped her up, shocked at how light she was. He carried her out of the stable and laid her on the ground far enough away from the smoking building.

He unwrapped the tape from her wrists and ankles and helped her to sit up.

"Go!" she said as soon as she caught her breath. "There are horses in that stable."

"Are you sure you'll be okay out here?" He wanted to go for the horses, but he was afraid to leave Ruby.

"I'm okay. But I don't want those horses left to die. Please go!"

Noah fished his cell phone from his pocket. "Call Landry, tell her what happened. She'll know who to call."

Leaving Ruby on the ground, he ran back into the stable through the broken door. The lights didn't work, but he knew the layout of the building. Pulling his shirt up over his mouth, he felt his way to the big front door and shoved the bar out of the braces. He then pushed the big door open.

The horses screamed behind him as smoke poured out into the open air. They could sense freedom but couldn't get out of their stalls.

The stallion pawed at his gate and the other horses kicked at the sides of their enclosures.

Smoke billowed from a pile of rags on the floor near the back of the stable. Noah ducked low in the haze, his eyes burning, the smoke singeing his lungs. He opened the first stall door. Before he got it open all the way, the mare inside burst through, slamming the door wide-open, nearly knocking Noah over. She raced for the light, out into the open.

Moving quickly, Noah felt his way deeper into the building to the next stall door. This time he stood back when he opened the stall. The gelding inside whinnied and ran for the open air.

His stallion reared again, his hooves crashing into his stall door and knocking it halfway off its hinges.

When Noah tried to open the door, it jammed, the

hinges bent, and the stallion grew more frightened and desperate, pawing at the broken door.

While fighting to right the door and not get hit by the flailing hooves, Noah wrestled with the door, his lungs filling with smoke. If he didn't get out soon, he'd succumb to smoke inhalation. Finally, he yanked the latch free and the door fell open.

Before he could move out of the way, the stallion slammed into him, throwing him to the side into a pile of flaming rags, soaked in diesel.

The fuel penetrated Noah's shirt, the flames leaping out to catch him on fire.

Noah rolled across the floor, leaped to his feet and yanked his shirt over his head, throwing it to the ground. Then he stomped on it to put out the flame.

Returning to the tack room, he found the fire extinguisher and ran back into the stable. Flames shot up from the rags he'd rolled into. He aimed the hose at the blaze and let loose a burst of fire retardant spray. The flames twisted and sputtered.

After spraying it again, he quenched the fire. Coughing and hacking, he grabbed a rag from a shelf, covered his face and worked his way to the back door. He flung the bar free and pushed the doors open. A breeze whipped through the building, chasing the smoke out the other end.

Noah sank to his knees, breathing in the fresh air in huge gulps.

"Noah!" a deep voice called out. "Noah!" Footsteps pounded through the stable, coming to a halt behind him.

"Oh, thank God." Whit Adair bent with his hands on

his knees, coughing. "When I found Ruby out on the ground, she said you'd gone into the burning building and hadn't come out."

"Ruby?" Noah, staggered to his feet and turned toward the structure.

Whit clapped a hand to his back. "She's okay. Carson is taking her to the guesthouse. Landry called the fire department, they're sending a pumper truck out this way, but from the looks of it, you've already handled it."

"Yeah, let them come. And while we're at it, let's get the sheriff involved." Noah coughed, his throat burning but not nearly as hot as his anger.

Whit stood with his hands on his hips, his feet wide, staring at the stable. "What the hell happened?"

"Someone set that fire and trapped Ruby in there to die." He staggered around the building rather than go through the smoke again. Whit grabbed his arm and draped it over his shoulder.

"I'm okay," Noah insisted, unused to anyone helping him and not sure how to feel about it. But then his lungs felt like crap and he could barely see, his eyes burned so much. He let Whit guide him back to the guesthouse.

When they got close, Whit ducked out from under Noah's arm. "You got it from here?"

Noah nodded.

"Good. I need to find Carson and Derek. We'll round up the horses and get them into a pasture before the fire trucks spook them even more."

Noah trudged the remaining steps toward the guesthouse.

A crowd of Adairs had gathered inside.

So much for a security system. Hopefully, with all the people around, no one would try to get to Rachel. And now Ruby. He was beginning to think Landry was right. The Adairs were cursed. Anyone who tried to get close to them was destined to be hurt.

Georgia Mason, Ruby's stepdaughter, was by Ruby's side. The curvy redhead was more of a daughter to Ruby than Noah was her son, having grown up with Ruby as her mother. She held the woman in her arms, helping her to drink a glass of water.

Sirens wailed in the distance, growing louder the closer they came.

With Ruby being cared for, Noah stared around at the faces, searching for only one. When he didn't see her, his heart pounded and he started forward, ready to plow through the throng until he found her.

A hand on his arm stopped him before he could get started.

"I'm here." Rachel stood by his side, her face drawn and pale, her green eyes wide and worried. "Are you okay?"

He let go of the breath he'd been holding and his shoulders sagged. "I am now." He coughed, his throat raw and smoke singed. "I could use some water."

She slipped her arms around his middle and pressed her cheek to his chest.

He wanted to gather her into his arms, but he knew he smelled. "I'm covered in soot."

"I don't care. And I don't care if you don't want me to hug you. I just have to." Her arms tightened around his middle and she buried her face against his naked chest, her tears making sooty tracks down his torso.

He wrapped his arms around her and held her, resting his cheek against the top of her clean, sweet-scented hair. He'd never smelled anything as good as Rachel at that moment.

Her hands splayed across his back, her fingers curling into his skin. With each breath she exhaled, the movement of air across his chest made his groin tighten exponentially. In that moment he felt he was in the right place. The only place he wanted to be.

They stood locked in that embrace for a long time, but not long enough.

Soon, people clapped him on the back and congratulated him for saving Ruby, the horses and the stable.

Noah didn't care. He was holding Rachel in his arms. The rest of the world faded into insignificance.

When the first responder truck arrived with the emergency medical technicians, he was forced to let go of Rachel.

Landry touched his arm. "You need to let the EMTs check you out."

He wanted Rachel back in his arms. "I'm fine."

"Yeah, and smoke inhalation is nothing to mess around with." Landry handed Sophia to Rachel. "Tell him."

"Please, let them check you out." Rachel held the little dog, smoothing a hand over her shivering body. The concern in her eyes warmed Noah's heart.

Landry lifted Noah's hand. "Noah, have them look at those burns on your arms, too."

Until she'd mentioned the burns, Noah hadn't felt them. The adrenaline rush of putting out the fire had wiped the reason he'd stripped off his shirt completely out of his mind.

Rachel ran her finger along the outsides of the injury. "Oh, babe, you definitely need to let the EMTs look at that."

"Okay," he relented. "But don't go anywhere."

Rachel smiled. "I won't."

The EMTs loaded Ruby onto a stretcher. Before they could wheel her away, she made the attendants stop.

One of them found Noah and brought him back to the woman. "She won't let us load her into the ambulance until she talks to you."

Noah took Ruby's hand in his. "You'll be all right. Let them take you to the hospital and check you out."

"I will. I just want you to know how much I love you." She cupped his cheek with her other hand. "Thank you for saving my life." Ruby curled her fingers around the back of his neck, drawing him close to her. She brushed her lips across his cheek. "I've wanted to do that for a very long time." She smiled and let him go. "Okay," she said to the EMTs. "I'm ready."

They loaded Ruby into the back of an ambulance. Georgia climbed in with her. Carson appeared in time to promise he'd be right behind them.

An EMT appeared in front of Noah. "Sir, you need to go to the hospital, as well."

"I'm not going anywhere," Noah insisted.

"Sir, you have second-degree burns on your arm and smoke inhalation isn't something to ignore. It can be very dangerous."

"I'm fine. I just need a shower and clean clothes."

Landry appeared beside him. "Typical, stubborn

Adair." She pointed to the ambulance. "Go to the hospital."

He shook his head. "I can't leave Rachel here. I won't."

"Then she can go with you. At least let them hold you long enough to make sure your throat doesn't swell shut or whatever could happen because of the amount of smoke you breathed. You won't be much good to Rachel if you're dead."

Landry's last statement finally got through to him. "Rachel comes with me."

"I'm sure that can be arranged. I'll keep an eye on Sophia. Whit can follow and bring you both back when the doctor releases you."

Derek stood beside Landry. "I can come along to provide security for the two of you and Ruby." He raised Landry's hand to his lips and pressed a kiss to her knuckles. "I think we need to consider hiring bodyguards for Ruby and Rachel."

"I'll take care of Rachel," Noah insisted.

"We still need someone to watch out for Ruby. I'll get ahold of Kate O'Hara. She'll have some connections she can recommend and know who to trust."

Noah had met Kate. She was his aunt and the former vice president of the United States. If anyone knew who to hire for protection, it was Kate.

Rachel handed Sophia off to Landry and walked with Noah to the back of the second ambulance. Noah refused to lie down on the stretcher, preferring to climb in the back of the vehicle on his own. He reached for Rachel's hand and helped her up, then settled her on a bench seat before he sat on the stretcher. The EMT slid onto the bench beside Rachel and the back door closed.

"Sir, put this on." The EMT handed him an oxygen mask.

"I don't need it," Noah insisted.

"Noah." Rachel laid a hand on his uninjured arm. "Please."

Noah took the mask and held it to his face. He had to admit he could breathe easier.

The trip to the hospital was made in relative silence. The EMT checked Noah's vital signs, then called in the information about his patient to the staff physician on call.

An orderly met them at the emergency room door with a wheelchair, insisting that Noah sit in it to be wheeled into the hospital.

Already impatient and ready to be back in his house, getting the shower he so desperately needed, Noah frowned all the way back to the examination room. Rachel had to stay in the lobby of the emergency room while they cleaned and dressed his wounds and checked his throat and lungs for negative effects from the smoke. All the while, Noah's eyes remained on the door, as if by staring at it he could see all the way into the lobby.

Whit and Derek had promised to watch out for Rachel, while Georgia and Carson went with Ruby. He prayed his half brothers were true to their word and watched over the two most important women in Noah's life.

He caught himself on that thought. He barely knew Ruby. Hell, he didn't have to know her long to realize she was genuine. She hadn't cared about being left out in the open as much as she feared for the horses.

Emmaline would probably have let the horses die rather than try to save them at the risk of her own life. Perhaps there was more to genetics than he'd originally thought. He'd always had an instinctive love of all animals. He didn't get that from Emmaline.

"You're lucky, Mr. Scott. The burns were only second degree. As long as you're breathing easily, I see no need for you to stay overnight."

Noah slid off the table and stood. "Good, then I can go home."

The doctor grinned. "After the nurse gives you discharge instructions on what to do if you experience any troubles breathing."

Fifteen minutes later, armed with three sheets of instructions, his wrist band and a hospital gown to wear home, he emerged from the examination rooms into the lobby. He scanned the room, his heartbeat speeding up when he didn't see Rachel, Whit or Derek. He spun in a 360-degree circle, searching desperately.

A hospital volunteer stepped up behind him. "If you're looking for Rachel, she and the two men with her went up to Mrs. Mason's room. Rachel asked me to let you know."

The woman gave him the room number and pointed to the elevator.

Noah figured he was being paranoid, but the longer he went without seeing for himself that Rachel was all right, the more anxious he became.

When the elevator stopped on the floor the nurse indicated, Noah tapped his toe, ready to leap out as soon as the doors slid open.

He passed the nurses station and loped down the hallway, searching for the right room number. When he reached it, he could hear voices and muted laughter through the door.

After a light knock, he didn't wait, pushing through the door into the room where five people gathered around the hospital bed.

His heart lightened, edging away the terror he'd felt when he'd seen smoke billowing from the stable. Had he been a minute or two later… His chest hurt at the thought, and he had to remind himself that he *had* gotten to her in time, that she *was* okay and he'd still get the chance to know her and love her.

"Noah, come in." Whit waved him forward. "Ruby was just telling a joke. The woman is amazing. Having been attacked and suffering from smoke inhalation, she's still able to cut up."

"My mother knows what suffering and heartache is, but she doesn't let it get her down." Georgia brushed the wispy graying hair back from Ruby's forehead.

Ruby held her other hand, smiling.

A lump settled in the middle of Noah's throat. This was his mother. The woman who gave birth to him, lost him and never gave up on him. She held out her hand. "Jackson—sorry. I know you prefer to go by Noah."

He walked to the side of her bed and took her extended hand, careful not to disturb the IV. "You can call me Jackson, if you like."

"No. You've been Noah all your life, there's no need

to change that. You're still my son, no matter what your name is." She coughed.

"Don't talk if it hurts," he said, squeezing her hand gently.

"No, I want to say something." She coughed again and shook her head. "You're an amazing man. I couldn't have asked for a better son if I'd raised you myself. And tonight, you're my hero."

His cheeks heated and his heart warmed. He hadn't known how important it would be to him to make a good impression on this woman until now. He just wished she hadn't had to go through what she had for him to prove he was worthy of her love.

"Now, go on, take your sweetie home. She's been through worse and she looks like she could use a good night's sleep," Ruby said.

Rachel leaned over the bed and pressed a kiss to the older woman's forehead. "I hope you feel better soon."

Ruby smiled up at her. "I already do. Now, all of you, shoo! I need my beauty rest."

One by one the others filed out of the room until Georgia was the last one to leave.

Noah slipped his free hand into Rachel's as they pushed through the swinging door. Now that he had her in his sight and hands, he could relax.

"I like Ruby," Rachel said. "She's warm, caring and funny. You're lucky to have her."

"I just learned who she is. I wouldn't know." Though he said the words, he knew already the woman was real and loving and everything a boy or man would want in a mother.

He had so many questions for the woman who'd

raised him, and part of him couldn't hate her. She'd loved him all his life, caring for him and being there when he needed her. Until now.

He'd called multiple times since he'd learned the truth. Those calls had gone unanswered, and unreturned. He'd left messages on her voice mail and nothing.

Noah wanted to sit with her, face-to-face, and ask her why. Why had she hidden him when she knew he belonged to someone else? Why had she kept the secret for so very long?

The more he thought about Ruby and Emmaline, the more he wanted answers. Perhaps it was time to find Emmaline and get those answers.

Chapter 10

Rachel leaned against Noah in the backseat of Whit's vehicle. As soon as they'd gotten in, he'd draped his arm around her and pulled her close. She remained in his embrace all the way back to Adair Acers. It was night and the events of the day had taken their toll.

Noah measured their progress along the winding road by the twists and turns, wishing the miles away so that he could get her back to the guesthouse where he had control of who moved in and out of contact with Rachel.

He felt responsible for her safety, telling himself it was out of obligation. He refused to let feelings get in the way.

Whit dropped Rachel and Noah at the guesthouse, where Landry handed off Sophia and climbed into her SUV to drive back to the main house.

While Rachel settled Sophia on her blanket on the bed in the spare bedroom, Noah made a thorough check of the house and double-checked the alarm system, doors and window locks before he was remotely satisfied.

Rachel met him in the hallway. "You should take a shower and go to bed. You have to be beat."

He ran a hand through his hair and pasted a smile on his soot-stained face. The movement through his hair stirred up the charred scent of smoke. "I need to eat something."

Rachel wrinkled her nose. "Tell you what. You have that shower, I'll whip up something to eat."

"A sandwich would be fine. I think there are some deli meats in the refrigerator. Don't make it any harder than you have to. You're tired, too."

She pointed at the bandage on his arm. "Do you need to wrap your arm in a plastic bag to keep it from getting wet?"

He shook his head. "The doc gave me extra gauze and tape. I'll just replace it after a shower."

"I can help you with that." She sighed. "I'm glad you were there to save Ruby."

"Me, too." He stared down at her with tired eyes.

For a moment she thought he was going to kiss her. Noah stepped back. "I'll have that shower. I stink."

"Right. I'll make that sandwich."

"If you hear anything out of the ordinary, if you even *think* you hear anything, don't hesitate. Come get me."

She popped a salute, turned on her heels and marched to the kitchen before she fell into the man's arms and kissed him. Rachel was so tired she wasn't thinking straight. Now was not the time to be throwing herself at the man.

He must have left the bedroom and bathroom door open. She heard the shower come on and the sound of water hitting tile. Part of her wanted to join him and spend the next thirty minutes rubbing soap all over each other's bodies. The other part wanted to play it safe, not fall any deeper in love than she already was. Giving her whole heart could get her hurt really badly. The kind of pain a bandage or a pill couldn't cure. Especially if he never forgave her for spying on him, and never loved her in return.

She found bread in the pantry and the deli meat and condiments in the refrigerator. In minutes, she had made a sandwich for herself and two for Noah. He was a big man and he hadn't eaten for over twenty-four hours, too busy saving her life and his mother's.

She pushed thoughts of the incidents to the back of her mind, not wanting to relive the terror of suffocating over and over. The important thing to remember was that she and Ruby were alive, thanks to Noah, and she planned on staying that way.

By the time she'd set the table with the sandwiches, condiments, iced glasses and the pitcher of tea Landry had prepared earlier, the shower had been shut off.

Rachel checked on Sophia, fast asleep on the bed, curled into her blanket. She barely raised her head when Rachel ran her hand across her back. The only indication the animal was awake was the quick flicking of her stump of a tail in appreciation for the attention. Poor little dog. To be displaced twice and then surrounded by strangers had to be wearing on her nerves. "We'll be okay," Rachel whispered. She patted the dog once more and turned toward the door.

Wanting to be in the kitchen when Noah came out of the master bedroom, she hurried from the spare room and ran into a broad, naked chest.

Noah reached out and steadied her. "I'm sorry, I didn't see you coming."

"I should have been watching where I was going."

They laughed softly.

"We are a mess, aren't we?" Rachel said.

"Yes, we are." Noah motioned her to take the lead while he followed, pulling a T-shirt over his head. He wore clean jeans and a plain white cotton T-shirt and padded barefoot through the house.

Rachel's pulse quickened and she tried not to turn back and stare. The man was sexy no matter what he wore or didn't wear. His dark blond hair was damp and spiked and the soot had been washed away. He smelled of aftershave or cologne. Gauging by the shadow of stubble on his face it was probably cologne.

In the kitchen they took seats across from each other at the little table.

Rachel hadn't realized how intimate a kitchen table could be until she sat facing Noah, within easy reach of his hand. She lifted her sandwich and bit into it to keep from doing something stupid, like telling him she loved him. So tired she was loopy, she couldn't trust what might come out of her mouth, so she ate, though she really wasn't hungry anymore. Not for food, anyway.

She hungered for Noah's touch. Ever since he'd kissed her down by the creek, she hadn't been able to get him out of her mind. No. To be honest, it had been before the kiss. She'd been falling in love with him since the first riding lesson.

God, she was pathetic.

"Is your head hurting?"

"No, why?" she asked, straightening in her chair.

"You're frowning, like you're in pain."

She was. The aching, soul-wrecking pain of unrequited love. "No, my headaches have pretty much gone away."

"I'm glad. Thank you for making the sandwiches." He'd polished off one and was working on the other. "I've been thinking."

"What about?" She took a tiny bite of her sandwich and chewed, waiting for him to go on.

"There have been three attacks in the past twenty-four hours. Two against you, one against Ruby. The way I see it, there's one common denominator."

"We're both female?" Rachel offered.

"Okay, two common denominators." He grinned. "You're both female, and you've both been hanging around me."

"Does this have to do with the curse Landry mentioned?"

Noah shrugged. "Something like that, only I don't believe in hocus-pocus. Someone is after you and Ruby because of me."

Rachel considered his statement. "That's an interesting theory. Any reason you can think of why someone would be after me and Ruby because of you?"

"I don't know, but I'd like to find out."

"I take it you have a plan in mind?"

"Maybe. The only person I can think of who might feel threatened by either one of you is Emmaline."

"You think your mother—aunt—is targeting people who are getting close you?"

Noah nodded. "I think so."

"If she's aiming for people who are getting close to you, why hasn't she tried to hurt Landry, Whit or Carson?"

"They aren't a direct threat. Landry hasn't been kissing me or trying to take the place of my mother. Nor have Whit and Carson."

Rachel's lips twisted into a smile. "I can't see Whit or Carson trying to replace your mother or kissing you."

"Do you see where I'm going with this?"

Rachel tilted her head to one side. "Actually, that's not a bad hypothesis."

"Thank you."

She set her sandwich on the plate and leaned forward. "So how do we prove it?"

"We find Emmaline."

Rachel sat back, crossing her arms over her chest. "Any idea where she might be?"

"That's the problem. She disappeared when the DNA results were announced."

"Did you try calling her cell phone?" Rachel asked.

"No answer," Noah said. "She might have ditched the phone to keep from being traced."

"This is a big country. She could be anywhere."

"I bet she's really close by. If she's responsible for the attacks, she's closer than I like."

"How do we catch her?"

"I'm working on the idea still. At the very least we

can pay a visit to her house in Palm Springs and see if there's any evidence that could prove my theory."

"Would that be like breaking and entering?"

"It's only breaking and entering if you actually break in." With a grin, Noah pulled a set of keys out of his pocket and separated one from the rest. "I have a key."

Rachel's eyes widened and her pulse spiked. "Are we doing this tonight?"

He shook his head. "No way. I'm beat and you've been through a lot today. We should get a good night's sleep and head out in the morning." Noah ate the last bite of his second sandwich and rose from the table. He gathered his plate and hers and carried them to the sink, filled it with water and washed the dishes.

Rachel cleaned the table and joined him at the sink with a dry towel. "Not only do you rescue damsels in distress, you do the dishes, too?"

"When you're raised as an only child, you do a lot of things."

When Noah handed her a wet glass, a spark of electricity arced between them where their fingers touched. Rachel fumbled and almost dropped the glass, heat rising in her cheeks. They worked in silence, bumping hips and arms, the tension building until the last dish was cleaned and placed in the cabinet.

Her entire body tingling with awareness, Rachel practically ran for the spare bedroom, gathered a nightgown, panties and her toiletries and walked across the hallway to the bathroom. She reached for the doorknob. Her hand stopped halfway there and began to shake. The trembling spread from her hand up her arm and into her body.

"It's only a bathroom," she whispered. No matter what she told herself, she couldn't open the door.

Noah stepped up behind her. "I took the shower curtain out earlier today. You'll have to take a bath. If you want, I can go in first."

She nodded, her feet stuck to the floor and her vocal cords locked around a giant lump lodged in her throat.

Brushing past her, Noah entered the bathroom, opening the door wide so that she could see inside. He hadn't lied about having taken the shower curtain out, even removing the curtain rod.

Stopping in front of her, he tipped her chin up and swept the hair off her face and behind her ear. "If it helps, the master bedroom has a walk-in shower with a glass door, no curtains and no tub."

She gazed into his eyes, anchoring her thoughts on him to shake off the panic attack threatening to consume her. "I'm a grown woman. I shouldn't be this afraid."

"You're a grown woman who almost died twice in less than twenty-four hours. You're allowed a little post-traumatic stress." He pulled her into his arms and stroked his hand down her back. "You can skip the shower altogether."

She rested her cheek on his soft cotton T-shirt. "The walk-in shower would be nice."

He led her into the master bedroom and took her as far as the doorway to the large bathroom. "Are you going to be all right?"

She nodded and forced a smile. "Thanks." Quickly, before she made more of a fool of herself, she stepped through the door and closed it behind her. She stared around at the gray stone tile on the floor and the speckled gray-and-white granite countertops.

The shower was a large walk-in style, tiled in a darker gray than the flooring with oiled-bronze fixtures. Nothing in this bathroom reminded her of the one in her town house. It didn't even smell like the one at her place. This one had the reassuring scent of Noah. His soap. His cologne. His strength filled the room.

With steady determination, Rachel pushed past her unreasonable fear and stripped out of her clothes. Taking a deep breath, she stepped into the shower and turned on the faucet. When the water heated to the perfect temperature, she ducked beneath it, willing the warm spray washing over her body to soothe her irrational panic. She risked getting soap in her eyes, refusing to close them for even a second.

By the time she dried off, her eyes stung from the soap and tears of exhaustion. How would she sleep if she couldn't close her eyes?

Rachel dressed in her nightgown and panties, combed the tangles from her wet hair and brushed her teeth. By the time she left the bathroom, she was so tired, she could barely put one foot in front of the other.

Noah wasn't in the master bedroom, but she could hear him talking and assumed he was on the phone. Slowly, she trudged to the spare bedroom. Sophia wasn't on the blanket where she'd left her. Rachel glanced around the room and peered under the bed.

"Looking for someone?" Noah appeared in the doorway, carrying the little Yorkie. She rested easily on his arm, content to be held.

"There you are." Rachel reached for the dog, her fingers skimming across Noah's bare arm. The connection sent an electric shock through her system, awakening her tired body to his gorgeous presence.

Shifting Sophia to her arms gave her something to hold on to rather than reaching out to Noah.

"Do you need anything else before we call it a night?" he asked.

She needed him. With a sigh, she answered, "No."

"If you get scared or think you hear anything…"

"I'll let you know."

"Okay, then." For a moment, he swayed toward her, close enough he could bend and claim her lips. At the last moment, he stepped back. "Good night, Rachel." He didn't wait for her to respond, but pivoted on the balls of his bare feet and left the room.

"Good night, Noah," Rachel whispered, stroking Sophia's soft hair.

For two people standing so close together, they couldn't have been further apart.

Rachel pulled back the comforter on the bed and settled Sophia on her blanket near the footboard. Finally, she crawled between the sheets, resting her head on the pillow, staring up at the ceiling. She leaned over to turn out the light on the nightstand, but she couldn't. If the lights were out, she wouldn't be able to see if someone was coming. Lying back against the pillow, she dragged the sheet and comforter up to her chin.

As she lay in the golden glow from the table lamp, her heartbeat quickened. She was exhausted beyond anything she'd ever felt, but every time she tried to close her eyes, her pulse raced and she imagined every noise was someone sneaking through the house.

Five minutes passed, then ten. Her eyelids drooped and, for a moment, she drifted off. No sooner had she let go, her feet slipped from under her and she was falling, the shower curtain tangling around her body, blocking her vision and choking the air from her lungs.

Rachel jerked awake with a gasp, sat up straight and dragged deep breaths into her lungs. Her heart pounded in her chest and she shook all over.

Sophia crept across the comforter to nestle against her, whining softly.

Noah burst through the open doorway wearing only a pair of boxer shorts. "What happened?"

"Nothing," Rachel managed to say, her teeth chattering, belying her words. "I just fell to s-sleep."

Noah shook his head. "Nightmare?"

She nodded, her bottom lip trembling. "I'm not a wimp, damn it." A single tear rolled down her cheek and plopped onto the sheet. "I'm an independent woman. I've lived by myself for years. This can't be happening to me." More tears slipped down her cheeks and her body quaked with silent sobs.

"Hey." Noah crossed the room, sat on the side of the bed and gathered her into his arms. "You're going to be fine."

"When? I feel like I'm falling apart and I can't stop it." She buried her cheek against his skin, fighting the sobs and the tears and failing miserably.

"You have to give yourself time to get over it," he said, rocking her and stroking her hair.

"But I'm so tired I can't think, and every time I close my eyes, I'm suffocating again."

Noah's hand stilled. Then he was shifting her out of his embrace. "Scoot over."

She glanced up at him, wishing he would take her back into his arms and hold her. Instead, she shifted to the middle of the queen-size bed, shoving Sophia over with her.

Noah slid between the sheets and held open his arms. "Come here."

"You don't have to stay. I'll manage."

"Shut up and come here." He slipped his arm beneath her and rolled her into his arms. "There. Now isn't that better?"

She lay in the crook of his arm, her cheek resting on his chest and her hand over his heart. The steady thump beneath her fingertips provided a soothing rhythm. "Are you sure we aren't hurting your injuries?"

"Not at all. Now, close your eyes," Noah's deep, rich voice commanded in a low, easy tone.

She shook her head, her eyes so wide she had to blink to keep them from drying out. "I can't."

"Try it." His hand traced a circle at the small of her back, again and again, the motion at once comforting and erotic.

Rachel braced herself mentally and closed her eyes. The sensation of falling and being smothered didn't flood over her. "They're closed."

"Good, then maybe you can loosen your hold on me. You have some sharp fingernails."

She jerked open her eyes and uncurled her fingers. She'd left little marks in his skin where she'd dug her nails in. "I'm sorry."

"I'm okay. I'll be even better when you go to sleep.

Try again. This time without claws." He lay back on the pillow and closed his own eyes as if showing her how easy it would be.

Conscious of her fingers now, she flattened them on his chest and slowly closed her eyelids.

She lay there still and stiff, her mind racing, trying to skirt the terrible memory from the morning.

"Think of something that makes you happy," he said, his chest rumbling beneath her ear.

"Like what?"

"What makes you happy?"

She tore her thoughts from what frightened her and scrambled for one that made her smile. "Horses."

"Good. Are you riding one or are you feeding it?"

"I'm watching it race around the pasture in the distance," she said. A forgotten memory from when she was a young girl resurfaced. "My parents used to drive by a horse farm when I was little. It was on the way to my grandparents' house. I remember seeing the horses running along the fences, their tails streaming out behind them."

"You love horses, don't you?"

"Yes." She smiled, her lips moving against his skin. "One time there was a colt racing alongside his mother. It was the most beautiful thing I'd ever seen."

"Sounds wonderful."

She tipped up her head to gaze into his eyes. "What about you?"

"I remember when I was eight. We lived outside of a small town. My mother—Emmaline—had to drive me to the private school in town each day. We drove past an historic chateau. It was surrounded by lush green pastures. There was a beautiful black stallion that lived there. So many times we'd pass and he'd be racing across the field, mane and tail flying. He was big, thickly muscled and powerful. I learned he was of a French breed called Percheron."

Rachel loved the way Noah's voice took on the French pronunciation so effortlessly. It was smooth and completely sexy.

Noah went on, as if from far away. "I vowed that one day I'd have a farm or ranch and raise horses."

"And now that your dream has come true?"

"Dream?" He snorted softly. "Sometimes I think it's more of a nightmare."

"All of it?"

His arm tightened around her. "Not all of it. I will always love working with the horses at Adair Acres."

Rachel held her breath.

Noah continued. "If things hadn't worked out the way they did, I might never have known Landry, Whit and Carson are my siblings." His voice dropped even lower. "And I might not have met you." He tipped her chin up.

Rachel opened her eyes and stared into his. "And then I went and broke your trust," she whispered.

"There is that." His thumb brushed across her bottom lip. "The problem is that ever since I kissed you, I haven't been able to get you out of my mind. All I want to do is kiss you again."

"What are you waiting for?" she dared to say, her breath catching and holding. Her gaze shifted to his lips and she swiped her tongue across suddenly dry lips.

Chapter 11

Noah groaned.

When Rachel's gaze dropped to his mouth, it was bad enough. When her tongue slid along the seam of her full, lush lips, he was captivated. He bent to claim her lips, deepening the contact and wanting so much more than just a kiss.

She slipped her hands up his chest to curl around the back of his neck, bringing him closer.

One of her legs skimmed along the back of his calf and up to his thigh.

Noah rolled her onto her back and pinned her wrists above her head. "Why can't I resist you?"

"Why even try?"

With a growl, he trailed kisses from her temple, across her cheek and along her jawline. Releasing his hold on her hands, he moved lower, tasted her neck, nibbled at her earlobe and tongued the pulse beating erratically at the base of her throat.

As he sank lower still, he shifted the hem of her nightgown up over her breast, exposing one of the lovely globes. He drew it into his mouth, rolling the nipple between his teeth until the tip tightened into a tiny nub.

Rachel moaned and arched her back, offering more.

He sucked it deeper into his mouth. She laced her fingers through his hair and guided him to the other breast, lifting the nightgown up to give him full access.

He leaned back, grabbed the garment and dragged it over her head, tossing it to the floor.

Rachel bunched his shirt in her hands and pulled it higher, then tugged it off. She ran her fingers over his bare skin, sending delicious sensations throughout his body.

He lay down on top of her, sliding his chest over her bare breasts and downward, flicking his tongue over her distended areolas.

She raked her fingernails across his back, dragging deep enough to make an impression but not break the skin. Every cell in his body on fire, Noah worked his way down her torso, licking, kissing and tonguing her skin, raising gooseflesh along the way.

She shivered and moaned again, parting her legs for him to slip between. When he reached the elastic of her lace panties, he hooked it with his fingers and dragged them off her legs.

"Yes," she said, her voice husky with desire. Then she leaned up. "Protection?"

With a muttered curse, Noah rose from the bed, his

chest heaving as though he'd been in a marathon. "I didn't come to your room to do this," he said, gritting his teeth in an attempt to cool his ardor.

She lay naked against the sheets, her body pale and beautiful as she stared up at him. "Please, don't stop now."

As if his inner beast had been unleashed, he lunged forward, gathered her in his arms and carried her to the master bedroom, laying her on the bed. He dug in a drawer in the nightstand and pulled out an accordion of foil packets, tossing them on the bed.

Rachel chuckled, her face flushed with more color than he'd seen throughout the day. "Think we'll need all of those?" She sat up and reached for the waistband of his boxer shorts. Then with her gaze locked on his, she stripped them off his hips and down his legs.

Noah stepped free of the shorts and kicked them to the side. He stood before her naked and so aroused he was afraid he'd scare her. Cupping her chin, he lifted her face. "We don't have to do this. You've been through so much. Just say the word and it stops here."

"I believe being with you...like this...is the only thing keeping me sane. Please, make love to me." She reached out, placing her hands on his hips, drawing him close.

She rested her cheek against his erection, sliding it over him, turning so that her lips brushed across the tip.

Noah drew in a sharp breath, his hand rising to her head, lacing into her damp hair.

When her fingers curled around his shaft, he thought he might come undone then. He gritted his teeth, fighting to maintain his control.

Rachel's hands slid up and down his member, dropping low to fondle him and back up to curve around the tip.

He stood rigid, so wound up he was afraid if he moved a single inch, he'd throw her on her back and drive into her so fast and hard, he'd forget to be careful, to take it slow and give her the attention she deserved.

Rachel slid her tongue along his length.

With a groan, Noah bunched his fingers in her hair.

When she took him into her mouth, he thrust his hips, driving his shaft into her warm wetness.

She dug her fingers into his buttocks guiding his movements, encouraging him to go faster and deeper until he bumped against the back of her throat.

"I can't…take…much more," he groaned, his hands gripping her head, holding her still.

She drew him in one last time, sucking hard before she pushed him away. Then she grabbed the string of condoms, ripped one free, tore it open and rolled it down over him. Her movements were swift and jerky, as if she was too aroused to take it slow and easy.

Then she took his hand and scooted back on the bed, bringing him with her.

Noah lay down over her, nudging her thighs apart, positioning himself between them. When he drove into her, she raised her knees, dug her heels into the mattress and met him thrust for thrust, her moans and sexy murmurs arousing the animal in him.

Tension built, rising like a tide, filling him with a kaleidoscope of sensations until he was pushed up and over the top. Noah thrust into her one more time, burying himself deep inside her slick channel.

Rachel wrapped her legs around his waist and dug her heels into his buttocks, her arms around his neck, her cheek pressed against his.

For a long moment, Noah held the position, his member throbbing inside Rachel. When at last he could draw in enough air to fill his lungs, he relaxed, rolled to his side and took Rachel with him.

He touched her lips, brushing a gentle kiss across their slightly swollen softness. "Sleep," he whispered, pressing his lips to her eyelids. "I'll take care of you."

Her body softened against his and she nestled closer, resting her head at the bend of his shoulder, her cheek against his chest. She spread a hand across his torso, her supple fingers warm on his skin.

He stroked her drying hair, again and again, until her breathing grew more regular and finally she slept.

For a long time, Noah lay with Rachel in his arms, his mind churning over the events of the past couple months. He'd gone from being an only child to a man with three siblings, an inheritance, an aunt who had claimed to be his mother and his mother who had been searching for him all his life.

The father he thought was dead had actually been the uncle he'd spent a summer with when he'd been a boy. The man had been murdered in his office and the murderer had yet to be caught.

Now his newfound mother had almost died in a deliberately set stable fire and the woman he was falling hopelessly in love with had been attacked twice and almost killed.

When he put it all together like that, he knew everything had to be related. Whoever had killed his biological father, Reginald Adair, was now trying to kill his birth mother and Rachel. The key factor had to be that they were connected to him.

Everything he'd learned so far pointed to the one person who stood to lose him.

Emmaline.

He prayed the trip to her house in Palm Springs would give them some clue as to her whereabouts. If she truly was the one who'd tried to kill Ruby and Rachel, he had to find her before she succeeded. She could be Reginald's murderer. Noah couldn't let her kill again.

Rachel didn't know how long she slept. The strong arms around her and the warmth of a body beside her allowed her to relax. Being so close to Noah, knowing how strong and brave he was, guarded her against the horrible nightmares that lurked in the back of her mind.

Several times in the night, she felt as though someone was watching her, someone waiting in the shadows to find her alone.

As long as she was with Noah, the shadowy menace remained at bay. She slept through the night, warm and safe, waking only when the morning light crept through the gaps in the window blinds to nudge her awake.

Rachel lay for a moment, loving the feel of Noah's naked body against hers. His chest rose and fell in a slow, steady rhythm.

She didn't want to move and disturb him, preferring to enjoy the freedom of studying him while he was unaware.

Her gaze swept over his strong jaw before shifting

downward to his broad chest, the muscles hard, defined and sexy as hell. Even asleep, he was gorgeous and exuded latent power, spring-loaded for battle should a threat arise. Her perusal crossed over his torso to the six-pack of abdominal muscles and lower still to the triangle of hair surrounding his jutting member.

Her breath caught at the sight of his erection, full, thick and ready for action.

Unable to resist, she smoothed her hand down his chest, across his belly and wove her fingers into the curly nest. His member jerked and he stirred.

Noah's arm curled, bringing her closer against him, his hand cupping the underside of he breast. "Don't go there unless you mean it," he said, his voice raspy with sleep.

A smile spreading across her lips, she curled her hand around his staff and slid it upward and back down. "Any doubt about my intentions?" she asked.

"Mmm. None whatsoever." He pulled her on top of him, settling her legs on either side so that she straddled him. "You get to do the work this time, while I sleep."

She swatted his chest. "Sleep? Not on my time, you won't."

He winked at her. "Guess you'll have to convince me to stay awake so that I don't miss anything."

She eased her bottom down his thighs and wrapped both hands around him, sliding up and down his shaft in slow, sensuous movements.

Noah lay with his eyes closed. Despite lying on his back against the sheets, for all appearances asleep, his body tensed beneath her, his thighs tightening.

Rachel bent to kiss the tip of his shaft.

His fingers bunched the sheet and his hips rose slightly.

With a smile, she dropped down over him, taking his full length into her mouth, wrapping him in warmth and moisture.

All pretense of sleep vanished. His eyes opened and he pulled her off him, twisted and laid her on her back, settling between her legs.

"Woman, you make a man want to wake up in the morning."

"Good. I was afraid I might have lost my touch from last night."

"Far from it." He captured her lips with a soul-searing kiss, his tongue sweeping across hers. Then, as if on a mission to conquer her, he stormed her body with his flicking tongue, tweaking fingers and tender nips to her lips, her neck, her breasts and lower.

He slid his hand down to the apex of her thighs, parting her folds to stroke the sensitive strip of flesh between.

Rachel arched her back off the bed. "Oh, yes!" she cried out.

He dipped his finger in the juices at her core and swirled his wet finger around that nerve-packed zone that had her body humming, the sensations leaping to a crescendo.

One more flick and she catapulted over the edge, calling out, "Noah!"

He chuckled as he climbed up her body, slipped a condom over himself and settled between her knees, his member poised at her opening. "Ready?"

"Oh, yes!" Lifting her knees, she pressed her heels into the bed and met his thrust.

He drove into her in a long, delicious glide, filling her channel, stretching her so beautifully a moan rose up her throat and she dug her fingers into his buttocks.

When he started to pull out, she held him there, reveling in how he made her feel so complete.

He held steady for only a moment, and then he was thrusting into her again and again, the rhythm increasing in tempo. His jaw tightened. He slammed into her one last time, throwing back his head with a groan.

Rachel held him inside her, basking in the warm afterglow of sex. The sun edged around the blinds, bathing their glistening bodies in a golden glow befitting the intensity of the passion they'd just shared.

Noah dropped down beside her, maintaining their intimate connection. He stroked her arm and reached up to brush a strand of her hair back behind her ear. "That was better than breakfast."

Rachel laughed out loud. "I should hope so."

He grinned. "Hey, for a hungry man, that's saying something."

"I suppose it is time to get up." If she could, she'd have stayed in that bed until all was right with the world again.

An insistent yip from the floor beside the bed brought her out of the warm afterglow and back to the life of responsibility.

"That's our cue." Noah slipped out of her, rolled off the other side of the bed and stood.

Rachel stared, enjoying the ripple of his muscles as he stretched.

When she rose, she remembered her hair had been wet before she'd gone to bed. God, she must be a mess. She turned her back to him, shoving her hair back from her face, finger combing it into some semblance of order.

Hands circled her waist and drew her back against a hard, sexy body. "Do you have any clue what you're doing to me?" His member nudged her bottom, hard and persistent.

She laughed. "I could give it a good guess." She turned in his arms and wrapped her arms around his neck. "I think we're going to go through your supply at this rate."

With quick efficient fingers, she rolled fresh protection over him.

He scooped her up by the backs of her thighs and carried her into the bathroom and straight into the shower.

Rachel twisted the handle and a cool spray washed over them. She didn't notice how cold when it was so hot between their two bodies.

Noah leaned her back against the tiled wall and lowered her over him, filling her all over again. This time he moved in a slow, steady rhythm, seeming in no hurry to get there.

Rachel had never had sex in the shower before Noah. The beauty of it helped shove the horror of the day before from her mind.

On the slow rise to climax, her heart swelled with so much emotion she could barely contain it. This man was truly the only one for her. If she had to spend a lifetime earning back his trust, he was worth it.

Together, they reached the peak, rocketed over the edge and floated back to earth in the warm, wet spray of the shower.

Noah set her on her feet and they spent the next few minutes soaping each other's hair and bodies, learning all the curves and edges.

When Rachel finally turned off the water, it had cooled.

They spent several more minutes drying each other with soft, fluffy towels. By the time they were through in the bathroom, Rachel's belly was rumbling.

"I'm about ready for that breakfast. How do you like your eggs?" she asked. Wrapped in a towel, she headed down the hallway to find clothes to wear.

"Naked."

She stopped, turned and smiled at Noah.

He leaned in the doorway, his towel in his hand, a leering smile on his lips. "Wanna skip breakfast?"

Rachel laughed, warmed inside by his desire. "I would, but I'm afraid if I don't take Sophia out soon, I'll be cleaning up after her."

She turned back to the spare bedroom and let the towel fall to the ground before ducking into the bedroom.

"You're killing me, woman," Noah called out.

Rachel laughed, feeling happier and more in tune with her body than she had her entire life. She wanted to freeze time, stay in the guesthouse and never come out. The thought of stepping past the security system and out of sight of Noah made her shiver. Would they ever get beyond the threat looming over them?

As she dressed in jeans and a short-sleeved cotton

blouse, she prayed they would find some evidence that would point to Reginald's murderer and to the person responsible for the more recent attacks.

If it was Emmaline, the sooner she was behind bars, the better for everyone.

Slipping on a pair of tennis shoes, Rachel snapped her fingers for Sophia and headed for the front door. "I'm taking Sophia out," she said, loud enough to be heard through the house.

"Wait for me."

"I won't go past the porch."

"Rachel, just wait."

Sophia turned circles in front of the door, wiggling so much Rachel was afraid she'd wet the floor before they got her outside.

"I'll go through first."

Rachel laughed. "I think Sophia will be first."

"Let me rephrase. I'll be the first human through the door." He disabled the security system and opened the door. Sophia shot out between his ankles.

Rachel dove to catch her, but too late.

Noah grabbed her arm, stopping her from chasing after the little dog. "Stay here," he said. "I'll go after Sophia."

Rachel frowned. "I'd like to see the morning sunshine, as well."

"Then let me check first to make sure it's clear."

Waiting hadn't always been one of her strengths, but after two attempts on her life, she wasn't chancing it. She stood behind the door while Noah made a cursory check of the yard and surroundings.

Rachel was starting to feel like a prisoner, not because of Noah but because of the threat to her life. She'd be happy when they caught the culprit. In the meantime, she had to wait.

"Okay." Noah opened the door and held it for her.

"Did you find Sophia?"

"She's around the side of the yard, sniffing at a tree." He led the way around the house toward the stable.

At the corner of the building, Rachel spotted Sophia, headed toward one of the pastures containing several horses. "Sophia!" she called out.

The Yorkie stopped and turned toward Rachel for a moment, then continued on toward the pasture.

Having spotted Rachel and Noah headed their way, three horses trotted toward the fence.

Afraid the horses would crush the little dog beneath their hooves, Rachel ran after Sophia.

Noah followed. "Sophia! Stay!"

The dog seemed hell-bent on making it to the pasture fence before the humans could catch her. Unfortunately, the only thing separating them from the horses was a split-rail fence. Sophia could slip right under it.

"Sophia!" Rachel cried out as the little dog ran under the fence, barking at the horses as if she were as big as they were.

The horses ground to a halt and dropped their heads as if trying to figure out what the noisy little creature was. Their nostrils flared, they sniffed and whinnied. One of them danced sideways, another pawed at the ground. The third lifted her front hooves and dropped back to the ground, tossing her head.

Rachel raced forward, afraid for Sophia and angry

at herself for not putting the dog on a leash before letting her outside.

Noah sailed past her, vaulted over the railing and ran for Sophia.

Sophia, the silly dog, knew no fear or common sense about animals bigger than her. She rushed toward the horses, barking like a screaming banshee.

The nearest horse reared, its hooves coming down so close to the Yorkie Rachel nearly had a heart attack. He reared again, pawing at the air.

Rachel reached the fence and watched in horror as the scene unfolded.

Noah dove for Sophia, grabbed her, tucked her in his arm and rolled to the side as the horse's hooves landed on the spot where Sophia had been a second before.

Rachel collapsed against the fence and released the breath she'd been holding.

A loud popping sound echoed behind her and something stung the back of her right shoulder. The pain was quick and intense, but Rachel didn't think much about it as she watched Noah duck out of the middle of the horses, carrying the frightened terrier.

When he reached the fence and handed her the dog, she nearly wept with relief. "Sophia, you bad girl." Rachel hugged the dog to her. "Mrs. Davis would have been devastated if she came back to find her little dog had been crushed by horses' hooves." She smiled over the top of the dog's head at Noah. "Thank you."

He nodded, brushing at the dust and grass stains on his jeans and shirt. "We'd better get back to the house. I'd like to go to Palm Springs sometime today."

When Rachel turned toward the house, she winced.

Now that the dog was safe, her adrenaline had abated and the stinging on the back of her shoulder made itself known. She reached over her shoulder to check for what might be causing it and felt something warm, wet and sticky. When she brought her hand back to the front, it was covered in blood.

Chapter 12

"What the hell?" Noah spun her around, his heart dropping to the pit of his belly when he saw that the back of Rachel's shirt was drenched in blood. "What happened?"

Rachel shook her head and swayed. "I'm not sure. I felt something sting my back, but I thought maybe a wasp or something had stung me."

Noah picked at the blouse, examining the wound. It appeared as if something had skimmed across her skin, leaving a long, thick, surface scratch that was bleeding along the length of the line. When it dawned on him what it was, his heart skidded to a halt and then raced ahead. "That's no wasp sting, babe. That's a gunshot wound."

"It can't be." She tried to look over her shoulder at the injury. "It didn't feel that bad."

"Only because it glanced off your shoulder."

She gave a shaky laugh, her body starting to tremble in Noah's hands. "A flesh wound?" She tried to joke, but then her face blanched and she swayed toward him. "Maybe we should go back inside."

Noah slipped his arm around her, steadying her. "Where were you when you felt it?"

"I was standing at the fence, watching you as you were almost trampled to death by horses." She clutched Sophia with her uninjured arm. "I don't know. It all happened so fast."

"Let's get you inside." He led her toward the guest-house, looking behind him several times before they reached the door. Once inside, he set the alarm system and pulled out his phone, hitting the number for the sheriff's department. As he waited to be connected with the detective working the arson case from the night before, he led Rachel through the house to the bathroom and made her sit on the counter.

While he reported the incident, he pulled the first-aid kit from beneath the counter, wet a clean washcloth and worked the buttons loose on Rachel's shirt.

The sheriff promised to have an officer and a paramedic out there in less than fifteen minutes.

Noah ended the call and handed the phone to Rachel. "Call Whit and tell him what happened. I'd like him and Carson here when the sheriff arrives. We need to find the shooter."

"Don't you think he'll be long gone by now?" Rachel asked.

"Probably." Noah peeled the shirt off her shoulders, careful where the blood had congealed and stuck the shirt to her wound. "That makes two breaches of security on the ranch. We need to shore up the fences or cameras so that this doesn't happen again, or if it does, we have the footage to identify the attacker."

Rachel nodded, wishing he was taking off her clothes for much better reasons than because she'd been shot.

"I don't think we should go to Palm Springs," he said behind her, dabbing the clean cloth across the wound.

The motion burned. Rachel gritted her teeth and focused on what Noah had said. "We have to go."

"It's not safe for you outside and I can't leave you here."

"You don't have to leave me here. I can go with you. As long as we're together, I'll be safe."

"I can't risk it. Whoever's doing this had to be close by, watching us. He, or she—" Noah's jaw tightened "—took a shot when I wasn't close to you."

"All the more reason to make him think we're staying in the house all day. When the sheriff and your brothers arrive, we can sneak out and escape in Whit's vehicle." Rachel turned to face him. "It'll work. Whit can stay for twenty or thirty minutes, then take your truck back to the main house."

Noah didn't want to expose Rachel any more than he had to, but what she was suggesting made sense. At least they could throw the attacker off the track for a little while and maybe come up with some evidence the detectives could use to help solve the cases. "Okay."

Rachel grinned and made the call to Whit, she told him what had happened and that Noah wanted him and Carson there when the sheriff arrived.

"I'll be right over," Whit said.

"Oh, and, Whit?" Rachel caught him before he ended the call. "Wear a hat."

"Huh?"

"Just do it," Rachel insisted.

"Okay," he responded, sounding confused.

Noah finished cleaning Rachel's wound and applied antiseptic ointment and a bandage. He was helping her into a bright red, button-up shirt when Whit and Carson arrived.

Rachel waved him to the door. "I can dress myself."

Noah opened the door to the two men and Landry, smiling at Whit's big straw cowboy hat.

"We were at the main house discussing the situation," Whit said, removing the hat as soon as the door was closed behind him.

"And how we could beef up security around the ranch," Carson added.

"Perfect," Noah said. "Whoever got in did so twice."

"That worries me," Landry said.

"Worries *you*?" Noah pinched the bridge of his nose. "I don't know how much more Rachel can take. We're up to three attempts on her life. She's not a cat with nine lives to spare."

"I don't know—I'm a third of the way there." Rachel entered the room.

Landry rushed forward and took Rachel's hands. "Are you okay?"

Rachel nodded. "It was just a flesh wound. Nothing serious."

"Nothing serious?" Landry stared at her as if she'd lost her mind. "Someone shot at you! You could have been killed." She wrapped her arm around Rachel's waist and hugged her.

Rachel's lips twisted. "Thanks. I was trying not to think about that."

Noah almost laughed at the sarcasm. Rachel was handling the gunshot wound better even than the incident the day before when she had nearly been suffocated. He felt as if he was coming apart at the seams.

He clenched his fists, wishing he could find the person responsible and rip him apart.

Whit waved his cowboy hat. "Why did you want me to wear a hat?"

Rachel glanced out the window. "I'll tell you after we talk to the sheriff."

A paramedic fire truck and a sheriff's vehicle pulled up in front of the house and the sheriff got out. The paramedic dropped down from the cab of the truck and unloaded a medical kit, while the sheriff's deputy got out of his car, carrying a notepad.

The men surrounded Rachel as they went out to greet the sheriff and take him to where Rachel had been standing when she'd been wounded.

While Noah shielded Rachel with his body, the paramedic checked her wound while the Adair brothers and the sheriff searched the grounds in the direction from which the bullet could have come.

Despite being an effort much like finding a needle in a haystack, they discovered the expended cartridge and secured it for evidence.

They returned to the house to discuss what would happen next. When the sheriff had all the information he needed, he left.

Noah faced his half brother, Whit. "I need your shirt and your hat."

"My shirt?" Whit handed him the hat and hesitated with his fingers on the buttons of his blue chambray shirt.

"And the keys to your SUV," Rachel added, then turned to Landry. "I need your shirt and sunglasses."

"What's going on?" Carson asked.

Noah took Whit's hat and pulled his T-shirt over his head. "We figure we're being watched pretty closely. I need to leave as Whit Adair in order to throw our pursuer off our trail. It's the only way to get away from the house without being followed."

"Where are you going?" Landry asked.

Noah glanced at Rachel. His gut told him he could trust his half brothers and sister, but just in case... "We're going to look for evidence."

Whit, Carson and Landry stared at Noah as if waiting for him to continue.

Rachel stepped up beside Noah. "It's best if he and I are the only ones who know where we are going. That way no one can let it slip."

"I don't think any of you are responsible for what's been happening to Ruby, Rachel and Reginald, but I can't be too careful."

Whit's lips thinned. "I understand. I don't like it, but I understand. If Elizabeth was the one being shot at, I'd probably err on the safe side, too."

Carson nodded. "I'd feel the same if it was Georgia. So many people we should have trusted have failed us." He stuck out his hand. "I hope that one day you can find it in your heart to trust your brothers."

Landry stepped forward. "And sister."

Noah nodded. "While we're gone, is anyone watching over my—Ruby?" As much as he wanted to, he still couldn't see her as his mother when he barely knew the woman.

"Derek contacted Aunt Kate. She got hold of a former secret service agent who'd worked protecting her when she'd been in office. He's living in California and will be here by noon. In the meantime, Derek and Georgia are at the hospital guarding Ruby."

"Good."

Landry smiled at Rachel. "Come on, let's swap shirts. You two need to get out of here while the going's good." She led Rachel to the spare bedroom.

"I'm having security cameras installed around the stable," Carson said. "What happened to Ruby and Rachel shouldn't have. If there had been cameras in place, we might have caught the culprit after the incident last night. Rachel wouldn't have taken a hit today."

Noah had it on the tip of his tongue to tell Carson and Whit what he suspected. Part of him didn't want to believe Emmaline could have committed all the crimes. How could one older woman be so ruthless and cunning? Until he had evidence, he didn't want to accuse the woman or turn her nephews against her for no reason. She'd been his mother all these years. Despite the lies, she'd always loved him and he'd loved her. After thirty-seven years, he couldn't turn off those feelings that quickly. The longer she remained in hiding, the more convinced Noah was that she was guilty.

Unless she was being held captive by someone.

Try as he might, Noah could think of no other person who would target Ruby and Rachel.

Whit unbuttoned his shirt, stripped it off and handed it to Noah. Noah gave him the T-shirt he'd been wearing.

By the time he had the chambray shirt on and buttoned, Rachel and Landry emerged from the bedroom.

Rachel wore the lightweight teal pullover sweater Landry had arrived in and Landry wore the bright red blouse Rachel had worn outside when she'd given her statement to the sheriff. Rachel had pulled her hair back in a ponytail just like Landry had worn when she'd come into the house. Landry had let her hair fall loose around her shoulders.

"Ready?" Noah asked.

Rachel nodded.

"No, wait." Landry dug in her purse and unearthed her sunglasses. "You'll need these."

With a smile, Rachel accepted the sunglasses and slid them onto her nose. "Thanks."

"Okay, then Whit and Landry are leaving." Landry gave Rachel a gentle hug to keep from hurting her injured back. "Be careful."

"We will."

Whit and Carson shook hands with Noah and hugged Rachel. "Call if you need help getting out of a tight situation."

"We will." Noah clamped the straw cowboy hat on his head and pulled it low over his eyes.

He stared across at Rachel. With the sunglasses and her hair pulled back, she could pass for Landry. "Let's go."

They walked out the door and into the sunshine. If Emmaline was watching for them to leave the ranch, as long as she thought they were still in the guesthouse, she might stay.

Noah hoped she didn't get tired of hanging around Adair Acres and decide it was time to return to her house.

Rachel kept her head down with the sunglasses snug against her face as she hurried toward Whit's SUV.

Noah clicked the key fob, releasing the locks as they arrived at each side of the vehicle.

He'd wanted to shield her with his body, but Rachel had insisted Whit would have no need to shield Landry since she hadn't been a target and she was his sister, not his lover.

Noah hadn't liked it, but agreed it made sense and he let her walk out alone, far enough away from him that a decent shot could take her out.

In the sunlight, Rachel tried not to think of herself as a target. Instead, she focused on making it to the SUV alive and getting in as if she hadn't a care in the world. Once inside, she breathed a sigh, until she glanced out the windows and realized they were only glass, not bulletproof glass. If someone did have her in their crosshairs and if the ruse hadn't worked, nothing would stop a bullet from piercing the windshield and hitting her.

Noah turned the key and the engine started. He glanced her way as he shifted into Drive and headed down the drive toward the gate. "You okay?"

Though her hands shook and she doubted she'd ever feel safe again, she nodded. "I'm fine."

Noah drove toward the gate leading off the property. The idea was that if they hurried, they could be in Palm Springs by early afternoon, investigate the house and be back on the road before dark.

They headed north on the highway to Palm Springs. For the first hour, Rachel glanced back several times looking for any sign of being followed.

"You can relax," Noah said. "I've been watching in the rearview mirror. I think your idea worked."

Rachel leaned back in her seat. "Thank God."

"Why don't you sleep? We still have another hour and a half before we get there."

"I'm not sleepy," she insisted. Despite her denial, after several minutes staring at the road in front of her, Rachel's eyelids drooped and soon she drifted off.

Noah's hand on her arm woke her. "We're entering Palm Springs now."

"Okay. Thanks." She yawned, rubbed her eyes and sat up.

Noah turned into a gated community and entered a code on a keypad. The gate swung open and he drove through. The security guard in the gatehouse didn't blink as they passed through.

Rachel admired the beautiful large homes on the street. "Did you live here with Emmaline?"

"For a short time before I moved to Adair Acres."

"When did she move here?"

"I suppose she got lonely after I'd grown and moved out on my own. She moved here shortly after I left home, wanting to be closer to her brother. I was moving around quite a bit in Europe."

"Sounds wonderful. Why did you come back?"

"Emmaline had a fall, broke her hip and needed help getting around. I came back to the States to live with her until she recovered."

Rachel smiled. "A good son."

His lips thinned but he made no comment.

"Why do you still have a key?"

"She wanted me to feel like it would always be my home. I was welcome anytime."

"Were you close to her?"

Noah hesitated, his gaze on the house at the end of a cul-de-sac. "I was as close as she'd let me."

"What do you mean?"

"She was my mother. I didn't know any different and she loved me like I was her own."

"I feel there is a *but* in there."

He pulled into the driveway and shifted the SUV into Park. "Emmaline didn't share her feelings with me. She kept me fairly secluded as a child. I grew up in France, away from the rest of the Adairs. She didn't take me to visit, and the only time I saw any of my extended family was when my grandparents came to visit. She never invited Reginald or his children to come stay with us."

"Sounds lonely."

He shrugged. "You don't know what you don't have. I didn't realize how lonely I was until I got a taste of what growing up in a family with siblings was like."

"The summer you stayed at Adair Acres?"

Noah nodded. "I was a teen and the others were

younger than me, but it was nice to have someone to ride with, to swim in the creek, to talk to at the dinner table. When Emmaline had recovered enough from her surgery, I didn't want to go back to France. As soon as I was old enough, I took jobs all over Europe, established myself as a businessman. Speaking a variety of foreign languages made me a valuable asset to a number of corporations. I was on the road most of the time.

"Emmaline was for all intents and purposes alone in France. She moved back to the States twelve years ago to be closer to Reginald." He shoved the driver's door open and climbed down.

Rachel joined him in front of the SUV. The sun was shining down on them and any curious neighbor could glance out their window. "Are you sure this is a good idea to enter the house in broad daylight?"

"Absolutely." Noah strode up to the door. "I was here long enough to meet most of the neighbors. I ran a business out of the house, until several months ago when Reginald was shot. In his will, he'd left a share of his estate to me, his nephew, Emmaline's son." Noah snorted. "That's when I moved into the guesthouse. Don't worry. The neighbors know me here. I've been here recently enough they won't be suspicious."

"What if Emmaline comes back and they say something about your visit?"

"I can leave a note on the counter for Emmaline when I leave. Remember, she's the one who has disappeared. I could be here looking for her, worried that I haven't heard from her. Besides, she must know by now I have a lot of questions for her."

He stuck the key in the lock and twisted it. Before

he opened the door, he turned to her. "Let me go first. If by some slim chance she's here, I don't want her to blow a hole in you." He shook his head. "Another hole."

"You'd rather let her blow a hole in you?" A shiver rippled down Rachel's spine. "I don't like that idea any better."

"I don't think she'll hurt me." Noah didn't wait for her approval. He stepped forward, entering the house of the woman who'd lied to him all of his life.

He searched one room after the other, quickly determining the house was empty. Once he was certain it was safe, he stood in the living room. "Okay, let's see if we can find anything that looks like evidence." He nodded toward the master bedroom. "We can start in her room."

Rachel knew they could cover a lot more ground if they split up, but Noah wouldn't hear of it. He wanted her close to him so that he could protect her. It made her feel good and sad at the same time. She didn't like that her life had become so dangerous that she couldn't move about on her own. She valued her freedom and the sense of peace.

Noah started by going through the drawers in Emmaline's dresser, looking beneath all the clothes, stacks of papers and old greeting cards. There were no hidden drawers in the dresser chest of drawers or nightstands.

Rachel went through a bookcase in a corner of the bedroom. It was filled with leather-bound books and photo albums. She pulled the books out and leafed through the pages. She wasn't sure what she was looking for but didn't want to leave one page unturned. When she got to the photo albums, she sat on the floor and turned page after page, staring down at a small boy, seeing his progression from toddler to grade school to high school and graduation. He stood with Emmaline in some of them, his light blond cap of hair a stark contrast to her rich brown hair. In most of them he was playing alone, either on a swing or standing near a field in the French countryside.

He was a beautiful little boy and he appeared to be happy. Rachel wondered what his children would look like. Would they have the blond hair from Ruby's side of the family or the rich dark hair of the Adairs?

"Ruby would love to see these photos." Rachel's heart ached for the woman who'd had her son stolen from her. "She missed all of this."

He didn't respond, his head under the bed as he reached for something. When he emerged, he had a long plastic box filled with papers. He sat on the floor beside the bed and opened it.

Rachel set the photo album back on the shelf and finished going through the others and the books and then stood.

"Look at this." He held up a document.

Rachel walked over to him and sat beside him. "What is it?" She took the paper from him, her pulse kicking up as she read the description of the item.

"It's a sales receipt for a rifle and a scope," Noah confirmed.

Rachel shot a glance at him. "Your mother was a gun enthusiast?"

"Not when I was living with her. She never kept one in her house." His face was grim as he lifted another receipt out of the box and handed it to her. "This one is for a .40 caliber handgun."

Rachel gasped. "I read in the paper that Reginald had been shot in the chest at point-blank range with a .40 caliber bullet."

Noah nodded. "The crime-scene investigators pulled the bullet out of the wall behind him. They said most victims shot at close range like that usually know their murderer."

"Just because she has a receipt for a couple of guns doesn't make her an expert shot. Granted, if you're shooting someone with a pistol when he's standing right in front of you, you're bound to kill him. But a rifle shot from far enough away you can hide…" Rachel shook her head.

Noah held up a business card advertising a gun range offering gun-handling lessons. "You know where we will be headed next?"

Rachel nodded. They would pay a visit to the firing range. She hurried back to the photo albums and leafed through until she found one of the most recent photographs of Emmaline.

Noah joined her. "I snapped that photo six years ago when I took her to San Francisco for her sixtieth birthday."

Rachel handed the photo to him and he tucked it into the pocket of his shirt. She could tell it was hard on him to realize the woman he'd thought was his mother could be a murderer. He obviously still had feelings for her. How could he not?

Rachel laid a hand on his arm. "I'm sorry all this happened to you."

His brows furrowed. "I'm sorry you're caught in the middle of it. If Emmaline is the one responsible for a murder and four attempts, she needs to be found and put away."

"Do you think she's lost her mind? After all those years knowing she had Reginald's son, she had to have been plagued with a heavy amount of fear and guilt."

"I hope so."

"And she had to have been in a pretty unstable frame of mind when your grandparents brought you to her to raise. I could see how losing her baby would make her all that more determined to keep a gift like you. A healthy baby boy to fill the void created by the loss of her own son."

"Depression doesn't excuse her actions. She had no right to keep me." Though his words were harsh, the expression in his eyes spoke louder. He cared for the woman, even though he had to stop her.

They spent another hour going through the rest of the house. They found a locked gun safe in the study and framed photos of Noah throughout the house.

"I never realized how creepy it was that she had so many pictures of me hanging all over the house," Noah commented as he slowly walked down a hallway covered in picture frames.

"It's not creepy." Rachel touched his arm. "She loves you."

As his last stop, he climbed the steps up into the attic. Rachel followed him. A few old pieces of furniture stood around, collecting dust, along with a couple of file boxes and an antique steamer trunk with the name Adair inscribed on a faded brass plate.

Rachel went through the file boxes and found only old taxes records.

Noah headed straight for the trunk. "I remember this. My mother kept it in her bedroom when we lived in France. It always had a lock on it and I wasn't allowed to look inside. I remember dreaming that it held a pirate's treasure."

"It's not locked now." Rachel walked across the dusty wooden floor to stand beside him.

Slowly, he lifted the lid and stared at the contents inside.

On top was a yellowed wedding dress covered in clear plastic. Moving it aside, Noah lifted out a Dodgers baseball cap that he recognized as the one his uncle Reginald had sent him after his visit to Adair Acres. As he dug past ribbons and trophies from his school days, he found an old photo album filled with pictures of Emmaline and her husband as young adults in Europe, happy, carefree and appearing to be in love.

"What happened to Emmaline's husband?" Rachel asked.

"She told me my father died in a car crash before I was born, when she was pregnant with me."

"Wow. Not only did she lose her child, she lost her husband while she was pregnant with that child. No wonder she didn't want to give you back to your rightful parents. In her mind, they had each other. She had nothing."

Noah moved the photo album aside and lifted out a large leather-bound book and opened the cover. It appeared to be a scrapbook of newspaper clippings and magazine articles. As he read the captions, his heart ached and burned for the woman who'd called herself his mother for thirty-seven years.

"Oh, my God," Rachel said. "It's a scrapbook of the search for Jackson Adair."

Chapter 13

Rachel held the scrapbook in her lap in the front seat of Noah's pickup, turning over page after page. "Emmaline had to have been consumed by fear and guilt to collect all of this."

Noah sat in the driver's seat, stone-faced.

"I can imagine how conflicted she was, in constant terror of someone discovering the truth and taking you away from her." Rachel's chest ached for the women. "There must be fifty articles from various newspapers and magazines just for the first year after your abduction. And there are some in a variety of foreign languages."

Reginald Adair's younger face was plastered over many articles, his jaw tight, his determination apparent in the way he held himself. Rachel could see a lot of him in Noah, if not the actual facial structure then the determination and strength.

Some of the articles led the readers to believe Reginald had murdered his son and was covering it up with a kidnapping plot and a desperate plea to find him.

The scrapbook was a media history of Reginald's attempt to find his missing son. Every year there were fewer and fewer articles, but the bereaved father kept fighting.

"Noah, your father never stopped trying to find you. Even last year he hired an agency to look into your disappearance." Rachel pointed to the article. "Emmaline found the article on the internet and printed it out to add to her collection."

Noah shook his head. "How could I have been so blind?"

"How could everyone have been so blind? Who would have guessed a member of your own family would steal a baby and give him to another member of your family?"

Noah pulled into the parking lot of the firing range and shifted into Park, making no move to get out of the truck. "It makes you lose faith in the human race."

Rachel wanted to cry for the man who'd been lied to all of his life. "Oh, babe, you can't lose faith. Not everyone is like that." Although she wasn't a good example, having lied to him to get close enough to spy on him. "Some people lie for really good reasons, maybe to protect someone from harm. And some lie out of desperation and broken hearts."

"Why can't people just tell the truth?"

"Sometimes the truth hurts too much," she offered.

"Other times, the truth could be dangerous. Think about the witness protection program."

"That's different. And it really doesn't matter." Noah pushed open his door. "How I was raised and by whom is the past. Let's go get some answers relevant to what's happening now." He rounded the truck, helped her down and they entered the building together.

Rachel could only imagine how hard it was for Noah to believe the woman he'd known and loved as his mother could be a killer. She wished none of this was happening and that she could take away Noah's pain.

The front reception area held the pungent scent of gunpowder and cleaning oil. The banging sound of rounds being fired could be heard behind a wall.

"May I help you?" A tattooed woman with long salt-and-pepper gray hair secured back in a ponytail smiled as they entered.

Noah retrieved the photo from his pocket and held it out to the woman. "Has this woman been here for lessons or to use the range for practice anytime in the past six months?"

She reached for the photo, a brightly inked bird of paradise curled around her forearm. She wore a plain black tank top with a skull emblem silkscreened on the right breast. "Who is she?"

Noah replied without hesitating. "My mother. She's been missing for a couple weeks and we're worried about her."

Rachel stood beside Noah. He hadn't lied. Emmaline had been his mother for thirty-seven years. She was missing and they were worried about her. But there was so much more to the search than just finding a woman who'd disappeared. They were looking for a potentially dangerous woman who could have murdered someone.

"I don't remember seeing her, but I've only been working here for a couple weeks, filling in for the woman who usually runs the front counter, while she's on maternity leave."

Noah nodded toward the rear of the building. "Could any of the instructors recognize her if she'd been here?"

"Maybe." The woman shrugged. "Go on back, but wait behind the yellow line while the shooters are firing."

Rachel led the way, Noah right behind her, his hand at the small of her back. She'd never been to an indoor firing range; nor had she fired a gun other than the ones used at the carnivals and arcades. Not that she was against them, just that she'd never had the opportunity or thought about firing a gun for sport or target practice.

The back of the building was set up in lanes with targets at the end and little chutes for the shooters to stand in. There was just enough room for one person to move his arms and position himself to fire a handgun. The shooters in their positions wore headphones for ear protection and stood with their feet wide, or with one positioned forward, and fired at the targets.

A couple of men dressed in cargo pants and black tank tops, their hair military short and their arms inked with dragons and eagles waited for two shooters to finish firing. When the shooters emptied their guns, they dropped the clips, pulled the bolts to the rear and reeled their targets in, then waited for the instructors.

The men in the black tank tops moved forward and

critiqued the way the shooters held their weapons while firing, the way they stood or the way they pulled the trigger.

Rachel watched in fascination, wishing they had time to get in a little target practice.

Noah leaned close to her and asked, "Have you ever fired a gun?"

She shook her head. "Never."

"We'll have to fix that."

Her lips curled upward at his words. That kind of talk made her believe he wasn't so ready to have her out of his life. They might actually spend more time together at a similar shooting range closer to San Diego.

The first instructor finished his critique and stepped back to where Noah and Rachel stood while the shooter attached a fresh paper target and sent it downrange.

"Mark Jameson." The man in the black tank top stuck out his hand to Noah.

"Noah Scott." They shook hands.

Then instructor turned to Rachel with a friendly smile and held out his hand to her. "And who is this?"

"I'm Rachel Blackstone," she said, and took the man's hand.

He had a firm grip and held his shoulders back like a man who'd been in the military.

Noah presented the photograph. "Have you seen this woman?"

Mark stared at the photo, his brow creasing. "I have. She came in for several weeks learning how to fire her handgun. Said she was living alone and wanted it for protection." He shook his head. "She liked firing it so much she bought a rifle with a scope and learned how to fire it on our outside range." He grinned. "She was pretty danged good for a woman her age."

Rachel's stomach knotted and the gash in her shoulder stung at the thought of Emmaline Scott practicing her aim so that she could shoot innocent people.

"When was the last time she was here?" Rachel asked.

The man scratched his head. "Seems like it's been several months. Maybe back in November of last year?" He shrugged. "I remember her because she reminded me of my mother. My mom was a feisty old woman. Miss Addy showed a lot of gumption to learn to fire a gun so late in life and she learned quickly."

"Addy?" Noah asked.

"Addy Smith." Mark handed the photo back to Noah. "Why do you want to know about her? Has something happened to her?"

"She's been missing for a couple weeks and we were getting worried about her." Noah tucked the photo back in his pocket and held out his hand. "I found your business card in her things and thought I'd check it out. I figured it might be a long shot."

Mark shook his hand. "I hope you find her. She seemed like a nice lady."

Noah and Rachel left the building in silence.

Rachel settled into the passenger seat of the truck, a cold chill washing over her. Sure, she felt sorry for the woman who'd lost her husband and her newborn, but what left her feeling cold and a little frightened was the notion that if Emmaline had shot Reginald, it hadn't been out of self-defense or in the heat of passion. It had been cold-blooded, premeditated murder.

* * *

Noah drove for the first hour without speaking, his brain churning with everything he'd learned about the woman he'd always known as his mother. The more he thought about her the more convinced he was that something wasn't right in her mind, and that it stemmed all the way back to when she'd lost her family.

Over the years, she'd held it together because she'd had him to care for. But the sickness had been there and followed her, growing and spreading.

When he'd moved out of her house in France, he'd been back often to visit, knowing she was alone. The more involved he became in trade and the import-and-export business, the less time he had to visit.

He'd been thrilled when she decided to move back to the States to be closer to her brother, Reginald. It meant that he would finally make it back to visit the one place he'd felt the most at home—Adair Acres. His mother would also be closer to family if she needed help. Except she wouldn't accept help from Reginald when she'd fallen and broken her hip.

Noah had returned to the States to help her and she'd made it too easy for him to move in with her and work his business from her home.

Looking back, he could remember how clingy she'd been, even after she had fully recovered from her hip injury. He'd stayed until he'd received news of his uncle's death and the subsequent filing of the will of which he'd received a copy. He was shocked and pleased to discover he'd inherited a share of Adair Acres. Knowing his mother was well enough to function on her own, he'd moved to the guesthouse of the estate.

He felt sick knowing he'd inherited property from a man his mother most likely murdered.

"This has to stop," Noah said.

"What has to stop?" Rachel turned in her seat and stared at him.

He shot a glance at her, tallying the attempt on Ruby's life and the three attempts on Rachel's. She'd survived all three, barely. The next attempt might take and she'd be dead. He couldn't let that happen, even if it meant sending Emmaline to jail for the rest of her life.

A heavy weight settled on his chest. Emmaline had loved him, cared for him and done so much for him out of love. But it didn't change what he needed to do.

"We have to stop Emmaline," he said, his determination set.

Rachel nodded. "I agree, but how? She's managed to slip past everyone. She's been in hiding since your DNA test."

He nodded, a plan forming in his mind. "We have to draw her out."

"What do you mean?"

"So far she's been the hunter, watching, waiting and attacking when she knows she has her victim alone."

Rachel trembled next to him. "True. But we never know when she's going to attack. How can we catch her if we don't see her first?"

"We go on the offensive. We don't wait for her to come after you or Ruby. We set a trap that she will be sure to show up for."

Rachel's pretty brows furrowed. "How do we do that?"

"Who is she obsessed with?"

"She wants to kill me and Ruby," Rachel offered. "I'm not sure about Ruby. I wouldn't use Ruby as bait, but I'd be willing to set a trap for Emmaline."

He smiled at her offer. "Granted she's gone after you and Ruby, but why?"

With a shrug, Rachel stared at him. "Beats me. Unless you're right and she's threatened by us, thinking we might take you away from her."

"Exactly. What has always been her greatest fear?"

Rachel's brows rose. "Losing you. What are you thinking?"

"We need to make her think I'm dying."

Her frown deepening, Rachel asked, "How do you propose doing that?"

"I can stage an accident that will be big enough to be publicized on radio and television. I'll be taken to the hospital. The news reporters will report that I'm not expected to make it."

Rachel raised her hand to her chest. "If she sees the news report, she'll come out of hiding to see you before you die."

"That's the idea."

Rachel's lips twisted into a wry smile. "You do realize that's lying."

Noah's mouth firmed into a thin line. "Yeah. I don't like doing it. But you were right. Sometimes you have to lie to protect the people you care about. I understand that now." He reached across the console and took her hand. "I can't let her hurt any more people. If I have to lie to make that happen, I will."

"You realize it has to be convincing? She's been

watching us closely. What kind of accident do you propose?"

"I could fall off a horse and break my neck."

Rachel nodded a moment and then shook her head. "Although your injury might be enough to bring her in, it won't be big enough to be newsworthy. It has to make a bigger splash for the television crews to cover."

Noah thought about it. "You're right. It needs to be exciting, something that gets all of San Diego and possibly even California and maybe national networks to pick up."

Rachel leaned forward. "Exactly. We don't know where she's staying and what kind of access she has to the news. We have to hit as many media sources as possible to insure maximum coverage."

"You're very good at this."

She smiled. "Thanks. It comes with years of practice. I've been involved in enough philanthropic efforts to know what gets public attention."

"How about a fiery crash?"

"That might do it." She caught her bottom lip between her teeth. "As long as you don't get injured for real. The idea is to bring her out, not to kill you."

"After I blew up at you, I'm surprised you still care."

"You had a right to be mad at me. Your world has pretty much turned upside down. If I had found out I'd been lied to all my life, and that I missed growing up with the mother and father who loved me dearly and wanted me to be a part of their lives to the point they spent their existence looking for me, I'd be mad, too."

"Yes, but you weren't responsible for what Emmaline and my grandparents did."

"No, but I shouldn't have spied on you." Rachel stared down at her hands. "It was wrong."

Noah stared at her bowed head and realized something. "If you hadn't agreed to spy on me, you wouldn't have asked for riding lessons, and I wouldn't have had the opportunity to get to know a very pretty, and loyal, green-eyed socialite."

Her lips quirked. "I enjoyed being your friend. I'll miss our rides."

"Who says you have to quit coming out to ride at Adair Acres?"

"I don't know if I can keep coming. We've gone way past friendship and I don't think we can go back to just friends." She didn't look at him, turning her face to stare out the passenger-seat window. "At least *I* can't."

"I don't want to go back either, but I'm not sure I'm ready for more. I'm still trying to sort out who I am." Again he reached out to take her hand.

"I understand." Rachel slipped her hand in his. "Just promise me that when this is all over, we sit down for a long talk."

"Agreed." He squeezed her hand and returned his to the steering wheel. "For now, we need to plan a spectacular crash. We'll need a vehicle."

Rachel glanced at the interior of the truck they were riding in. "It wouldn't be fair to crash Whit's SUV. How attached are you to your truck?"

He shrugged. "My old truck has stood by me like a champ. I don't think I've had to make any major repairs on it since I bought it."

"I hate to trash a good vehicle. Is there one that you're ready to send to be recycled?"

"For it to be believable, I have to make sacrifices. Besides, I can afford another truck." He nodded. "It's decided, I'll use my truck. I'll need to do a little research to find out what makes the biggest fireball."

"I can talk to a friend of mine on the local news crew. She's always covering my charity auctions and events. I know she's been chomping at the bit to get something juicier. I can tell her that I have an event I'm staging at Adair Acres and ask her to meet me there on the day we stage the accident. That way she'll be on her way out with a cameraman."

"Tomorrow."

"What about tomorrow?" Rachel shot a glance at him. "You want to do this tomorrow?"

He nodded. "The sooner the better. I'd do it tonight, but we need time to put things in place, coordinate with the parties involved and make it look as real as possible." Noah grinned. "I think this will work."

"We can crash the truck and make it light up like the Fourth of July, but how do we get the emergency medical technicians to take you seriously when you're smiling like the cat that ate the canary?" She laughed out loud, her face happier than it had been in days.

Noah wanted to keep that happy smile on her face. The sooner they caught Emmaline and got her off the streets, the sooner all their lives returned to normal.

"I can fake a back injury," he offered. "They will load me up and take me to the hospital."

"I have friends and acquaintances at the hospital. I might be able to get them to cover for us, but it could be dicey getting you into an ICU room. They don't like tying up space in the ICU with people who don't need it."

"I've made enough money in my business—I can afford to make a healthy donation to the hospital." He raised his brows.

Rachel shook her head. "Let me work it from the inside. I have a doctor friend who was Special Forces before he decided to dedicate his life to preserving life rather than taking lives. He might be willing to help us stage the hospital side of this effort."

Noah shoved a hand through his hair. "It's starting to sound too complicated. Too many things could go wrong. If we involve too many people, word might leak out."

"Then *we* stage the accident. Only you and I can know it's fake until it's plastered all over the news."

Noah nodded. "Deal."

"Once we have you at the hospital, your family will be there, we can let them in on the secret."

The rest of the drive back, they planned where the "accident" would take place and when.

Rachel made a call to her friend on the local San Diego news crew and arranged for her to show up the next day at Adair Acres. She asked the reporter to text her when she was on the way so that Rachel would be on her way there at that time.

By the time they made it back to San Diego, the plan was set.

"We're going to stop at the San Diego Police Department to pass on the information we found at Emmaline's house and the firing range," Noah announced.

"Are you going to tell them what we're planning to do?"

"I don't want to pass on too much and have it leak out." Noah knew, in order for this plan to work, it had to look real.

"It would be nice if we had police backup at the hospital for when Emmaline shows up."

Noah scratched his chin, his eyes narrowed. "Yes, it would."

"Do you want me to wait in the truck?" Rachel asked.

"Hell, no. I'm keeping you with me as much as possible."

"And tomorrow?"

"I'll have Whit or Carson with you. You can follow behind him so that you're there soon after my truck goes over the cliff."

She gave him a crooked smile. "Thanks. Nothing like watching a truck go over the cliff. Promise me you won't go with it."

He winked. "I promise."

They stepped out of the SUV and entered the police station, where they were escorted back to Detective Grant.

Rachel laid the scrapbook on his desk and Noah gave him the receipts for the guns and the business card for the firing range.

Detective Grant pinched the bridge of his nose and shook his head. "Tell me you didn't break into Emmaline Scott's home and take these items."

"We didn't break in," Noah said. "I happen to live

there when I'm not at Adair Acres. I lived there for more than a year and I have my own key."

The detective's stiff shoulders loosened. "Okay, then. You have the method she could have used in the murder of Reginald Adair and the subsequent attempts on Ruby Mason and Miss Blackstone. What could possibly be a sixty-six-year-old woman's motive?"

Noah jabbed a thumb toward his chest. "Me."

The detective stared at Noah. "What do you mean?"

For the next fifteen minutes, Noah went over the story of his abduction as a baby and how Emmaline was involved, showing him the contents of the scrapbook. When he was done, he added, "Why else would someone want to kill Reginald, Ruby and Rachel? It fits."

"If I recall, Mrs. Scott had an alibi," the detective said. "You. She said she had dinner in Palm Springs with you that night Reginald was killed. How could she have killed Reginald and had dinner with you two hours away?"

"Did she mention it was a late dinner? I'd been working all day and late into the evening. She came into my home office and asked me to go to dinner with her. We did."

"So she could have had plenty of time to kill Reginald and make it back to Palm Springs to have dinner with you." Detective Grant nodded. "The situation bears looking into. We need to bring her in for questioning."

Noah couldn't have agreed more. "Problem is that since the DNA test results came back identifying Reginald as my father, Emmaline's been missing."

"But you think she might be the one responsible

for the attempt on Mrs. Mason and Miss Blackstone," Grant stated. "Which means she's probably close by."

"Looking for her next opportunity." Noah glanced at Rachel. "I've assigned myself as Rachel's bodyguard. Ruby is still in the hospital and at risk. She has a bodyguard, but if Emmaline shows up to finish off Ruby, there need to be people in place to catch her."

"I can have a police officer positioned outside the hospital room, but that won't do much more good than having the bodyguard there."

"Exactly," Noah agreed. "You need someone there undercover, watching."

"I'll see what I can do."

"If you can have more than one undercover at the hospital tomorrow, I'm planning a visit to Ruby," Rachel said. "It would be a perfect opportunity for Emmaline to try and kill two birds with one stone."

"I'll do that." The detective made a note on a pad in front of him. "I won't guarantee we'll catch her. She might not show up in such a public place."

"True." Noah nodded.

"I have a gut feeling that Emmaline's grasp on reality is slipping. She's getting more desperate. She'll show up," Rachel stated with confidence.

Grant nodded. "I'll put two men undercover as nurses or janitors at the hospital."

Satisfied they would have backup, without giving away their plot, Noah hooked Rachel's elbow and led her from the hospital and back to the truck.

"You're a clever man, Noah Scott." Rachel grinned. "You could get good at lying."

His jaw tightened. "I don't plan on doing it after this is all over."

"Not even a little white lie to keep from hurting someone's feelings?"

"Well, maybe a little white lie if the outfit you're wearing makes you look a bit funny." He held the door for her to climb up into the truck.

She paused as she stepped onto the running board, turned and faced him. "Life is entirely too complicated, isn't it?"

"There's nothing complicated about this." He curled his fingers around the back of her neck and kissed her.

What started as a simple brush of his lips across hers turned into a knee-wobbling, soul-defining moment.

When he stepped back, he stared at her full sensuous lips and glazed eyes and marveled at the beauty of this woman.

"Oh, baby," she said, touching her fingers to her lips. "That was way more complicated than you can imagine." She reached out, grabbed his shirt and pulled him back to her, kissing him again. When they broke apart, she slipped into her seat and closed the door.

Noah stood for a moment longer, staring at her through the window before he rounded the truck and sat behind the steering wheel. "When this is all done, we're going to uncomplicate things, once and for all."

She shot him a glance, her lips quirking in the hint of a smile.

Noah suspected simplifying anything between Rachel and him might be a hopeless cause, but it would have to wait until they captured Emmaline. Until that time, his real mother and this amazing woman beside him were still in danger. He prayed the events of the next day proved successful and no one got hurt in the execution of them. Come tomorrow, he planned to have Emmaline in custody.

Chapter 14

Later that evening, Rachel emerged from the master bathroom in a pale green nightgown with matching panties that were so sheer as to leave little to the imagination. She'd chosen them for a reason.

She was done spending her nights alone. If the man in her thoughts was of the same mind, they'd share a bed that night and whatever else came along with it.

Noah had let her go first in the shower while he checked the windows and doors and armed the security system. She'd assumed he hadn't wanted to shower with her or he'd have said something. Granted, he'd only went in with her last time because she'd been so traumatized by her experience in her own shower. Or so she told herself.

Noah had given her lots of indication that he was

interested in her. But was he only interested in casual sex or something that lasted longer?

Rachel wanted the whole issue with Emmaline to be settled so that she could get to the part where she and Noah untangled and determined just what their relationship would be.

God forbid Noah should decide the best way to simplify was to end it?

Her heart slowed and she gulped, trying to dislodge the lump in her throat. She wasn't ready to end what they had between them. She wanted it to last a lot longer. A lifetime, if she had her choice.

Since Noah wasn't in the master bedroom, she felt silly standing around waiting for him. She'd rather be in the big bed with Noah. Not having been invited, she didn't want to just crawl in. The ideal situation would have been for him to already be in bed when she walked through. With her in the sheer nightgown, he would be so captivated that he couldn't resist asking her to stay.

Rachel sighed. Who was she kidding? She plodded down the hall to the spare bedroom, crawled beneath the covers, wincing as her injured shoulder brushed against the sheet. She hadn't even tried to apply new bandages, hoping Noah would volunteer to do it. Since he'd done so much for her already, she didn't want to ask. Instead, she turned off the light on the nightstand. She couldn't handle his rejection if he found her in his bed and didn't want her there.

She lay in the dark, the door slightly ajar, her gaze on the sliver of light pouring across the floor from the hallway.

When a shadow passed, blocking the light, Rachel held her breath.

The shadow kept going, leaving her alone in her bed.

So much for Noah being attracted to her.

Rachel closed her eyes and willed herself to sleep. As soon as she started drifting off, the nightmares returned. Lying in bed with her eyes open would do her no good. The sound of the shower coming on got her mind off being smothered and on Noah standing naked beneath the spray.

Her body burned and her nipples tightened at the thought of Noah running his soapy hands over her breasts.

Great. Now she was lying awake for an entirely different reason, and even more frustrated. Rachel rolled over and pressed her pillow over her ears. After a few minutes, she realized she wasn't going to sleep any better that way and pushed the pillow aside. She lay on her back, staring up at the ceiling, wishing she were brave enough to march into Noah's room and ask him if he wanted her in his bed.

For a moment she lay there considering the notion. Her body on fire, she kicked back the sheet.

The beam of light from the hallway widened and a tall, dark figure wearing nothing but boxer shorts appeared in her doorway.

"Are you asleep?" he whispered.

She swallowed hard, willing her pulse to slow. "No."

"Good." Noah strode across the room, scooped her up in his arms and carried her into the master bedroom to the bathroom.

"Let me take care of that wound so that it doesn't get infected."

"I could have walked in here by myself," she muttered, disappointed he hadn't taken her straight to bed.

"If you had walked in here yourself, I wouldn't have had the opportunity to show off my strength, now, would I?" He pulled a first-aid kit from beneath the counter and laid out tape and gauze. In a few short minutes, he had her properly bandaged. "Better?"

Highly frustrated and disappointed were the words she would have chosen. "Yes," she grumbled.

He tipped her chin up. "What's wrong?"

"Not a thing." She forced a smile to her stiff lips. When she scooted to the edge of the counter to get off, he blocked her move, scooped his hands beneath her bare thighs and carried her into the master bedroom, where he laid her on the bed and crawled in beside her.

A thrill of excitement rippled through her as she lay against the pillow, staring up into his bright blue eyes. "You didn't bring me in here because you felt sorry for me, did you?" She held her breath, waiting for his response.

He snorted. "Hell, no." Then he pressed a kiss to her forehead and each of her eyelids. "I wanted you in my bed. The thought of you sleeping down the hall from me just wasn't going to work." He leaned back, frowning. "Are you okay with this?"

A smile spread across her lips and she wrapped her arms around his neck. "More than okay." She pulled him close and kissed him. "Much more than okay."

Noah gathered her into his arms and held her close,

leaning his cheek against the top of her head. "I'm worried about tomorrow."

"Then don't do it. There has to be another way to find Emmaline rather than putting yourself in a dangerous situation."

He smiled and tucked a lock of her hair behind her ear. "I'm not worried about me. I'm worried that you will be in danger. While I'm out staging a wreck, you'll be exposed."

"I plan on being right behind you." She cupped his cheek and brushed his lips with hers, loving how right it felt. "I could ask one of your brothers or sister to ride along with me, if it would make you feel better."

"Mmm. Yes. That would be a good idea. I'll call in the morning and see if Whit or Carson can keep you safe while I'm being injured."

"Good. Now can we think about something else?" She trailed a kiss along his jaw and nibbled his earlobe.

"I'm all ears." He winked. "What did you have in mind?"

She leaned up on her hand and shoved him over onto his back. "This." One kiss at a time, she trailed a path from his lips, across his stubble-covered chin down his neck to his chest. There, she tongued a small brown nipple, making it bead into a tight little bud.

Noah lay back with one hand behind his neck, the other skimming across her back and up under her nightgown. "And by the way, this nightgown is almost as good as seeing you naked." He tugged it up over her head and tossed it across the other pillow. "Almost. Naked is better."

She laughed and nipped him.

"Hey! That was a compliment."

"And so was my little nibble." She grinned and worked her way down his torso, loving every ripple of his taut abs and the arrow of dark, curly hair widening down to the base of his stiff member. Wrapping her hands around him, she stroked, massaging the length of him.

Noah's body grew more rigid with each touch. "Babe, I'm not going to last at that rate."

She held out her palm. "Protection?"

He leaned over to the nightstand, grabbed the leftover condoms from the previous night and handed her one.

Rachel tore open the packet and applied the contents, smoothing it down his length.

When she was done, Noah gripped her arm, dragged her up his body and then rolled her over onto her back. "My turn."

"Don't take too long, I won't last at his rate," she said, her voice breathy, her pulse humming through her body. Parting her legs, she guided him between them and bent her knees. "Please."

He slid into her wet channel, burying himself all the way. For a long moment he stayed deep inside her and she reveled in the way he filled her so completely.

In a slow, easy motion, he moved in and out of her, building the rhythm and pace until he was pumping faster and faster.

Rachel dug her heels into the comforter and rose to meet his every thrust, her heart racing, her soul on fire with lust, tingles spreading from her core outward.

Noah thrust one last time and held, his body rigid, his member pulsing.

Rachel finally remembered to breathe and sucked in a long, steadying breath and let it out. "This is much better than sleeping alone," she whispered.

"Damn right." Noah dropped down beside her, pulling her into his arms, spooning her body with his.

In the aftermath of lovemaking, Rachel lay satiated, replete and incredibly sleepy. *I love you, Noah Scott*, she said to herself, still too unsure of his feelings to speak the words aloud. She lay in his arms, absorbing his strength and confidence that all would work out for the best. She prayed they would and that no one got hurt in the process.

Noah lay for a long time, loving the feel of Rachel's naked body lying next to him, her curves pressed into his harder planes. The scent of her shampoo and the musk of their sex wrapped around him.

He could stay this way for the rest of his life and be completely satisfied. No longer angry that she'd lied about spying on him, he understood her reasoning and probably would have done the same.

He snuggled close, his arm tightening around her middle, brushing against her full breasts. Just that little bit of contact made him want to make love to her all over again.

Her breathing was smooth and steady. The woman had been through so much, she deserved to sleep.

Noah closed his eyes trying not to think about every detail of the mission for tomorrow. Unfortunately, he couldn't turn off his thoughts. It was well into the early morning before he finally fell into a troubled sleep.

He woke early but remained still for a long time, listening to Rachel breathe.

She lay against the pillow, her dark hair fanned out around her. Long, silky lashes made little crescents on her cheeks.

When the drama and danger was over, he'd make things right with Rachel. Other than the lie she'd told him to spy on him, she was an innocent, caught in a crazy woman's crosshairs.

After a while, he slipped out of the bed, pulled on a pair of jeans and padded barefoot into the kitchen.

Though it was early morning, he placed a call to Whit. "Whit, this is Noah."

"Everything okay?" Whit's voice was gravelly as if he'd just woken.

"Yeah. I need you to do something for me."

"Name it."

"I need you to come stay with Rachel this morning while I run into San Diego."

"I can do that."

He arranged the time and ended the call.

By the time Rachel appeared in her very sheer night-gown, pushing her hair back from her face, Noah had scrambled eggs and toast ready.

"Is that toast, I smell?" she asked.

"Yes, it is. But if you want to eat, you have to put on more clothes. I don't think I can sit across from you without attacking you in that outfit."

She raised an eyebrow at him. "Same to you, buddy.

How can a girl concentrate on food when you're bare chested?"

"Point taken." He set the plates of food on the table and hurried to the master bedroom, grabbed a T-shirt from a drawer and dragged it over his head. He met Rachel in the hallway.

She'd changed into a pair of jeans and a soft pink short-sleeved sweater. "Better?" she asked with a smile.

"No, but less distracting." He rested his hand at the small of her back and guided her back to the table.

They ate in silence, each buried in his or her own thoughts of the plot that was about to unfold.

When they'd finished their meals, Rachel helped Noah clean dishes. He liked that they worked well as a team. He washed, she dried. In tune with each other, like a married couple.

As the hour neared, Whit arrived and the mission began.

On schedule, Rachel's cell phone rang. She answered and gave Noah a slight nod, indicating Brenna Trace, the news reporter, was leaving the city at that time.

Dressed in old jeans, sturdy boots and a leather jacket, Noah collected his keys. "You two stay safe. Try not to stand out in the open for long periods of time."

Whit stretched. "I've got nowhere to go. I'm hoping there's a game on the television."

Fully dressed, Rachel followed Noah to the door. "Be careful." She leaned up on her toes and kissed him. "We'll be right behind you."

"How are you going to convince Whit you need to be out on the road?"

She smiled. "I've got that covered."

Noah looped his arm around her waist and pulled her to him. "I meant it. When this is all over…you…me…we're going to figure *us* out." Then he claimed her mouth, kissing her long and hard.

Whit cleared his throat behind them. "Sorry, didn't know you two were making out."

Rachel laughed, the color high in her cheeks. "See you soon."

Noah left the guesthouse and climbed into his truck. This would be the last time he drove the truck. He patted the steering wheel. It was just a method of transportation. The important thing was to get Emmaline to come out of hiding long enough to capture her.

For a long time he'd resisted the idea that Emmaline could be a murderer, but all the evidence was sure pointing toward her. The fact she'd isolated him and kept the secret of his birth parents from him and her family for thirty-seven years still astounded him.

Noah pulled away from the house, looking back in the rearview mirror.

Rachel stood in the window, her brows furrowed in a worried frown.

He wanted to take that frown away, to give her the peace and happiness she deserved. He prayed she'd be okay while he was out crashing his truck.

Noah drove through the gate and out onto the winding highway that lead into San Diego. He knew the exact point at which he needed to drive the truck off the side of the road. It was in a sharp curve where the shoulder dropped into a steep, rocky gully littered with giant boulders at the bottom. He would get the truck going fast enough around the curve, then he'd drive it over the edge and jump out before it tumbled down the hill.

Easy, right? As he neared the curve, his pulse quickened and he braced himself for the jump.

Rachel paced the living room floor for only two minutes after Noah left before she walked to the kitchen counter and lifted a stack of papers she'd left there. "Oh, no."

Whit had just settled on the sofa and hit the power button on the television remote. "What's wrong?" The television blasted them with a commercial. He turned down the volume.

"The papers Noah was supposed to take are here on the counter." Rachel held up the stack of papers.

"If you call him before he gets too far, he can come back to get them."

She lifted her cell phone and punched some random buttons, held it to her ear and waited. It didn't ring, nor did she expect it to, since she hadn't actually dialed anyone. She waited long enough to be convincing then hit the end call button.

"He must be out of cell range." She grabbed her purse and the papers. "Come on. If we hurry, we can catch him before he gets all the way to the city."

"You heard Noah, it's not safe out there. When he realizes he doesn't have those papers he'll be back." Whit remained seated on the sofa.

Her heart pounding, Rachel paced the room. "We really need to catch up to him. These papers are important."

"What are they?"

She stared down at the documents, thankful to realize they were some of the information they'd brought back from Emmaline's house. "We think these might be evidence the police can use. It's very important Noah has these or his trip to town is a waste of time."

Whit's brows lowered. "That important, huh?" He seemed to be considering it.

"Really important." She walked to him and held out her hand. "Come on. I know we can catch him."

"What about the shooter?"

"We'll run out to your vehicle and I'll stay low in the seat as we leave." She crossed her finger over her chest. "Promise."

"Okay, then. Let's go catch Noah." Whit took her hand and let her pull him to his feet. Then he strode across the floor to the front door. "Me first."

He stepped outside, leaving the door ajar enough that Rachel could peer out. After a moment or two of scanning the surrounding area, he turned. "Let's go." He held his arm wide.

Rachel ran out, slamming the door behind her.

With Whit's arm around her shoulders, his broad shoulders providing a shield for her body, they ran to the vehicle and he helped her into the passenger seat.

Rachel glanced out the window. As promised, she ducked low in her seat. A bang sounded and something pierced the front windshield.

"Holy smokes!" Whit threw himself into the driver's seat. "Someone just put a bullet through my window."

"Go! Go! Go!" Rachel cried out.

He cranked the engine and pulled out onto the driveway leading toward the gate.

Rachel glanced up at the hole in the glass and felt the blood drain from her face. If she'd been sitting up, the bullet could have gone right through her forehead.

Another shot hit the back window.

Whit swerved back and forth as he put more distance between his vehicle and the crazy person firing at them. He pulled his phone out of his pocket and threw it her way. "Call 911 and report that shooting."

She did, knowing their response would fall right in with the plan. By the time they headed toward Adair Acres, Noah would have crashed his truck and they would need an ambulance. Having the sheriff there with flashing lights when the reporter showed up would be even better.

Rachel made that call, reporting a shooting at the ranch. When she ended the call she said, "They're sending someone out now."

"We should go back and wait on them."

"No!" Rachel shook her head, scrambling for the right words to keep Whit on track to find Noah. "Whoever is shooting at me might still be there. And I need to get this information to Noah. It's a matter of life and death." She sat up straight and twisted in her seat to see behind her. "My life or death."

Whit raised a hand. "Okay. We'll get that info to Noah, then I have to go back and meet the sheriff at the ranch."

"I'll call Carson and see if he can be there when the sheriff arrives."

"Good. We'll probably pass the authorities on their way out to the ranch."

Rachel was banking on it. Preferably at the site of Noah's crash.

He'd pointed out the spot where she could expect to find the crashed vehicle. It was a couple more miles away.

Rachel sat forward, her gaze on the horizon. She lowered her window just enough to hear noises outside and she waited for the explosion and subsequent plume of smoke to rise.

Chapter 15

Noah gripped the door handle and opened it just slightly as he pressed his foot to the accelerator. At thirty miles per hour, the wind rushed in.

It was not going to feel good, jumping out of the truck with it rolling so swiftly, but he had to make sure it rolled all the way down the hill at sufficient velocity to make it crash hard into the boulders below. The crash had to have enough of an impact to rupture the full gas tank and send a ball of flame and smoke high into the air.

So far he'd passed no one on the road. If the reporter had left San Diego when she said she was going to, and she hadn't stopped anywhere along the way, she should be about five minutes from his location.

As he neared the curve, pulse pounding, he gritted

his teeth, pointed the truck at the bare shoulder without a guardrail and hit the gas.

The truck barreled toward the precipice.

Noah stayed in the seat as long as he could. When the front wheels flew over the edge, he flung the door wide and launched his body out as far as he could.

He landed on the curve of the shoulder, hit with his shoulder and rolled to the edge. Unable to get his feet under him, he toppled over the edge, sliding in gravel and small rocks in the same direction as the careening truck, bumping down the hill toward the huge boulders.

With nothing to grab hold of, he tumbled, slid and rolled down the hillside, banging against rocks. His thigh slammed against something sharp and jagged, ripping through his jeans. Pain shot through his ribs and his head bounced against something hard, making him see stars.

A loud crash of metal on stone sounded below him.

In the back of his fall-addled brain he knew he had to stop, had to keep from falling right into what would come next.

Arms flailing, searching for purchase, he found a root jutting out of the side of the rocky hill. Grabbing hold, he used the last of his strength and consciousness to hold on to it as a loud explosion rocked the ground beneath him.

A huge fireball leaped into the air and heat surrounded him, the pungent scent of gasoline and smoke filling his nostrils.

Noah buried his face against the rocky slope and held on, his sight threatening to fade into a hazy darkness.

* * *

The sound of the explosion ripped through the interior of Whit's vehicle and a bright puff of flame and smoke rose above the horizon.

"What the hell?" Whit took his foot off the accelerator, the vehicle slowing.

"Noah," Rachel whispered, and then spoke louder. "That could have been Noah. Hurry!" Her heart in her throat, she prayed he'd made it out all right, wishing they hadn't gone through with this plan after all. It was too dangerous. She rocked in her seat, her gaze on the cloud of smoke over the rise ahead.

As they rounded a bend in the road, she could see the spot Noah had indicated and the tire tracks leading over the edge.

"Stop!" she screamed.

Whit slowed and pulled onto the shoulder, out of the way of traffic that might pass by.

Before he could shift into Park, Rachel threw open her door, leaped out of the vehicle and ran toward the edge of the drop off. "Noah!" she cried out. When she saw the truck at the bottom of the hill engulfed in flame, her stomach knotted and she pressed her fist to her mouth to keep from crying. "Noah!"

Whit joined her at the edge. "Oh, my God. Noah!"

Rachel scanned the shoulder of the road and just over the edge. Noah was nowhere to be seen. "Dear God, what happened?" She started over the edge, her feet slipped in the gravel and she lost her balance.

Whit grabbed her arm and jerked her back from the edge. "Call 911 while I get a rope."

He ran back to the vehicle and unearthed a long

length of rope. After tying it to the trailer hitch on the back, he threw the rope down the hill.

Rachel dialed 911 and reported the accident and the location.

"We have a sheriff's vehicle on that road now," the dispatcher said. "I've notified the fire department."

Whit started down the hill as Rachel ended the call.

"I'm coming with you," Rachel said, bending to grab the rope.

"Like hell, you are. Stay put and wait for the rescue units. We need someone to wave them down."

She didn't like standing around, not knowing whether or not Noah was okay.

While Whit eased down the slope, his feet slipping out from under him on the loose rocks and gravel, Rachel held her breath and dialed Landry.

"Hey, sweetie, what's happening?" Landry asked with her bright and cheerful voice.

Her first instinct was to burst out crying, but that would do no one any good at all. "There's been an accident. It's Noah." She gulped back the sob climbing her throat.

"Where? What happened?" Landry demanded.

She gave her friend a quick description of the scene. "Let the family know. Whit's here and the fire department is on the way."

An SUV rounded the corner and slowed to a halt. Along the side of the vehicle was an advertisement for the local television station. Brenna Trace, the news reporter, climbed out of the passenger seat. Her cameraman slipped from the driver's side and grabbed his camera out of the backseat.

Rachel could have laughed if she didn't feel more like crying. The plan was working out just as they'd discussed. With one exception. She didn't know whether or not Noah was alive, or if he hadn't made it out of the truck and was not part of the burning inferno. Tears welled and threatened to blind her.

"Rachel, honey!" Brenna raced toward her, microphone in hand. "What happened?"

"I don't know," she managed to get out. Noah had to be okay. He was somewhere nearby. "We saw the explosion and saw the truck down there."

"Oh, dear Lord. Do you know who was driving?"

The tears bubbled up and over, sliding down Rachel's face. "Noah Scott."

Brenna frowned. "Noah Scott? Isn't he the missing Jackson Adair?" Her frown cleared and her brows rose. "Wow." She stared down the hill as she stood beside Rachel. "Did he make it out?"

"I don't know," Rachel said, and this time her words came out on a sob.

"Who's on the rope?"

"Whit Adair. He's l-looking f-for Noah."

Brenna slid an arm around her shoulders. "Oh, honey. I'm sorry."

A shout rose from down below. "I found him!" Whit's head popped up and he waved.

Rachel leaned over the edge, searching the ground beneath Whit. The steep slope made it impossible to see what Whit was looking at. Her breath caught in her throat, and, dying a thousand deaths inside, Rachel waited for Whit's next words.

"He's alive!"

Rachel sagged against Brenna. "Thank God."

Then everything started happening at once.

The sheriff pulled up, lights flashing. A few short minutes behind him, a first responder fire truck arrived and men dropped to the ground, grabbed ropes, a stretcher and mountain-climbing gear. Within minutes, they were over the edge and rappelling down the slope to where Whit clung to his rope next to Noah. While the rescue crew stabilized Noah, one of them helped Whit climb back up to the top.

An ambulance arrived and the paramedics unloaded a stretcher.

Landry, Carson, Georgia, Derek and Elizabeth arrived. Elizabeth ran to her husband, Whit, and hugged him.

"He's alive," Whit announced. "Unconscious, but alive."

Relief warred with concern. Noah hadn't said anything about sliding down the hill. And he was far too close to the burning vehicle for Rachel's comfort. He'd said he'd fake a back injury or something to make sure the ambulance took him to the hospital. Could he fake being unconscious?

Rachel doubted it. Which meant he'd suffered some serious injuries in his fall down the hill.

The minutes dragged by as the rescue team loaded Noah onto a board and strapped him in. Then, so slowly Rachel could almost feel her hair grow, they pulled him up the hill to the road.

Rachel dropped to her knees beside him. "Noah?"

He didn't blink, didn't twitch or anything to indicate he was pretending to be unconscious, and that wasn't fake blood on his forehead, cheeks, arms and legs. His jeans were torn and he looked like he'd been tossed in a rock tumbler.

"Oh, baby, what happened?" she whispered, smoothing a lock of his blond hair off his blood-encrusted forehead.

The emergency medical technicians loaded him into the back of the ambulance.

When the driver started to close the back door, Rachel stopped him. "Wait, I want to ride with him."

"Are you a family member?" he asked.

She shook her head, her heart dropping into her belly. "No." She wasn't anything to him. But she loved him. Didn't that count for something?

"Sorry, ma'am." The driver closed the door and rounded to the front. The ambulance pulled out on the road, the bright flashing lights turned on, and they drove away.

Landry slipped her arm around Rachel's waist. "Come on, we'll follow behind them and get there at the same time." Her friend led her to Whit's vehicle and they climbed in. Whit slipped behind the steering wheel and they drove past the fire trucks.

Firemen worked on extinguishing the blaze and keeping it from spreading. Brenna Trace stood with her back to the smoke, a microphone in her hand. She faced the cameraman filming her live report of Jackson Adair's brush with death.

Dread threatened to overwhelm Rachel. They couldn't get to the hospital fast enough to satisfy her need to know Noah was all right.

"What happened?" Landry asked.

Rachel stared out the window. "He went to town to talk to the police about the case."

Landry shook her head. "I don't understand why he would leave you."

"He didn't leave her alone." Whit glanced at his sister. "Noah asked me to come stay with Rachel while he made a trip into San Diego."

"And you just happened to find a couple bullets to put through your window?" Landry pointed to the bullet holes and the splintering crack leading outward from the small holes. "Carson, Derek, Georgia, Elizabeth and I were on our way over to run interference with the sheriff on the shooting incident when Rachel called. When did you get these?"

"Whoever our shooter is was back and shot at Rachel when we ran from the house to the vehicle," Whit explained. "Didn't Carson tell you?"

"Yes, I just wanted to hear it from you." Landry smiled at her older brother. "I like to yank your chain on occasion, brother."

Whit glared at her. "There's nothing in the least humorous about this entire situation. Rachel could have been killed. Noah was injured badly, just how badly, we don't know yet."

"Sorry." Landry swiveled in her seat to glance back at Rachel. "You didn't tell us what you found in Palm Springs. Did your trip yesterday to Aunt Emmaline's house reveal any new information?"

Rachel hated lying to the Adairs. Landry had been her friend for so long she was like a sister. With Noah unconscious, she had to make sure his effort hadn't been in vain. She nodded. "We found a scrapbook filled with newspaper and magazine articles of Reginald Adair's attempts to find Jackson."

Landry's brows rose. "Interesting."

Whit glanced at Rachel in the rearview mirror. "That proves nothing."

Looking down at her hands, Rachel continued, "We also found receipts for two guns. A rifle and a .40 caliber handgun."

Landry clapped a hand over her mouth. "Aunt Emmaline bought guns?"

With a nod, Rachel went on to tell them about their visit to the firing range and what they'd learned there.

"For heaven's sake, the woman is sixty-six years old," Whit exclaimed. "How does she get around to make the shots she does?"

"I know that one," Landry said. "Derek found four-wheeler tracks out behind the stable."

Whit's frown deepened. "Any one of us could have left them there."

"Derek checked the tire patterns. None of our ATVs have that particular pattern."

"Okay, maybe you two have something with the ATVs, but Aunt Emmaline always seemed so nice."

"Oh, yeah. She was nice when you saw her, which wasn't often, because she always had to get back to her son." Landry's lips tightened. "A son she kept from his rightful family." She pounded her fist into her open palm. "We missed out on getting to know our brother all these years because she was too busy hiding him to let him be with family."

Her gaze on the back of the ambulance in front of them, Rachel sighed. "Whether Emmaline is Reginald's murderer or not, we gave the information to the police department in San Diego. Based on what we'd found, we knew that Emmaline would need to be brought in for questioning."

"How are you going to do that when she's been missing for so long?" Landry asked. "Do you have a plan?"

"The plan is in place." Rachel sat back in her seat and stared out the window at the vehicle carrying the man she cared so much about. "If things go as we predict, she should be in custody soon."

Landry cast a frowning glance back at Rachel. "How?"

Rachel stared into Landry's eyes. "Who is the one person Emmaline loves so much she might consider killing others to keep him to herself?"

"Noah," Landry answered. "So?"

"If the child you loved so insanely was injured and lying at death's door in a hospital, where would you be?" Rachel asked.

Whit answered, "With the child."

Landry's eyes widened. "You think she'll risk being caught to visit Noah in the hospital?"

Rachel hoped so. Otherwise, everything Noah had gone through to stage this production would be for naught. "Yes."

"So, the accident—" Landry started.

"Was staged." Whit's jaw hardened.

"Why didn't you tell us?" Landry exclaimed.

"We needed it to look real for the news reporter."

"How did you do that?"

"She was on her way out to interview me about a

charity project I was going to do in conjunction with Adair Acres."

"What project?" Landry shook her head. "It was a ruse to get her out here."

"The crash had to be big enough to make it interesting on camera. I'm pretty sure the cameraman got some good footage of the fireball. As we left, the news reporter Brenna Trace was filming with the smoke in the background. At the hospital, one of my friends is a doctor in the ICU unit. We will have him declare Noah as critical and barely holding on."

"When that hits the news, Emmaline will be beside herself with worry." Landry smiled. "Brilliant."

"Except for the part about being critically injured for real. I take it Noah didn't plan on being as incapacitated as he ended up," Whit stated.

"No." Again, Rachel's eyes filled with tears. "I thought he would just set the truck in Neutral and push it over the edge. It looked like it was going fast when it crashed. God, I hope he'll be all right."

"We do, too," Landry said. "I kind of like having another older brother. Somebody to keep Whit in line." She winked at Whit.

They arrived at the hospital behind the ambulance. Whit dropped the ladies off at the emergency room door and drove away to park.

Without one of the big Adair men to keep her safe, Rachel felt exposed. The exposure didn't scare her nearly as bad as the possibility Noah wouldn't wake up. She had to see Noah and make sure he was okay. Hooking Landry's arm, she hurried inside the hospital.

Noah had been taken into the emergency room.

Landry marched up to the information desk. "My brother was brought in just now. We'd like to be with him."

"Are you both family?" the woman at the desk asked.

"I'm his sister," Landry repeated, and pulled Rachel up beside her. "And this is his fiancée. I guess that makes us family."

"I'll let the doctor know you're here." The woman stood and disappeared behind a door leading into the examination rooms. When she returned, she said, "He's been taken into Radiology. They promised to let me know when he's been moved."

Rachel stepped forward. "Is he okay?"

"Ma'am, I can't tell you that. The doctor will know more when he has the radiologist's report."

"Can you at least tell me…is Noah conscious?" Rachel asked, her voice catching.

The woman looked at her with compassion in her eyes. "No."

Rachel's chest tightened. She turned away from the desk and paced across the waiting room and back to Landry.

Whit entered. "What's the news on Noah?"

"He's still unconscious. They've taken him to Radiology for a CT scan." Landry turned to Rachel, a frown pulling her brows low. "Are you okay?"

"Noah has to be all right." Standing around would not help her pass the time. She had to set the rest of the plan in place. If…no…*when* Noah woke, he had to know the plan was in motion. "If you'll excuse me, I have to take care of something." She nodded to the two, left the waiting room, and stepped into an empty hallway. She pulled out her cell phone and dialed the number for Christopher Rice, the doctor she knew on staff at the hospital. She had his personal number, having helped to raise the funding for new radiology equipment for the trauma center. The same center caring for Noah as she stood waiting for Chris to answer. Chris had been so impressed by her successful efforts in fund-raising that he'd told her to call him anytime.

After five rings, Rachel had given up and reached for the end button.

"Hello?" a voice said.

"Dr. Rice, this is Rachel Blackstone." Rachel held the phone to her ear, relief making her knees weak.

"Rachel? What's wrong?"

She glanced around to make certain she was alone before she spoke. "My…f-fiancé, Noah Scott, has been injured and they brought him to the trauma center."

"Fiancé? Congratulations. I didn't know you were engaged."

"It was all kind of sudden." She almost laughed at the irony of the lie. "Anyway, he's been involved in a terrible auto accident and is unconscious."

"And Noah is at the hospital now?"

"Yes. They have him in Radiology." She took a deep breath and continued. "The last I heard, he was still unconscious."

"I'm not on call tonight. But I can come in and consult with the doctor on call."

"I'm afraid for him. He could have swelling in the brain. He could d-die. I won't feel comfortable unless he's got someone watching him through the night."

"If he's still unconscious and he has a lump on the

back of his head, we'd want to keep a close eye on him, anyway. And since it's after normal hours, ICU for the night would be a safe bet," Dr. Rice said. "I'll check in with the doctor on duty."

"I appreciate anything you can do to help."

"And if the CT scan comes back with any kind of anomalies, I'll come in."

Rachel swallowed hard. "Thank you."

"Rachel?" Dr. Rice said.

"Yes?"

"Noah's in good hands. I know the doctor on call. He's good. And he cares."

"Thanks. I feel better already." She ended the call and returned to the waiting room. When Noah woke, he'd be in the ICU. She was glad she hadn't had to tell Dr. Rice the whole story. Noah's actual injury negated the need to. Now, if only Noah would come to and tell her everything was going to be all right, Rachel could relax.

Until he regained consciousness, she couldn't rest, and her thoughts no longer centered on Emmaline Scott.

Noah was the man who held her heart. He had to wake up.

Chapter 16

Carson, Georgia, Derek and Elizabeth had joined Whit, Landry and Rachel in the emergency room waiting area. The shiny, clean floors and the scent of disinfectant made Rachel's heart pound and her hands grow clammy. Every noise made her jump and look around, praying for someone to come out and tell her what was going on.

"We already heard about the crash on the radio as we were driving in. They made it sound really bad," Derek said.

"How's Noah?" Carson asked. "The news reporter said he was taken to the hospital comatose."

Rachel wrung her hands. Noah's injuries weren't supposed to be real. "We haven't heard much. They took Noah in for a CT scan. He hasn't come out of it yet."

"Damn…" Carson sighed. "What happened?"

"From the look of it," Rachel said, "he lost control of the truck in the curve, and it went off the road."

"He looked pretty beat-up," Whit confirmed. "He must have gotten out of the truck near the top of the road and fallen all the way down to where I found him."

Derek crossed his arms over his chest and glanced around the waiting room. "I hate hospitals."

Rachel knew what Derek was feeling. She didn't like the itchy, twitchy feeling she got when waiting to hear the prognosis for someone she cared about. As much as she disliked the waiting room, though, she wouldn't budge from it until she got to see Noah.

One by one, Whit pulled Derek and Carson aside and filled them in on the plot to trick Emmaline into showing up at the hospital.

Glad she'd shared the information with Whit, Rachel could concentrate on Noah and receiving any information she could get about him. She paced the length of the waiting room and back, unable to settle for more than a minute at a time.

After the word got all the way around to the family, Landry joined Rachel near a window. "The guys agreed to hang around the hospital and keep an eye out for Emmaline. With them and the additional police officers, we should be able to catch her."

"Good." Rachel didn't care. If she didn't hear something about Noah's condition soon, she'd fall apart.

"You really are upset about Noah, aren't you?" Landry slipped an arm around Rachel's waist.

"Yes. He wasn't supposed to be so badly injured."

"From what I've learned about the man, he won't

let this beat him. He'll be up within twenty-four hours and back on the ranch the next day, feeding horses and mowing pastures. He's an Adair. It takes a lot to get one of us down." Landry smiled and hugged Rachel close. "He'll be okay."

"I hope you're right."

"Do you love him?" Landry asked.

Rachel swallowed hard on the lump of tears lodged in her throat. She nodded, unable to speak.

"I have a feeling he loves you, too."

Rachel couldn't deny the chemistry between them, but love? She didn't dare to hope, and she wasn't worried about that now. Whether they figured things out between them was pushed way to the back burner until Noah woke up. If he didn't love her and chose to walk away from their relationship, she'd be okay, as long as she knew he was alive and well.

Noah Scott, Jackson Adair, whatever name he chose to go by, was a good man and deserved to live a long and healthy life. With or without Rachel Blackstone.

But she'd rather he lived it with her.

"Check it out." Georgia Mason, Carson's fiancée, pointed to the television in the corner of the room. "They've already got a segment on the news about the accident."

Rachel hurried over to the screen and listened as Brenna Trace reported on the accident involving Noah Scott, recently revealed as the missing Adair heir, Jackson Adair. A grainy old film clip appeared on the screen with a young Reginald and Ruby Adair pleading with the public to help find their missing baby.

The cameraman had gotten to the accident scene in

time to capture the drama of the burning truck on film, and Brenna did a good job sensationalizing the event with, "Jackson Adair was taken to the trauma center and is listed in critical condition. Our thoughts and prayers are with the Adair family as they wait to see if he pulls through. We'll keep you posted."

Hearing the news report and seeing the fire all over only made Rachel worry even more. The film footage of the fire and the paramedics lifting Noah up onto the stretcher made the entire incident look really tragic.

Rachel resumed her silent pacing, twisting her hands together and struggling not to cry.

An hour and a half after Noah had been brought into the hospital emergency room, Rachel and the others were finally told that he had been moved to ICU. This information came from one of the nurses. The doctor would be with them soon to give them an update. They were all asked to move to the waiting room outside of ICU.

Rachel wanted to call Dr. Rice and ask him if the move to ICU was because he told them to move him, or if Noah really was in danger of not making it through his fall. Was he that badly injured? She glanced at the clock. It was getting late, and she'd disturbed the man on his day off once already.

Instead, she led the way into the elevator that took them up to the floor where ICU was located.

Once they were all in the waiting room, it was another effort in waiting and trying not to climb the walls.

"He has to be okay," Landry said.

"Noah's tough. He'll be all right," Whit said.

Rachel paced.

Finally a doctor came into the room. "Are you all family members of Noah Scott?"

They all replied at once, "Yes."

It warmed Rachel's heart that they considered Noah family. A month ago, they'd thought of him as just a relatively distant cousin and maybe someone who was trying to horn in on the family inheritance where he didn't belong.

Rachel wrung her hands and willed the doctor to get on with his prognosis.

"Noah has suffered a head trauma. He's got a sizable lump at the base of his skull and he's still unconscious. The CT scan didn't reveal any internal hemorrhaging, but because it is nighttime and he hasn't woken, we want to keep him under close observation until he comes out of it. Hopefully, it's just a precaution."

"What's the worst-case scenario?" Carson asked.

The doctor frowned. "Bleeding in the brain, blood clot, stroke, brain damage. Do you want me to go on?"

"No!" Rachel cried.

"He's going to be okay." Landry slipped her arm around Rachel's shoulder. "Can we see him?"

"He's resting easy, and hooked up to monitors. He might not wake up during your visit," the doctor warned.

"We don't care what he looks like. He's family and we want to see him for ourselves," Whit said.

Rachel couldn't speak for the sob clogging her throat. Instead, she nodded.

"Only two at a time until visiting hours are over," the doctor said. "Once visiting hours are over, you'll need to leave a phone number where we can contact you if anything happens." The doctor left them to their thoughts and went back to work.

Landry glanced at her brothers. "Rachel and I would like to go first to see Noah."

Whit nodded. "I want to check on Ruby. When I spoke to her this morning, she said the doctor will probably release her tomorrow. They kept her a couple days to make sure the smoke inhalation from the fire hadn't damaged her lungs. I'm sure she'd appreciate a visitor." He gave Rachel a half wink, indicating he would also be checking with the bodyguard and the police force on duty to make sure everyone was in place.

"Thank you." Rachel stepped out into the hallway, her knees weak and her entire body shaking. "He's going to be all right."

"Yes. He is." Landry let Rachel lean on her as they walked to the ICU. "And I'm sure hearing your voice will make him want to come out of that coma."

"I hope so." Rachel could see him before they actually entered Noah's room. The walls were glass to allow the nurses on duty to see into the room and respond in cases of emergency.

As Rachel stepped into Noah's room, she was immediately overwhelmed by the amount of equipment, light and the smell of rubbing alcohol and antiseptic cleaners.

Noah lay in the bed, his face pale, a breathing tube affixed to his nose and an IV in his arm. His face was bruised, and one gash over his right eye had swelled and turned a deep purple.

Rachel's heart hurt for him. What had gone so terribly wrong when he'd set up the accident? She should have been there.

She closed the distance between her and him and took his free hand in hers.

"They say talking to a person in a coma helps," Landry offered, whispering as if they were in a library.

Rachel nodded, wondering where to start. "Hey, baby. Are you trying to get us all worried about you? Because if you are, it's working." She laughed, choking back a sob. Tears rolled down her face and dripped onto the sheet. "You're going to be all right. Landry tells me Adairs are tough. Nothing keeps them down. Since you're an Adair, we all think you should live up to that boast."

"That's right," Landry agreed. "Besides, I haven't had a chance to get to know you as my brother. You need to stick around a little longer."

Rachel stroked his hand while she stared around at the monitors measuring his blood pressure, pulse and heartbeat. Nothing was flashing and his heartbeat was strong and steady. But then the damage caused by head traumas wouldn't always show up on an EKG or pulse monitor. Strokes would come on suddenly, wouldn't they?

One minute he could be fine, the next…

Rachel bit hard on her lower lip, refusing to go any further in that scenario. Noah would be okay. He had to be. She loved him with all her heart.

Landry laid a hand on her shoulder. "Come on, my brothers will want to see him, too, before visiting hours end."

Not wanting to let go, Rachel held on until she had to release Noah's hand.

"The nurses will take good care of him," Landry assured her.

Rachel let her friend lead her out of the room. As she walked toward the waiting room, she gazed back.

Noah looked so alone, plugged into all those imposing machines, his face pale beneath the tan. Nothing moved but the green light of the heart monitor, displaying a somewhat reassuring, steady rhythm.

She didn't want to leave him. Every muscle and nerve cell in her body screamed at her to go back to him, to stay by his side until he woke.

Back with the rest of the family, Rachel collapsed into a chair and wrapped her arms around herself. The room was cold and she couldn't seem to get warm.

Whit and Carson paid their visit to the comatose Noah and returned within ten minutes.

Rachel glanced up, hope in her eyes. "Is he awake?"

Carson shook his head. "No."

She slumped in the chair and closed her eyes.

Please, please, please help Noah get better, she prayed.

The chair beside her creaked and she opened her eyes.

Whit sat beside her. "While you were with Noah, Derek and I spoke with the bodyguard Aunt Kate and Derek arranged to look out for Ruby." He shot a glance around the room and lowered his voice. "The bodyguard has been in contact with the policeman in charge of the undercover operation here at the hospital. He told me they have four men located at different positions in the hospital. All of them have been briefed and have a copy of Emmaline's latest picture. They're ready if she shows up."

Whit tilted his head toward Derek. "Derek insisted on stopping by to check in with hospital security. They gave him a radio to carry so that they could get in touch with him if something happens while he's in the hospital."

A little reassured that the people were in place to nab Emmaline, Rachel nodded. "Thank you." She nodded toward Elizabeth, Whit's pregnant wife. The woman stood by the window, her shoulders sagging. "You need to get Elizabeth home to bed. Derek, Carson and the police can handle capturing Emmaline."

Whit shook his head. "I'm as worried about Noah as the rest of the family."

"But there's nothing you can do. Noah has to get better on his own." Rachel patted Whit's arm. "Your beautiful wife needs to sleep. You don't want that baby coming prematurely."

Whit glanced across at his wife, a smile lifting the corners of his lips. "She is beautiful, isn't she?"

"Yes." Rachel's chest squeezed at the amount of love glowing in Whit's eyes as he stared at Elizabeth. "Take her home. Noah will be fine."

"Are you sure? I can have Landry take Elizabeth back to the ranch."

Rachel shook her head. "Just show up in the morning when Emmaline's in jail and Noah's up and shouting for his breakfast."

Whit hugged Rachel. "You're so much like family sometimes I forget you aren't—by blood." He kissed her forehead and stood. "Hey, beautiful," he called out to Elizabeth.

Elizabeth smiled at him, her hand smoothing over her baby bump, the dark circles under her eyes more pronounced with each passing minute. "What do you need, sweetheart?"

"I need to take you home, and get you off your feet."

She frowned. "I can't leave with Noah in the condition he is."

"Yes, you can." Whit was firm but gentle. "He's probably going to sleep it off like a hangover." He took her arm and led her toward the elevator, glancing over his shoulder. "Call me if anything happens."

The rest of the group nodded and Whit left with Elizabeth.

"I could use some coffee," Carson said.

Georgia jumped up from her seat. "I'll go with you."

Derek shoved a hand through his hair. "All this waiting around is making me crazy. I think I'll hang out in the hospital's security room. Maybe we can spot Emmaline when she comes through a door." He pulled Landry into his arms. "Can you two manage on your own for an hour or so?"

Landry kissed her fiancé. "Barely. Just don't be all night."

Once it was just Landry and Rachel in the waiting area, the room got really quiet.

The silence was as deafening as the noise of people moving around. Rachel couldn't take it. She wanted to be with Noah. "I'm going to the ladies' room," she said, and headed for the door.

"Do you want me to come with you?" Landry asked.

"No. I'll be all right. It's not far." Rachel left the room and walked down the hallway to the bathroom. Inside she took care of business, washed her hands and bent over the sink to splash water on her face. When she glanced up in the mirror, the circles beneath her eyes were dark and she looked tired. How she looked didn't matter. Nothing mattered as long as Noah was unconscious. Tears welled in her eyes and blurred the image in front of her. Sobs rose up her throat and she gave in to them, covering her mouth to keep from making enough noise to alert anyone outside the room.

When she'd spent her tears, she ran the water and splashed more on her face. For a moment she thought she heard something like a rumble of thunder.

With her eyes closed, Rachel reached for a paper towel to dry her face. She straightened and gave herself a good long look in the mirror. Her eyes were puffy and she looked like hell. But then her world was falling apart and the man she loved was in a coma. What did anyone expect?

Those darned tears welled again and she dashed them away before they could fall down her cheeks. She had to pull herself together. Noah didn't need a weepy woman to wake up to.

And he would wake. Rachel would accept no other option.

Squaring her shoulders, she opened the door to the bathroom, stepped out and was almost run over by one of the nurses rushing by.

Something was beeping loudly; the fire alarm started up and a flashing red light blinked on the wall.

One nurse was on the phone and all of the others ran toward one of the other ICU rooms.

Landry rushed at her, her eyes wide. "Oh, thank God, you're okay."

"Why wouldn't I be? What's going on?"

"There was a loud boom somewhere in the hospital. The nurses were all in an uproar and calling to find out what happened, then it seems the man in the other room went code blue." Landry stared down at her cell phone. "I can't get Derek, Whit or Carson on the phone or text. I don't know what's going on."

"Is anyone watching over Noah?" Rachel asked.

"I don't think so." Landry waved a hand toward the room full of nurses working over the other patient in ICU. "They seem to be busy."

Rachel gripped Landry's wrists. "You find out what's going on. Find Derek and let me know. I'm going to check on Noah."

"I can't leave you!" Landry said, her voice ragged.

"I need you to find out what's going on. That could have been an explosion. We need to know if the family is okay. Take the stairs. If there was an explosion, the elevator might not work, or it might stop while you're in it."

Landry nodded and ran for the stairs.

Rachel hurried toward Noah's room. None of the nurses stopped her despite being past visiting hours. They were focused on the man in the other room.

Noah lay silent amid the chaos of fire alarms, beeping monitor alarms and shouts from the nurses. Rachel stood beside his bed and took his hand. "Baby, if you're listening, now's the time to wake up."

She raised his hand to her cheek. "You promised me we'd figure things out. I can't do that on my own. We have to do that together. You and me."

Rachel stared down at his face. Had his brow twitched? Was he frowning a little?

"Come on, Noah. Like it or not, you're an Adair. You have to live up to the reputation of being tough as nails and bulletproof." She tried to sound strong, but her voice broke. "I love you, Noah. If you don't come back to me, who's going to give me the riding lessons I don't need? Who will I swim with in the creek? Who will I have babies with and grow old with? I don't want anyone else."

The muscles in his face jerked.

Rachel leaned forward. "Noah? Can you hear me?"

Nothing.

"If you can hear me, squeeze my hand." Rachel stared down at the hand she held and willed his fingers to curl around hers.

For a long moment, nothing happened. Then slowly, his fingers flexed and curled around hers.

"Noah!" she cried. Rachel leaned over him and kissed his lips. "Baby, you have to wake up. I love you. I don't want to live without you."

His hand tightened.

A noise behind her made her look over her shoulder in a brief glance.

A nurse in scrubs pulled the curtains around to block the view into the room. "All the noise and flashing lights are too much for Mr. Scott," she said in a gruff voice.

"Thank you. I'm glad someone has come in to check

on him." Rachel held his hand, staring at his face, praying for another sign he was coming around.

The nurse moved up behind her.

"I think he might be responding to my voice," Rachel said.

"Well, he won't be for long."

Rachel frowned and faced the woman. She wore a mask over her face like a doctor going into surgery and her hair was tucked under a surgical hat. All Rachel could see were the woman's bright blue eyes.

Before she could make the connection, the nurse grabbed her wrist and yanked her arm up behind her. Another hand curled into her hair at the base of her scalp and shoved her forward. Rachel's forehead slammed into the corner of the machine monitoring Noah's vital signs. She hit it so hard it split her skin.

Pain shot through her head and blood poured down into her eyes, blinding her. Rachel flailed with her free hand in an attempt to grab the person behind her.

The hand at the back of her skull gripped her hair, pulled her head back and slammed it downward, this time hitting her against the bed rail.

More pain ripped through Rachel and she swayed.

"You did this," the woman said.

"What?" Rachel gasped as the hand yanked hard on her hair, forcing her head to tip backward and stare at the ceiling. "What did I do?"

"Because of you, Noah crashed." Her attacker's voice was low and guttural, almost feral in its intensity. Crazy.

Emmaline.

"I wasn't even with him when he crashed," Rachel

croaked, her neck straining from the hand tugging her hair.

"If he hadn't been with you, he'd be all right. He got along fine without you."

With her arm twisted up behind her back the pain radiated through her shoulder, forcing her up on her toes to alleviate the worst of it. "Let me go. We can talk."

"Talking never accomplished anything." Emmaline jerked her arm higher. "I won't let you or anyone else take my son away from me."

"He's not your son," Rachel said through gritted teeth.

Emmaline yanked her hair hard, bringing tears to Rachel's eyes, and then shoved her face into the mattress beside Noah.

Rachel tried to scream, but her voice was muffled, her oxygen cut off by the pressure Emmaline applied to her arm and the back of her head. She struggled, but she couldn't work her arm loose. Surely the nurses would hear them soon and come running.

When Emmaline relaxed her hold on Rachel's hair, Rachel lifted her head enough to drag in some air. In her peripheral vision, she saw that the woman had closed the door to Noah's room and jammed something in the door lock to keep it from opening.

"Emmaline, please," Rachel gasped. "Let go of me. We can work this out."

"No." The older woman jerked her away from Noah's bed and shoved her across the room. "You can't have Noah. He's mine. I won't let you or anyone else turn him against me."

"You're doing a pretty good job of that all by yourself." Rachel fought through the pain in her arm and forehead, took a deep breath, braced her foot on the wall and shoved backward, throwing Emmaline off balance.

The woman released her hold on Rachel, her arms flailing as she fell backward.

Rachel fell, too, landing on her. As soon as she was down, she rolled to the side and onto her hands and knees, scrambling away from the woman.

Emmaline grabbed her ankle with a surprising grip and yanked her back.

Rachel's chest slammed into the floor, knocking the wind out of her long enough for Emmaline to jump on her back.

"Rachel!" Landry's voice could be heard through the door. "Rachel! Open the door!"

Rachel bucked, trying to throw Emmaline off her back. "Landry! Get help!"

"Rachel, what's happening?" Landry pounded on the door. "I'm going for help."

Sitting in the middle of Rachel's back, Emmaline grabbed her hair again and slammed her face into the tile floor.

Rachel knew if she didn't get out from under the woman, she wouldn't last much longer. No amount of bucking, rolling or kicking broke the woman's freakishly strong hold on her. Blood dripped into her eyes and her head hurt so badly she was seeing double.

Then something hit the floor with a crash. The IV stand lay next to Rachel, the IV spilling out on the floor.

"Get off her!" a deep, familiar voice demanded.

"No!" Emmaline screamed. "She's ruining everything. You love me. Only me. I won't let anyone take you away."

Rachel fought to surface through the dark haze threatening to take her down. "Noah?"

"One step closer and I'll kill her," Emmaline threatened.

Cold, hard steel pressed against her temple. Emmaline had a gun.

Chapter 17

Noah fought off the gray cloud that threatened to take him back into the darkness. His head hurt and his vision blurred, but he couldn't go back. He had to stay awake, aware.

The fire alarms had pierced the darkness first, bringing him back to the light. When a warm, soft hand had taken his and the soft soothing tone of an angel had spoken to him, he first thought he was struggling between the cacophony of noise in hell and the beautiful voice of an angel.

When something loud banged against the wall, he'd been jolted awake. His first clear vision was that of his mother holding someone's face against the mattress.

Rachel?

Noah struggled to sit up, knocking over the IV stand.

His head swam and his vision clouded, but as he steadied and his eyes focused, he could see the gun in his mother's hand.

His pulse ratcheted up. He couldn't let her kill the woman he loved. "Emmaline— Mother," Noah croaked, forcing words past his dry throat. "Don't do this. Don't hurt Rachel. She's not a threat to you."

"I heard her, she loves you. She'll steal your heart away from me." Emmaline pulled Rachel's hair, lifting her head off the floor. She pushed the gun into her skin. "I can't let that happen. You're *my* baby."

"I'm all grown up, Mother." Trapped behind the railing, Noah fumbled with the release button, afraid he wouldn't get the railing down in time to save Rachel. He kept speaking, hoping to talk Emmaline out of her plan to kill Rachel. "I'm not a baby anymore." He spoke in a calm, steady tone.

Apparently, Emmaline had tipped past the edge of sanity. Screaming at her wouldn't help the situation. He had to use rational, calm and soothing tones like he used on frightened animals. At least until he could get out of the confounded bed and grab Emmaline.

"You can't love anyone else. I love you the most." Emmaline sobbed, her dark hair, streaked with gray, slipping loose of the bun she usually wore. Her blue eyes shone bright and glassy with a maniacal gleam. "This woman, Ruby, Reginald…they don't love you like I do." She rocked, sitting on Rachel's back, her thin body rigid, her bony hand twisted in Rachel's hair. "That tramp mother of yours never would have fit in the Adair family. My parents saw that. That's why they took you from her and gave you to me. They knew if there was nothing to keep them together, the marriage would fall apart. And it did."

"Reginald blamed Ruby for leaving me alone," Noah pointed out.

"And he was right. She wasn't fit to be a parent." Emmaline's brows pressed low as she stared down at Rachel. "This woman isn't right for you. Can't you see? She'll poison you against me and take you away from me like the others have tried to for years. I'm your mother. I'm the one who raised you. I'm the one who loves you the most."

Tears streamed down her face.

Noah found the release button and guided the railing down so that he could swing his legs over the side. Every movement made him dizzy, but he couldn't let that stop him. He prayed when he stood that his legs would hold.

He knew he had to tell her what she wanted to hear. Anything to keep her calm and to delay her pulling the trigger on Rachel. "Mother, you're the only woman in my life," he lied, barely able to push the words past his lips. This woman had lied to him all his life. But, as Rachel said, she was consumed by her own lie and her grief after losing her husband and child. He had to play to her fears in order to keep Rachel alive.

Seeing Rachel lying on the floor, blood pooling around her forehead, broke Noah's heart. She'd started out as a friend he enjoyed spending time with, but somewhere along the line, he'd fallen in love with the bright, beautiful woman. He realized in that moment that he loved her more than he loved to breathe. He couldn't let Emmaline kill her.

"She loves you. I heard her say so." Emmaline glanced his way. "She'll make you love her more than me. Then she'll turn you against me. Can't you see? She'll take you away from me, just like Reginald tried. I have to stop her, just like I stopped him."

"No, you don't." Noah slid off the bed onto his bare feet. His knees wobbled but held. He was one step closer to saving Rachel. He had to get to her before Emmaline pulled the trigger and ended any chance he might have at a future with the woman he loved. "Hand me the gun, Mother. It's over."

"No." Emmaline shook her head, her eyes swimming with tears. "I only wanted to love you. You were all the family I had. I couldn't let you go."

"Hand me the gun, Mother. No one and nothing will change the way I feel about you. No one will take me away from you." He inched toward her, afraid sudden movements would make her finger tighten on the trigger.

Rachel lay on the floor, trapped beneath Emmaline, her body still, unmoving.

His heart in his throat, Noah swallowed hard and took another step closer. "You don't want to hurt anyone. Hand me the gun so I can hug you and hold you in my arms." He took another step closer.

"All those years Reginald searched for Jackson. I never let anyone know. I hid you in France. You were mine. Reginald went on to have three other children. He didn't need you. I did."

"So what happened?" Noah asked, hoping to distract her as he took another step across the room.

"He finally figured it out. I was supposed to be in

France, but I'd flown back a day earlier. He called me on the phone and asked me if I was really your mother. I knew then that he'd put the pieces together. I broke down and told him I was ready to come through with the truth. We arranged to meet that weekend since he thought I was still in Europe. I went to his corporate building that day and waited until everyone left his office." Her eyes glazed and the hand gripping the gun shook as she told the story.

Noah held his breath, close enough to lunge for her and the gun but afraid, with the way she was shaking, her finger would jerk on the trigger. "What happened when you told him?" Noah kept the conversation going, hoping to buy more time.

"He was angry. He couldn't believe members of his own family would be so deceitful to the people they were supposed to love. He wanted me to tell you immediately." Emmaline shook her head. "I couldn't. No one could know." She looked up at him, her eyes red, pleading. "I couldn't bear it if you hated me. So I shot Reginald in the chest and then I drove back to Palm Springs and had a late dinner with you. I shot him because he said that if I didn't tell you, he would. I knew it would make you hate me."

"I don't hate you." And he didn't. He pitied her. Like Rachel had said, the woman had lived the past thirty-seven years with an enormous lie and a burden of guilt. But he could never forgive her if she shot Rachel. "Hand me the gun, Mother. It's over. Everyone knows who I am."

"You're wrong. It's not over." Emmaline's eyes flared and her hand tightened in Rachel's hair. She let go of Rachel and lurched to her feet, stepping to the side, still aiming the gun at her head. "If I can't keep you as my own..."

Then she turned and shifted the gun to point at Noah. "No one can have you."

Noah hadn't expected this. He raised his hands. "Mother, you spent all your life keeping me safe, taking care of me and loving me. Do you honestly think you could kill me?" He shook his head and held out his hand. "Give me the gun."

"No. Life's not worth living without you." Emmaline's voice cracked and her body shook.

Rachel moved, her leg shooting out to knock into the back of Emmaline's, throwing her off balance.

The woman's hands flew upward, the gun went off.

Something nicked Noah's shoulder, but he didn't let that stop him. He lunged for Emmaline, grabbed her wrist and shook the gun loose from her grip.

She sagged against him, her body racked by sobs. "It was meant to be. My Noah died. You were meant to be mine. I couldn't give you back."

Worried more about Rachel, Noah pushed Emmaline to arm's length and captured both wrists in one hand. "I never was yours. But I won't forget that you raised me." He glanced at Rachel scooting across the floor to kick the gun toward the door, well out of Emmaline's reach should she get loose. He breathed a sigh of relief that she seemed okay despite the blood on her forehead and the bruise on her cheek.

Pounding sounded against the door. "Rachel?" Carson called out. "Can you open the door?"

Rachel struggled to stand.

Noah reached out to her and helped, still holding on to Emmaline's wrists.

Emmaline glared at Rachel, but Noah wouldn't let the older woman hurt her ever again.

"Can you get the door?" Noah asked, his legs weak. He wasn't sure how he was standing and his head hurt like crazy.

Rachel nodded, a smile spreading across her face. "Yes."

She walked toward the door, swaying slightly and pulled hard at a magazine jammed in between the door frame and the locking mechanism. When she finally got it out, she pushed the door open and a flood of people entered.

A man in scrubs carrying a pistol entered first, followed by another, dressed in a janitor's overalls. Derek entered third. Each of the men carried pistols and they were aimed at Emmaline.

Emmaline fell against Noah. "Don't let them take me away from you. You're all I have."

"Mother, you've committed murder. I can't protect you from that," Noah said.

The first undercover police officer snapped handcuffs on Emmaline's wrist and pulled her arms behind her back. "You have the right to remain silent…" He spoke in a clear, monotone voice, reciting her Miranda Rights.

Noah's heart ached as he watched the woman he'd always known as his mother being led away.

Nurses entered behind the police. "Sir, you might want to get back in the bed."

"Why?" he asked. "I'm fine."

"Noah, if for no other reason, you might want to get back in bed because your hospital gown is open in the back and you're flashing all of us." Carson clapped a hand on his back and chuckled.

Heat rose in his cheeks, but Noah was not to be deterred from his goal. He glanced around the crowded room, his heart beating faster. "Where's Rachel?"

Landry poked her head around Derek's body. "A nurse took her out into the hallway and got her a wheelchair. They've got a doctor on the way to examine her wounds."

"Move." Noah ploughed through the throng of police and family to get out into the hallway, where he found Rachel seated in a wheelchair, a nurse swabbing the blood away from her forehead with a gauze pad. "Rachel?"

She gave him a weak smile. "I'm okay."

Noah dropped to his knees beside her.

"Still flashing, buddy," Carson reminded him.

An older nurse brought him another hospital gown and draped it over his back with a smile. "A shame to hide such a sexy butt." She winked and stepped out of the way so that the rest of the family could gather around the two injured members.

"What happened?" Carson asked.

"I stepped away for five minutes." Landry threw her hands in the air. "I would never have left if I thought Emmaline could get past the security we had in place." She dropped to her haunches beside Rachel. "Honey, I'm so sorry."

Rachel patted Landry's hand. "Don't be. The plan

worked. We'll live and Emmaline can't hurt anyone else."

"And she confessed everything from killing Reginald to trying to kill Rachel and Ruby," Noah said.

"She did. Both of us heard her," Rachel confirmed, her gaze meeting Noah's as the nurse finished dressing her wound. "I'm so sorry."

Noah shook his head. "She brought it on herself."

"She's a sick woman," Landry said.

Rachel nodded. "Now that she's been caught, she'll get help." She frowned at Noah. "Shouldn't you be in bed? You almost died in that accident."

He chuckled. "That was nothing compared to the thousand deaths I experienced while Emmaline had you at gunpoint." Noah reached for her hand. "It made me realize something."

Rachel placed her hand in his and let him draw her to her feet. "What's that?"

"That life can be shorter than you think. You have to grab for all the happiness you can before it's over or snatched away from you." He pulled her into his arms, holding her gently so as not to reinjure anything. "I'm grabbing for you, Rachel."

She smiled tremulously, touching a hand to her bandaged forehead. "I'm a mess."

Carson snorted. "Noah's no prize. The poor man's dressed in a hospital gown."

Derek piped in, "Good grief. Kiss her already."

Noah claimed her lips, kissing her softly. "I'm afraid I'll hurt you," he said.

"I'm afraid you'll stop kissing me." She cupped his

cheeks in her palms and brought him back to her lips. "Please don't stop."

"Never." He kissed her again.

She opened her mouth to him, allowing him to slip his tongue inside to caress hers.

"See, Rachel, I told you he had it bad for you." Landry slipped her hand into Derek's and she leaned against him. "And the best part is that we're all family."

Carson hugged Georgia close. "Come on. We should let Ruby know what's going on. She'll be glad to know Noah's safe and Emmaline won't hurt either of you again."

Noah glanced up. "Tell my mother that I'll be by to see her as soon as I can."

"We will," Georgia said. She walked up to him and kissed his cheek. "I always wanted a big brother. Glad you're part of my family." Then, hand in hand, she and Carson left ICU.

Landry smiled at Derek and leaned into his embrace. "We'll just leave you two alone. If you need us, we'll be making out in the waiting room." She winked and led a willing Derek away.

Though Noah's heart ached for the woman he'd known all his life as his mother, he was equally filled with joy that the beautiful woman he loved was safe. He felt he'd come home, to the only place he wanted to be. In Rachel's arms.

When the dust settled and the mess of the ICU room was cleared, Noah insisted Rachel see a doctor to make sure she hadn't suffered head trauma from her fight with Emmaline.

Noah refused to leave her side until she'd been through a CT scan and thorough examination. In record time, the doctor plastered a bandage on her forehead, gave her an ice pack for the cheek, a pill for the pain and declared her fit to go home.

Even though it hurt her cheek, Rachel couldn't stop smiling. With Emmaline's confession, they finally had Reginald's killer and the person responsible for the attempts on hers and Ruby's lives.

But that wasn't what had her smiling.

Noah was awake, alive and well. So well that he was cranky when the doctor insisted on keeping him through the remainder of the night. Fortunately, they moved him into a regular room where he could have a member of his family stay with him all night, if he wanted.

He'd asked Rachel to stay.

Her heart swelled with all the love she had for the man.

When the nurses gave her a hard time about not being a family member, he'd told her that he was Jackson Adair and if they wanted to see another sizable donation in the near future, they'd better let Rachel stay.

When they were assigning Noah to the new room, Rachel had asked if it was at all possible to place him close to Ruby.

They'd done better than that. They'd moved him into the room directly across the hallway from hers.

As soon as the nurse left him alone, Noah ducked out of his room into his mother's to prove to her that he was alive and well and not much the worse for wear.

Rachel followed, afraid to leave him for even a moment. The danger and fear of the day still lingered, making her pulse beat too fast and her stomach clench.

"Jackson—" From her bed Ruby cupped his face and stared into his eyes. "I mean Noah. I was so worried when I saw the news."

He smiled down at his mother. "I'm okay. Just a bump on the head. They did a CT scan and apparently I have the gene for hardheadedness inherited from the Adairs."

She laughed. "Yes, that would definitely be an Adair trait." Her smile brightened the room. "I'm just so happy to have you back in my life, and I'm blessed to get to know you as an adult and, I hope, a friend." Her smile broadened. "Now I have two children to love." She held out her hand to her stepdaughter.

Georgia stood on the other side of Ruby's bed with Carson. "Yes, you do. And your heart is big enough to handle it beautifully."

"I don't know..." Ruby pressed her hand to her chest. "Feels like my heart's about to explode, it's so full."

Noah frowned. "Should I call the doctor?"

Ruby laughed. "No, no. Don't do that, unless I could die of happiness."

The scene before Rachel made her own heart expand. She wished she could capture this moment forever.

A nurse entered the room and clucked her tongue. "Mr. Scott, you need to be in your own room. You and Miss Ruby need your rest." She gave them both a stern look. "Unless you *want* to stay another night in the hospital."

"Hell, no. One night in the hospital is more than I

can stand. Two would kill me." Noah kissed his mother's cheek. "See you tomorrow when we blow this joint." He winked, grabbed Rachel's hand and hurried back to his own room.

The nurse followed, insuring he did indeed get back in his bed.

Noah's scowl was so fierce Rachel would have thought the nurse would rush out of the room. But she didn't. Instead, she drew blood, gave him a pain pill and finally left Noah and Rachel alone.

"About damn time," Noah grumbled. He scooted to the side and patted the mattress. "Come here."

Rachel shook her head. "I can't do that. You're the patient."

"You look as beat-up as I do. Get up here."

She glanced toward the door.

"I'll deal with the nurse." He tugged on her hand. "Please. I won't go to sleep until you're here with me."

Rachel kicked off her shoes and crawled up beside him, stretching out on the narrow bed, her head resting on his chest. "Are you sure I'm not hurting you?"

"Positive. I've never felt better." He curled his arm around her and held her. "Now that I have you alone and no one is trying to kill you…"

Her heart slammed against her chest and she held her breath. Not knowing what he might say, she rested her hand on his chest and waited.

"I love you, Rachel Blackstone. I'd wait and do this over a candlelit dinner or on a beach at sunset, but I don't want to waste one more minute."

Tears welled and Rachel bit down on her bottom lip

to keep it from trembling. She couldn't remember the last time she'd cried so much.

Noah lifted her chin with his finger. "What's this? Wait a minute. Why the tears?"

She shrugged, one of the pesky tears slipping out of the corner of her eye to drop onto his hospital gown. "I don't know. All of the sudden I feel like crying."

"Well, don't," he demanded. "Or I'll feel like you don't want me to ask you to marry me."

Her eyes widened and more tears spilled from them. "Oh, I do!"

Noah grinned. "That's more like it. Get some practice in saying *I do*, because *I don't* want to wait long."

She leaned up on her elbow, her tears drying, a frown creasing her brow. "Are you going to ask me to marry you, or not?"

"That's my girl." He hugged her and kissed the top of her head. "Rachel Blackstone, you started out as my pupil, became my friend, turned into my enemy and then my lover. You're beautiful, intelligent and the woman I want to make babies with. I don't want to go another day without you in my life. Will you marry me?"

Rachel kissed his cheek, fighting back those confounded tears. "Yes!"

Chapter 18

"Rachel, I was worried about you. What took you so long in the bathroom?" Noah held out his hand. "Everyone is waiting on you to start the party."

"Have Derek and Landry arrived?"

"Yes, and they brought a surprise." Noah stared at Rachel's face. "Are you feeling all right? You're kind of green around the gills." He touched a hand to her cheek. "And you're a bit cool and clammy. Maybe we should skip the shower and take you to San Diego to the doctor."

"No way. I can't go. This is Elizabeth's moment. I'll be okay. I just need a cracker or piece of bread to settle my stomach."

Noah didn't like it. Rachel's lips were pale and she looked as if she might throw up at any time. "No, we need to get you to a doctor."

She straightened her shoulders, her chin tipping up. "You'd have to drag me kicking and screaming. Georgia, Landry and I put in a lot of effort to make this day special for Elizabeth. I'm not missing it." Her shoulders sagged. "I just need a cracker."

Rachel ran for the large kitchen in the main house.

The caterers had set out finger food all over the counters, ready to filter through the family and friends who'd gathered for Elizabeth and Whit's baby shower.

Noah followed close behind, worried that Rachel wasn't acting normal. He noted that when she saw the trays of food, her face turned as white as a sheet of paper. She rummaged through the cabinets until she found a box of saltines, ripped open a packet of them and stuffed two in her mouth at once.

"Are you sure you should be eating when your stomach is feeling bad?" he asked.

She chewed for a minute, then choked it down with a glass of water. "For some reason, food has been making me sick lately. The only thing I can keep down is saltine crackers."

He hooked her arm. "Come on. We're going to the doctor right now."

"Hey, you two. The party's outside and everyone is here." Landry entered the kitchen. "And I brought a surprise."

"I'm okay now," Rachel whispered to Noah, the color returning to her face, along with a smile.

Noah couldn't believe the difference from one second to the next. He'd cut her some slack until after the party, but then they were going to the doctor.

"What's the surprise?" Rachel asked.

"Kate and Patrick O'Hara flew in last night. They wanted to come out for a visit and it coincided perfectly with the baby shower."

Rachel clapped her hands. "That's wonderful." She turned toward the counters full of food and her face lost all color again. "Excuse me." Clapping a hand to her mouth, she ran for the bathroom.

Noah started after her, but Landry held out her hand. "I'll go check on her. Maybe you could help carry one of these trays out to the guests. The caterer is short-handed, but I told him we were all big boys and girls and could serve ourselves the *hors d'oeuvres* while they pulled the buffet line together."

"I don't mind, but Rachel—"

"Will be just fine. I'll check on her and bring her out when she's feeling better."

Noah hesitated. He really didn't want to leave Rachel when she was feeling bad, but Landry was stubbornly insistent. "I'll be back in five minutes if Rachel isn't out by then."

Landry smiled. "Fair enough."

Derek entered the kitchen as Landry turned to follow Rachel.

"Oh, good." She pointed to him. "Derek, sweetheart, could you please help Noah with the food?" She didn't wait for his response before following Rachel.

Derek's brows rose. "What's got her in a hurry?"

"Rachel isn't feeling well. She went to check on her." Noah lifted a tray. "Guess we better follow orders."

With a chuckle, Derek picked up another tray and followed Noah through the house to the patio.

"How's business at the agency?" Noah asked.

"Picking up. Didn't hurt having Kate Adair O'Hara's endorsement. Seems being the former vice president of the United States carries a little weight. She recommended the agency's services to some of California's elite. I've got more business than I can handle. I'm going to have to hire more staff and possibly open another office in San Francisco."

Noah grinned. "Too much business is a good problem to have."

They stepped out onto the patio with the loaded trays and were surrounded by hungry family and friends.

Georgia took the tray from him. "When are you and Rachel coming to dinner at our house?"

"As soon as you invite us," Noah responded.

"I didn't know family had to send out written invitations." She winked at him and set the tray on a table. "I'll arrange a date as soon as the painter is done with the interior."

"How do you and Carson like living in San Diego?" he asked.

Carson snuck up behind Georgia and slipped an arm around her waist. "We love it. I'm closer to AdAir's corporate offices and Georgia secured a position at the San Diego library."

"How's the work at AdAir Corp?"

Carson nodded. "I wasn't sure I'd like it, but I find it a challenge, and the work is never boring. Plus, Adair Acres isn't too far out to visit often enough to allow me that physical release you only get when ranching."

Noah nodded. "I love it. I thank my lucky stars every day that Reginald saw fit to leave a share of the ranch to me."

"Between you and Whit, this place is running like a fine-oiled machine. You're really good with the animals and he's got the vineyards and farming down to a science. Are you still running your import-and-export business?"

Noah nodded. "Yes. And it's going so well Rachel's been helping me with it."

"Speaking of Rachel…" Carson glanced around. "Where is she?"

Noah checked his watch. Five minutes had passed. He turned toward the house and had taken a step in that direction when Landry and Rachel came out, laughing and talking.

The color had returned to her face. She and Landry hugged and Landry kissed her cheek.

If Noah wasn't mistaken, he heard Landry say, "Congratulations."

Rachel hugged her and smiled. "Thanks." Then she turned to him and gave him the most beautiful smile, which seemed to rival the sunshine.

He hurried to join her. "What was all that about?"

"Attention!" Whit stood at the top of the steps leading down to the patio area. "Kate Adair O'Hara would like to say something."

Despite Kate's petite frame, she commanded attention with her piercing blue eyes, stylish haircut and regal bearing, a product of years of political service to her country. She frowned and waved Whit away. "Seriously? I left that title behind me. I'm Aunt Kate to you all." Her frown cleared and she smiled at the family and friends assembled. Patrick O'Hara, her husband, stood by her side, beaming proudly.

Kate slipped her hand in his and addressed the gathering. "I wanted to congratulate Whit and Elizabeth on the pending arrival of their baby. Our children are the most important legacy we can give this world. Whatever schools they go to, people they fall in love with and career paths they might take, love them for who they are and not for what they can do for you or bring to your family. Love your child as much as you can. You don't have any guarantees of how long you'll have him or her in your life." She leaned against her husband and together they joined the crowd gathering around Elizabeth and Whit.

Noah stood with Rachel in the crook of his arm.

Ruby walked up beside him and took his hand in hers. "She's right, you know. And you have to grab for all the love you can get. You never know how long you'll have it."

Noah turned to his mother. "Have you thought about my offer to come live at Adair Acres?"

She smiled up at him. "I have. And I think you and your fiancée need time to be alone together. I'm using the money Reginald left to me to purchase a property close by. Far enough to give you kids your space and close enough to get to know my grandbabies."

"What grandbabies?" Noah asked.

Ruby laughed. "The ones I expect you and Georgia to give me." She leaned around him to wink at Rachel. "I want at least half a dozen."

Rachel grinned. "We'd like to be married before we start baby production. Has Georgia agreed to your plan?"

Georgia joined them. "Have I agreed to what plan?"

Noah hugged his stepsister, still amazed at the fact

he had an entire family of siblings. "That you agree to give Mother half-a-dozen grandchildren."

"Six grandchildren?" Georgia shook her head. "I don't think so. Two would be optimal. Three would be a stretch, but six?" Her lips twisted. "Not hardly."

"Oh, I don't know." Carson draped an arm over her shoulders. "I'm okay with six."

"You and your next wife?" She leaned into him. "I'm good for two."

Georgia turned to Noah. "You have to do your part."

"Thank you, Aunt Kate." Landry took center stage on the steps, interrupting the side conversations taking place. "We all want to thank you for helping to celebrate the coming addition to the Adair family. And thank you, Elizabeth and Whit, for giving us a new baby and the opportunity to get together with family and friends."

All present clapped. Those closest to Whit and the very pregnant Elizabeth shook hands with or hugged the happy couple.

Landry cleared her throat. "I wanted to announce that Rachel has agreed to be my maid of honor next month. But the bigger announcement, and one I hope doesn't outshine our reason for being here in the first place—" she nodded toward Elizabeth and Whit "—is that we're adding another baby to the Adair clan."

A cheer went up and then died down.

"Who?" Whit asked.

Landry grinned and turned her gaze to Rachel and Noah.

Noah frowned and shook his head. "Not us. I think I'd know if Rachel was pregnant." He smiled down at her.

When she grinned up at him, he stared at her, shock making his stomach turn somersaults. "You're pregnant?" he asked. Stunned.

She nodded. "Landry had an early pregnancy test kit in the bathroom." Her smile spread across her face. "We're going to have a baby."

Noah's heart could have burst he was so happy. He grabbed Rachel around her waist and swung her around, then set her down.

Everyone laughed and clapped.

Noah glanced up at Landry. "I'm sorry, Landry, but Rachel can't be your maid of honor."

Landry's smile turned to a frown. "Why?"

"Because she's going to be a bride, as well. It's going to be a double wedding."

Landry's grin returned. "I'm okay with that, if Rachel doesn't mind sharing the spotlight."

"Yes!" Rachel flung her arms around Noah's neck. "I love you, Noah Scott."

"I love you, too, Rachel. But would you be terribly disappointed if you married Jackson Adair? Seems I like the sound of it, and, since I'm going to be part of this family, I might as well carry the name."

"I don't care what name you choose, as long as you choose me to share it."

Noah hugged her and held her close the rest of the evening, happy to have her to love and a family with whom he could share his happiness.

Life really was wonderful as an Adair.

* * * * *

If you love Elle James,
be sure to pick up her other stories:

DEADLY ALLURE
SECRET SERVICE RESCUE
DEADLY LIAISONS
DEADLY ENGAGEMENT
DEADLY RECKONING

Available now from Harlequin Romantic Suspense!

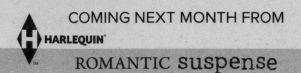

REQUEST YOUR FREE BOOKS!

2 FREE NOVELS PLUS 2 FREE GIFTS!

ROMANTIC suspense

Sparked by danger, fueled by passion

YES! Please send me 2 FREE Harlequin® Romantic Suspense novels and my 2 FREE gifts (gifts are worth about $10). After receiving them, if I don't wish to receive any more books, I can return the shipping statement marked "cancel." If I don't cancel, I will receive 4 brand-new novels every month and be billed just $4.74 per book in the U.S. or $5.49 per book in Canada. That's a savings of at least 12% off the cover price! It's quite a bargain! Shipping and handling is just 50¢ per book in the U.S. and 75¢ per book in Canada.* I understand that accepting the 2 free books and gifts places me under no obligation to buy anything. I can always return a shipment and cancel at any time. Even if I never buy another book, the two free books and gifts are mine to keep forever.

240/340 HDN GH3P

Name	(PLEASE PRINT)

Address	Apt. #

City	State/Prov.	Zip/Postal Code

Signature (if under 18, a parent or guardian must sign)

Mail to the **Reader Service:**
IN U.S.A.: P.O. Box 1867, Buffalo, NY 14240-1867
IN CANADA: P.O. Box 609, Fort Erie, Ontario L2A 5X3

Want to try two free books from another line?
Call 1-800-873-8635 or visit www.ReaderService.com.

* Terms and prices subject to change without notice. Prices do not include applicable taxes. Sales tax applicable in N.Y. Canadian residents will be charged applicable taxes. Offer not valid in Quebec. This offer is limited to one order per household. Not valid for current subscribers to Harlequin Romantic Suspense books. All orders subject to credit approval. Credit or debit balances in a customer's account(s) may be offset by any other outstanding balance owed by or to the customer. Please allow 4 to 6 weeks for delivery. Offer available while quantities last.

Your Privacy—The Reader Service is committed to protecting your privacy. Our Privacy Policy is available online at www.ReaderService.com or upon request from the Reader Service.

We make a portion of our mailing list available to reputable third parties that offer products we believe may interest you. If you prefer that we not exchange your name with third parties, or if you wish to clarify or modify your communication preferences, please visit us at www.ReaderService.com/consumerschoice or write to us at Reader Service Preference Service, P.O. Box 9062, Buffalo, NY 14240-9062. Include your complete name and address.

SPECIAL EXCERPT FROM

HARLEQUIN®

ROMANTIC suspense

Jack Colton wants Tracy McCain as far away from his son as possible. But when she becomes an assassin's target, the stakes have never been higher…

Read on for a sneak peek of
COLTON COWBOY PROTECTOR
the first book in the
COLTONS OF OKLAHOMA series.

"Excuse me."

Jack pushed to his feet, his knee cracking thanks to an old rodeo injury, and faced the woman at eye level. Well, almost eye level. Though tall for a woman, she was still a good five or six inches shorter than his six foot one. He recognized her as the woman he'd seen earlier lurking in the foyer, practically casing the main house.

"Are you Jack Colton?" she asked.

"I am."

"May I have a word with you?" she asked, her voice noticeably thin and unsteady. She cleared her throat and added, "Privately?"

In his head, Jack groaned. *What now?*

"And you are…?"

He suspected she was a reporter, based on the messenger bag hanging from her shoulder. He had nothing to say to any reporter, privately or otherwise.

"Tracy McCain." She added a shy smile, her porcelain cheeks flushing, and a stir of attraction tickled Jack deep inside. Hell, more than a stir. He gave her leisurely scrutiny, sizing her up. She may be tall and thin, but she still had womanly curves to go with her delicate, china-doll face.

"Am I supposed to know you?"

Her smile dropped. "Laura never mentioned me?"

His ex-wife's name instantly raised his hackles and his defenses. His eyes narrowed. "Not that I recall. How do you know Laura?"

"I'm her cousin. Her maternal aunt's daughter. From Colorado Springs."

Jack gritted his back teeth. Laura had only been dead a few months and already relations she'd never mentioned were crawling out of the woodwork like roaches after the light was turned off. The allure of the Colton wealth had attracted more than one gold-digging pest over the years. "You should know Laura signed an agreement when we divorced that ended any further financial claim on Colton money."

Tracy lifted her chin. "I'm aware."

"So you're barking up the wrong tree if you're looking for cash."

Tracy blinked her pale blue eyes, and her expression shifted, hardened. "I'm not after money," she said, with frost in her tone.

Jack scratched his chin and tipped his head, giving her a skeptical glare. "Then what?"

"I wanted to talk about Seth."

Jack tensed, his gut filling with acid. He squeezed the currycomb with a death grip and grated, "No."

"I… What do you mean, no? You haven't even heard what I want to—"

"I don't need to hear. My son is off-limits. Nonnegotiable."

Don't miss
COLTON COWBOY PROTECTOR
by Beth Cornelison,
available June 2015 wherever
Harlequin® Romantic Suspense
books and ebooks are sold.

www.Harlequin.com

HRSEXP0515

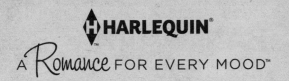

HARLEQUIN®

A *Romance* FOR EVERY MOOD™

JUST CAN'T GET ENOUGH?

Join our social communities
and talk to us online.

You will have access to the latest
news on upcoming titles and special
promotions, but most importantly,
you can talk to other fans about your
favorite Harlequin reads.

Harlequin.com/Community

HSOCIAL

THE WORLD IS BETTER WITH

Romance

Harlequin has everything from contemporary, passionate and heartwarming to suspenseful and inspirational stories.

Whatever your mood, we have a romance just for you!

Connect with us to find your next great read, special offers and more.

f /HarlequinBooks

🐦 @HarlequinBooks

www.HarlequinBlog.com

www.Harlequin.com/Newsletters

◆ HARLEQUIN®

A *Romance* FOR EVERY MOOD™

www.Harlequin.com